CHTHONIC

WEIRD TALES

OF

INNER EARTH

EDITED BY
SCOTT R JONES

Martian Migraine Press

print edition 2018

CHTHONIC
Weird Tales of Inner Earth

© 2018 Martian Migraine Press

edited by Scott R Jones

The Rats in the Walls by H. P. Lovecraft first published in *Weird Tales* (March 1924)
David Stevens's *Some Corner of a Dorset Field That Is Forever Arabia* first appeared in
Three-Lobed Burning Eye Magazine (Issue 25 July 2014) / Gemma Files' *The Harrow*
saw publication orignally in *The Children of Old Leech* (2014) / Ramsey Campbell's
The End of a Summer's Day first appeared in his collection *Demons by Daylight* (1973)
The Re'em by Adam McOmber first published in *Conjunctions* (Fall 2013) / Antony Mann's
Vault first published in *The Third Alternative* (1998)

Cover illustration "Anon XII" © Lucas Korte
Interior illustrations © 2017 Fufu Fruenwahl

National Library of Canada Cataloguing in Publication Data
ISBN (ebook) 978-1-927673-24-9
ISBN (print) 978-1-927673-25-6

martianmigrainepress.com

DELVINGS

THE CAVE YOU
FEAR TO ENTER...

little less than two hundred kilometers north and west of my home on Vancouver Island lie the Horne Lake Caves, a pristine cave system popular with everyone from seasoned spelunkers to school groups. With over one hundred rooms of various sizes distributed throughout the system, the caves are a geological treasure and a satisfying delve into the boggling abyss of Deep Time, for those inclined to experience such things.

As it turns out, I am not one of those people.

My wife and I visited the Horne Lake Caves a few years back, almost on a lark. It was summer, we were camping nearby for the weekend, and it seemed like an entertaining way to fill a few hours in the early afternoon. Certainly, we wouldn't be taking the long tour, or anything where we'd have to crawl or worm our way between masses of implacable rock. Just a few rooms, a passage or two, and then back out into the light.

I barely made it forty meters in, friends. I'm a tall person and it wasn't long before I'd hit my head on a chunk of the planet, and then through the pain I heard the guide say "time to turn off our headlamps!"

1

and like a fool, I did, along with all the others. I thought I'd be OK, but before long a feeling began to bloom behind my ribs that quickly overrode any rational response I might have had. The darkness came, and it was total darkness, sure, but that wasn't the problem. The sandy ground was beneath my feet, still, and the dry, slightly musty but not entirely unpleasant smell of the living rock around me remained. So that wasn't it either; I wasn't disoriented or turned around at all. There was no danger of being lost in there. No, it was something more primal that welled up in me, then, some antediluvian ancestor within me that would rather be swinging from branch to branch than set paw in a cavern that rose to speak a warning. Something that said *this is not the place for you* and *there are things in the depths that you would* never *see coming* and then finally just *s c r e a m i n g s c r e a m i n g   s c r e a m i n g* and before you could say "who knew he was bathophobic?" I was in a profound panic. Very simply, I needed the sky. I had to get out, and I did.

There's a quote sometimes attributed to the great mythographer Joseph Campbell that has resonance here. Probably he said something like it in a more prolix fashion (as was his wont) and it was later trimmed down by admirers, but basically it goes like this: "The cave you fear to enter holds the treasure you seek." Well, Mr Campbell, I'm not sure I (or the proto-squirrel-monkey that lives deep in my DNA) would necessarily agree with you there... but I do happen to think that the dark tales collected in the fungoid caves, claustrophobic caverns, and midnight galleries of this anthology will constitute a treasure for seekers of the strange and wonderful in their fiction.

Within the pages of *CHTHONIC: Weird Tales of Inner Earth*, you'll find seventeen stories from a diverse group of international authors. Stories that plumb the depths of earth at least as deeply as they explore the human capacity for suffering and enlightenment. The demons and beasties that slide between the stones and tectonic plates of the planet feature in stories by Howard Lovecraft (his classic *The Rats in*

THE CAVE YOU FEAR TO ENTER...

the Walls), John Linwood Grant's *Where All Is Night, and Starless*, Tom Lynch's *The Writhe*, and the very special *Pugelbone* by Nadia Bulkin.

Themes of the mythical Hollow Earth itself (so much sexier than those dull Flat Earth conspiracy types!) inform the crushing *Volver Al Monte* by S. L. Edwards, Orrin Grey's mesmerizing story of fate and choice in the realms below, *Hollow Earths*, and the gritty *A Song for Granite Khronos* by Aaron Besson. *Tending the Core*, a fine and deceptively light fantasy by Adam Millard, will leave you unsteady on your feet. Belinda Lewis' *The Dragons Beneath* introduces us to a queen on a mission to retrieve a treasure for her people. But it is Gemma Files' *The Harrow* which will have you squirming to escape that which ever burrows beneath, even as your third eye is opened (surgically!) to their beauty and wonder.

As below, so above, the kabbalists are known to say, and in keeping with that eternal truth, we haven't neglected tales of eruptions into our world of things best kept out of the sunlight. Dark family secrets and ancient aboriginal cities burst from the land and the subconscious alike in Christopher Slatsky's chilling *Tellurian Façade*. Sarah Peploe checks us into a hip London hotel with very unusual management in *UNDR*. Antony Mann's hapless protagonist learns just how far below the literally rich veins of modern banking reach in *Vault*. And the master himself, Ramsey Campbell, provides us with a paranoiac tale of a caving tour gone terrifyingly wrong in *The End of a Summer's Day*. (Yes, that one *is* difficult for me to read, thanks for asking!)

In the end, though, we all go below. We enter the cave we fear, finally. In Scott Shank's *Nivel Del Mar*, those depths promise not death, but life, health, and something almost beyond comprehension. *The Re'em* by Adam McOmber takes us to a valley not only below but somehow outside of the earth we know, where dreams and desire clash. Finally, David Stevens' *Some Corner of a Dorset Field That Is Forever Arabia* gives us the secret history and fantastic death of a famous English colonel. I count this last as a jewel in *CHTHONIC*, and I think you will, too.

The cavern mouth awaits, as does the cistern with hidden depths, the tunnel that twists and writhes, the abyssal space that hums with unknown activity. Note the faint glow to the walls as you descend: mere phosphorescent fungi... or something more peculiar? There is a sound of rushing water that you can't place, and the suggestion of drums and strange flutes in the deep. The rock vibrates beneath the soles of your feet, and your headlamp flickers, fails. But then, you knew it would, eventually. This place is not for you, but here you are.

Welcome to *CHTHONIC*.

Scott R Jones
2 February 2018
Victoria, BC

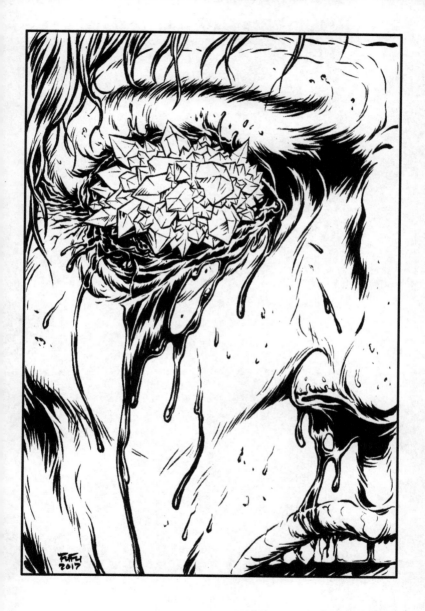

WHERE ALL IS NIGHT,
AND STARLESS

JOHN LINWOOD GRANT

arch, 1919, Inner Hebrides

MThe agent tells me that the house is built on solid bedrock. It has three rooms, with bare stone walls forming a kitchen, a bedroom and a parlour. A failed farmhouse for a failed farm. The last owner died in the war, childless, and his wife soon after, in 1918. The agent has no record of how or why. He has a florid, anxious face—a Lowland Scot, desperate to please and yet ill-informed about the Western Isles. I have neighbours on the other side of the island, a handful of crofters, but he knows little about them. A boat brings supplies once a week.

"Nae so fine a place for a lassie." He shakes his head, a sudden burst of conscience, perhaps. "And if your faither takes bad..."

I take out my cheque book, and let my pen speak for us. He swallows his doubts.

"Aye, well, there's nae a snib on the isle, I'll wager."

I stare until he realises.

"No locks, Miss Allen. So I dinna have a key to gae ye."

Our business done, he trudges to the small jetty. The sky is turning dark with promised rain, and he's eager to be away. My father sits in his wheelchair, waiting for me.

"Inside, then," I say. There is grass, wiry grass, under the wheels of his chair, but the soil is thin. I make him comfortable in the parlour, which will be his.

"Soon," my father mutters.

I have waited almost two years, and seen him through four hospitals and recuperation homes. The urgent need I once had has been mellowed, and now I can wait. I can feel that his story is coming, the words which have been trapped inside him since the blast which shook the spires of half of Europe.

We settle, and for a week I let him inspect our new home. He pronounces that we are on granitic gneiss, which seems to reassure him. The term means little to me, but I notice a change in him. He walks, only a few steps, but it is heartening.

Lieutenant Robert Allen, thirty nine years old, of the 183rd Tunnelling Company in Belgium. A tall, slim figure, easily missed in a crowd— except for the way his head cocks at any unexpected noise. Like a dog, a dog which cannot settle.

When they dragged him from the remains of a tunnel-mouth, they did not know what they had. He was recovered alone and in a state of exhaustion, raving, covered in blood. Those fingernails which he retained were ragged and torn. They had no explanation for me.

His commanding officer wrote a letter which betrayed more than I think he intended. "In the finest tradition of the Army," and "Work vital to our efforts,"—brown ink on cream paper—but in between, curious phrases concerning sudden action and "necessary haste". By which I have come to believe that a mine was blown before its due time, and that my father and the sappers were still at work when it was done.

They call his condition shell shock. He himself denied this when I sat by him in the early months. He promised to tell me the truth, one day, when he could. This lonely isle, I believe, is what he has been seeking.

A James McAllister calls, to enquire if we need seaweed for our vegetable garden.

He takes a nip of whisky, and offers to bring a hand-cart full of it over, and my father nods, accepts. Outside, McAllister turns to me.

"Hit bad, thon?"

"Flanders. But he's getting better."

"Aye. Mony a soul lost; mony a guid man broken."

He explains, haltingly, that he was on the fishing fleets, keeping the country fed. I praise his efforts, and am rid of him at last.

Father no longer drinks, but he holds up McAllister's empty glass, watching it glint in the morning light.

"Is this the day, Emma?"

I seat myself on the window-bench, watching his scarred hands re-arrange the cheap plaid rug over his knees. He might be one hundred and thirty seven, from the look in his narrow eyes.

"Only if you wish."

I take up the blank journal which has been ready since June 1917. I had it when I first sat by his hospital bed, and it has always been to hand. I had always wanted a record, from his own lips.

He puts the glass down.

"I … I think so."

Bending back the spine of the journal, I lift my pen …

▼▼▼

We didn't hate the Germans (my father began)—the Saxons, Prussians, Bavarians, any of their kind. We'd never seen them, except in photographs. We were tunnellers, sappers, and we were paid well. Tommy Atkins sneered at us, knowing the extra shillings we earned, but he feared us too. We drove shafts and galleries far beneath him, and at any moment we might bring destruction. Our mines ripped open the land without warning, tore through soft bodies as easy as hard clay, and more than one Tommy had been taken on the edge of an ill-timed blast.

If we worried our own troops, we worried the enemy more. We were masters under the earth. Clay-kickers, baggers and trammers, running our secret roads into the dripping dark, always further, always deeper. Miners from Cornwall, Yorkshire and Durham, Canada and Australia, the old hands from the copper shafts and the coal seams. Behind us came more sappers, and the Bantams, too short to pass a recruiting sergeant, but suited to die in shallow galleries and choke in pockets of poisoned night.

We were transferred to Flanders in the March of 1917. Hundreds, if not thousands, of our kind were at work there—the Australians were said to be under Hill 60, packing ammonal almost beneath the German trenches. I had only been a pit-head foreman, but I had education. They made me sew on a pip, and I was handed fuses and geophones, with the last word down there—how far, how quick, how deep.

Major Cartwright, once a geologist, had taken cores.

"There's a promise here, lads," he said, pulling at one end of his moustache. "They'll never get under us here. The Hun can't kick clay."

They could dig, of course, but they used shovels and picks which resounded through the thick earth, bounced off the chalk deposits and alerting our listening posts. We worked soft and quiet, the grafting tool cutting into the clay with little more than a soft, sucking sound.

"One hundred and twenty feet, no less," said Cartwright. "The Hun are at sixty or seventy, so we'll fox them."

We started where a gallery had been abandoned the previous November. We were to turn it and head for the lower end of a ridge held by the German Fourth Army. We knew that there were a great number of mines being prepared for something really big. We were to do our job and end with a chamber for the ammonal, tons of the stuff.

Thanks to pumps, the gallery had only an inch of water in it. We laid tracks to the incline shaft, so that spoil could be hauled up and timbers sent down. Twelve hours on, then twelve hours off. We ate, slept, and then trudged back to the main shaft, still aching. Sappers and soldiers sweated by the opening, hauling up spoil—we were cursed for not having to share their work, and cursed for causing it.

Once in the gallery, two or three candles were all we had to see by. Our domain was nothing but a single curve of wet, shadowed tunnel, more than a hundred feet of soil and rock above us. We felt its weight, and maybe we crouched more than we needed to.

By the second day, the lads had made a side chamber, and I knelt to use the geophone there, pressing the discs to the slick earth. No one moved as I put in the earpieces and began. For minutes there was nothing, and then I heard the tell-tale sounds—the sharp crack of a pick hitting rock, the crunch of what might be boots. Germans.

Listening is an art. Moving the contacts around, even on the chamber wall, I became fairly sure that the sound came from above us and to the north. It wouldn't intersect with our tunnel, not even close.

I scribbled down *Pickwork, strong, 10 degrees*, and sent the note back up to the next listening post. I moved further down, and tried again. Something muffled, further away and on a different bearing, which might have been an echo. It wasn't enough to report.

Morris began working the 'cross', angled on the boards so that he could drive the grafting tool into the clay face. Drive, twist and pull,

Jack Sleath catching the clay which came out, sliding it into Hessian bags. 'Pigeon' Brown was our regular Bantam, ready with rifles as we dug, or helping Smith, our trammer, to push the spoil wagon.

Every half hour I stopped to have a listen. The Saxons, or whichever poor sods they'd enlisted, would be counter-mining nearer the surface. It would be the Upper Gallery's job if they wanted to go for a camouflet and blow the German tunnel. I still thought there was a murmur further off, but I couldn't settle on it, so we pried open cans of bully beef and ate, pressing chunks onto biscuit.

"I'd kill for a kettle," said Morris. He was a closed-mouth Geordie, hard, but a good clay-kicker.

I nodded. "Hot, sweet tea."

Harry Smith scraped the last out of a bully beef tin.

"Any news from the 'phone, Allen?" In the filth and labour of mining, rank was pointless. Nor did I feel I deserved to be a lieutenant. I was still a foreman.

"I'm not sure. They may be cutting towards the north, hoping to find the Aussies. And then..."

They looked at me.

"Aye?" Morris narrowed his eyes.

"It's probably echoes. I thought—a couple of times—that there was something else, something further down on another bearing."

That had their attention.

"You mean they've cut below us?" Smith shook his head. "We're almost one hundred thirty feet now."

We'd taken the gallery down on a stepped gradient, to please Major Cartwright—a man who'd never been further than the head of the shaft.

The Germans could not be underneath us.

Our section now ran four hundred feet towards the enemy lines, and we'd started a chamber for the mine itself. The silence lay heavy on us. I lent a hand to the trammers when I could. Pigeon and a sapper from the rear unloaded the rubber-wheeled wagons when they came back, fitting the timber props together—no hammers or nails. Somewhere up there, the enemy was listening as well.

We were eight hours into a shift when a runner arrived. The ammonal was coming down to pack our chamber. It would take days to shift enough explosive to fill the space, and then we would have to tamp behind it with clay and sandbags, seal it off, only the fuse wires connecting that bulk of death to the living. I checked the canary, Jenny, our warning of a carbon monoxide build-up, and opened tins of pears for the lads, whose fingers were numb from the work.

"We're about ready," I told the runner, a pasty-faced private. Pigeon and Smith had started the back-breaking business of lifting sacks of spoil onto the wagons. I handed Sleath his tinned pears, slopping the thin juice. I saw his mittened fingers grasp the tin …

The world shook. A wave of fouled air hammered into us from the shaft end of the gallery, a deafening blast that lay Pigeon and the runner flat. I saw a set of timbers split, and a mass of clay slide to block half the width of the gallery. The runner's shriek penetrated my dulled senses, and I fell on him, clamping one hand over his mouth. Instinct for a tunneller. The water in the bottom of the gallery trembled, like the old gear we once used for listening, and was still again.

No one moved or spoke. After a couple of minutes—a couple of hours, it felt like—I got up, shot a warning glare to the runner. Pigeon was on his feet again.

"Check it out," I whispered. He nodded, and eased past the fall, heading for the main inclined shaft. I went round, but everyone was fine.

"Camouflet?" Sleath asked.

"They weren't near us." It was common enough for an enemy counter-mine to be used next to, or under, one of our tunnels. A pipe charge driven into the earth between us, fired so that it collapsed our diggings. But I would have heard them. "See what Pigeon finds."

We waited, and Sleath handed round his miraculously preserved tin of pears. Five minutes, staring at my watch by a relit candle, and the Bantam returned.

"It's the shaft."

An accident with munitions; a camouflet elsewhere which had triggered something. There was no way to tell. An entire section of the main shaft was blocked, right where our gallery hit it.

"Days," said Morris. "Days to excavate that."

I glared at him. "Might not be. If it's open further up..."

"If."

My team, the runner and a sapper who had been helping Pigeon. Seven men in a sealed pocket of night. I looked to Jenny in her cage. How much air, how much oxygen, did a pocket like this hold?

Seven men, breathing.

"You're the officer." Morris spoke, surly.

I turned to the sapper, a stocky man in his forties.

"What's your name?"

"Lambert. Sir."

"Morris, take Lambert. Find out if we could cut into the shaft and clear any of it. The rest of you, not a sound."

I took the geophone into the main chamber we'd dug. Distance was a bugger, which was why we had many listening posts. Triangulation.

There was digging—or something like it. It made no sense. Not from the inclined shaft, but south of us, and under, surely under. Like the times before, but not a muffled scratching or echo now, more a random hacking at rock. I'd not heard the Germans work like this.

The huddle of men looked at me when I returned.

"Someone..." I didn't know how to put it. "Someone's coming up."

"They've foxed us. The bloody Hun." Smith looked outraged. "I'd never have said they could beat us, going this deep."

"We'd better be sharp, then." I wasn't going to let them see my doubts.

Morris came back angry, and filthy. "Shaft's full."

"Any sign of what caused it?"

He shook his head.

"What are we going to do, Allen?" Pigeon looked at me with small, watery eyes.

I formed a smile I couldn't feel.

"They'll be on it now, our people. Hauling out the debris. Meanwhile, we have the Boche below us, God knows how. They'll have fresh air. We'll turn the tables and blast into their tunnel."

Purpose cut through shock. We cleaned rifles, and got bayonets ready. Most of these men were better with a knife than with a gun. I employed the geophone, moving along the gallery, until I had a definite bearing. The sounds were louder.

We always had a charge ready, for if I should blow the tunnel or organise our own camouflet—a metal pipe packed with ammonal, plenty of fuse wire and a detonator box. We hauled the cross to the right spot and had Morris cut down and south towards the enemy workings. If I was right, we'd break into the German tunnel, incapacitating—if not killing—their tunnellers.

And if we failed, better a swift surrender than choking to death where we were.

It didn't take long. The charge slid tightly into the hole, the long fuse wire dangling behind. The others began heaping sandbags over it all, to help direct the blast.

"Fall back, lads."

We crouched with weapons ready, and I turned the lever on the fuse box...

The second blast of the day shook more soil from the tunnel roof, and filled the gallery with fumes which bit at the back of the throat.

"Go," I urged.

We rose as one, Morris in the lead with his bayonet thrust out. He was through the ragged hole in seconds, scrambling down the slippery clay. I shone my torch for him, mindful of having no spare battery, and tried to keep my balance as I followed.

This lower tunnel was wrong. It varied in width and height, the roof coming down to less than five feet in places. There were no timbers, either. I began to think that someone had enlarged a natural fissure in the depths.

"It would explain the Germans," said Sleath, his voice low by my ear. "They found this, and had only to dig a proper access shaft to it."

"Must be that. Not seen Boche work this crude." Smith stroked the nearest wall, which looked as if it had been hacked at almost randomly.

Lambert, the sapper, had gone ahead with Morris. He ran back, his face crumpled by an emotion I couldn't read, and tugged on my shirt sleeve.

"Sir, please..."

I followed him twenty feet down the tunnel to where Morris had lit a candle. The squat Geordie stood over a body which lay face up. There was a broken pick at its side.

The uniform was German, badly torn and mouldering. It hung off a corpse which couldn't have been the result of our blast. The smell alone made me think this man had been dead for weeks. I saw a shrivelled face, lips drawn back thin from the yellowed teeth, and the gaping sockets where his eyes had been—no, the broken-edged holes, inches across. The bone had been shattered. There was only darkness inside the empty skull.

"Damned rats," I said.

The men said nothing, preferring to share the lie. No rat had done this.

Lambert pointed to where my torch lit the floor. "There are footprints. Somebody ran—maybe they heard us tamping the camouflet."

Despite the stink of the body, there was fresher air here. Jenny, lowered down to us in her cage, seemed unaffected. I had some mad dream of taking the Germans by surprise and rising up, finding the surface again, followed by a night-crawl back to our own lines.

It was a single file job, so much so that in places Morris had trouble squeezing this thick chest through. I allowed us one candle. We found a mattock abandoned fifty feet further along, and I checked the compass, which stuck a couple of times. I had to shake it to get a bearing. We were heading south-east. We were also still going down.

We made slow progress. An hour in, and no living soul, but where there was wet clay underfoot, there were impressions of feet—both booted and bare-footed. No rats. I stopped, and we shared out chocolate. Not long after, the fissure widened, and we hit a sight which paused us. The cavern ahead was low, but wider than a marshalling yard, with granite outcrops and thick pillars of a grey-green stone which glinted. Some kind of feldspar, possibly, and quartz.

We were below the clay.

Edging forward, the crystalline columns had their own light, a weak luminescence, which was barely enough to see by, but it spared our candles. Here and there, slender lengths of feldspar lay broken on the cavern floor. I thought of Goths and Vandals, the Germans diggers passing through and kicking out idly, destroying things which had been formed millennia ago...

"There's someone down here." That was Clough, the runner from HQ. "I can feel it. They're watching us."

"Aye." Morris had his rifle up.

We spread out as we crossed the centre of the first cavern, equipment clinking gently as we moved from one rock formation to another.

Water had flowed here once, enough to break through seams in the granite and expose fields of quartz and other crystals. We followed those forgotten floods, shifting in the semi-dark as we watched for the enemy.

Our spirits were hardly raised when, after pushing through a short narrow section which headed downwards, we came out into yet another, almost identical cavern. Off this ran dim openings, some no wider than the fissure we had first entered, others the size of railway tunnels. Sleath lit a candle, but its light seemed weak, as if the glinting, greenish columns absorbed and held it in their depths.

"Summat up with this," said Morris, his hand on a clustered mass of quartz. I touched it. It felt greasy, slick with something other than water. I wiped my hand vigorously on my trousers.

"The Germans made it through," I said. "We'll go a bit further."

We lost Lambert first. He was to my left, by an outcropping of granite which resembled a clenched fist. I heard a gasp, the clatter of his boot heels against the rocks, and Pigeon and I ran to the spot. There was no sign of the young runner.

We edged forward until we reached a narrow crevice in the cavern wall. There was utter blackness inside, with a smell of decay on the faintest of breezes.

"I could get in there," whispered the Bantam.

"And do what? The Germans have him. I couldn't follow you."

It seemed that they knew we were there. There couldn't have been many of them, or they would have rushed us. Maybe they'd sent up for reinforcements.

We re-joined the others, only to find that Smith too was missing.

"He went ahead," said Sleath. "We didn't know what we were walking into, Allen."

We waited a half hour, an evil half hour where there always seemed to be more breathing in the cavern than our own, and the slightest movement sounded like thunder. The glimmers and pale reflections from crystal to crystal confused any sense of distance or direction. I began to imagine that we were in the mouth of some monstrous dead thing, and that the outcroppings were its teeth, ready to crunch down.

Smith did not return. We tracked him, as best we could. My torch showed the occasional footprint in the dirt, and then, suddenly, dozens of them, a jumble of prints. In the middle of these was Smith's rifle. Beyond that there was bare rock again, unmarked.

"They rushed him, the bastards." Morris picked up the rifle.

"We go back," I said. "That's enough. We've lost the advantage."

Resistance was token—a few protests that we should try to rescue Lambert and Smith, but no idea how, or where, they had been taken. They felt the same fear that I did, at least in some form—we were not meant to be down here.

We would retreat into our own gallery. We would get hungry, but there'd be air from where the camouflet had blasted through, and we could guard the hole. Guard it long enough, hopefully, for our own tunnellers to clear that main shaft.

It seemed simple when we started back, but within half an hour the compass no longer gave a reliable reading, and the oppressive gloom of the caverns confused us all. We had taken the first opening behind us, but had gone wrong—this passage opened out into the largest cavern yet.

Titanic granite boulders were strewn across the chamber floor, half-embedded in growths of the same greasy, crystalline substance, more luminescent than before. And in that suffocating light we saw a work which no German had ever carved.

The granite roof, thirty feet above us, had been scoured smooth. Cut deep into the bare rock was a single twisting design, so intricate that I could make no sense of it. Writhing but motionless, it challenged the orderly, gleaming formations of quartz below and filled us with a sick feeling of intrusion.

"Christ, I can't stand this." Clough threw down his rifle and started to run for the nearest exit. I yelled at him, my voice reverberating around us, and then we saw them. The enemy.

Figures rose from behind boulder and outcropping, men in torn German uniforms or earth-stained shirts and ragged trousers. A few held picks, but most were empty-handed. A dozen, at least, and amongst them, two who were no strangers.

"Smithie!" Sleath stepped forward, but I grabbed him.

"Look, man," I hissed.

The faces around us were not those of men, not as I would have counted them. Where eyes and brows should have been, there were thick chunks of crystal, gleaming with the same weak light as around us. I thought of the corpse we had found. Smith's cheeks were streaked with trails of dried blood, and as he turned to stare at Sleath, the idiot-slump of his gaping mouth was only too apparent.

Pigeon raised his rifle, cursing, and fired at the nearest German... creature. The shot went into its chest, but it came on, looming over him before he could clear a jam in the breech. It held him, despite Sleath's attempts to help, and then they were charging us. A second one grasped Pigeon, pulling him to his knees. Morris thrust with his bayonet, cutting deep into the thing's back. It made no apparent difference.

I pulled out my revolver and shot one in the head, only to realise that it was Lambert, the sapper. Or had been. The bullet shattered one gleaming mass embedded where an eye should have been, and what remained of Lambert let out a shrill, wordless cry.

Morris was firing at every figure near him. Bullets whined and spanged off rocks, an unholy chorus. I was forced to Morris's side by more of them, helpless to stop Pigeon being dragged away, Sleath hanging onto one thin leg until he was overwhelmed. I emptied my revolver into their assailants, but the things barely staggered with the impact.

"The heads!" I was shrieking, a counterpoint to Morris's angry growl.

Geordie managed one shot into the face of a thin, shirtless figure, dropping it, and then he too was grasped as I reloaded. Another group had come up, noiseless, behind us. I fumbled, cartridges clattering on the ground, and felt hands at my ankles and thighs. Any hope that Clough had escaped was dashed by a glimpse of him on his knees by the entrance—and by the sight of a figure grasping two long fragments of grey crystal as others held the runner down, forcing his chin to his chest and tearing hair from the back of his head…

I saw no more, thank God, for a blow to my own head rendered me unconscious at that moment.

When sense returned, I was being held almost erect by half a dozen of them, Smith amongst them. The others were Germans, but no longer the Kaiser's men. They smelled of urine and self-fouling, of decay. They were filthy, their clothes rotting, and each had chunks of crystal, two or three inches across, driven in where their eyes should have been.

I saw the marks of rank on one, the jacket still intact but torn and flapping as it moved—and a smeared photograph, sticking out of the top pocket. More unbearable than anything was this picture—a smiling woman and a child—for it said that these had been men like us, soldiers, tunnellers, taken in these dreadful depths.

"Smith," I called out, but drool ran from his slack lips, and he paid no heed. As they dragged me on, I saw Morris's body. He had my discarded revolver in his hand, and a bullet hole in his temple. A better end than the rest of us had found.

I looked away, up to the cavern roof. We were passing that terrible carving which moved and did not move. Passing, but moving on a curious, circling path, as if we should not walk directly below it. I was pushed with the mob, unable to avoid contact with their greasy, clammy flesh, until the far opening came in sight.

As with the seal on the roof, no natural force had made this gaping mouth. I judged it to be forty feet across, and twenty deep, outlined by carvings which lacked sense or meaning. Ropes of granite twisted around what might be symbols, but they seemed to slide into the other, and I was forced to look away, to stare into the blackness beyond.

No gleam of crystal, no single reflection from the main cavern. Utter darkness, that dreadful moment when the candle fails and you are alone in the tunnel, blind.

At any moment I expected to be driven to the ground, for my skull to be breached and for my humanity to be lost, but the figures urged me forward, to the edge of the opening. Hands, whole or rotting, thick-fingered or claw-like, clutched at my shoulders, my hips, and held me there, immobile…

Beyond the sinuous carvings around this entrance, deeper than I could guess, something stirred...

If, in church, I had ever felt the presence of God, then this was His counterpart—not Lucifer, nor any Biblical adversary, but the antithesis of deity. A knowing void, an impossibility.

I felt it reaching into me, and in the process, I felt also the way in which it caressed the ones who held me, controlled and nurtured them. It saw me, through those crystal mockeries of eyes. From it came a questing, a need. This void shed monstrous thoughts as it wormed its way into the galleries of my memories, tunnelling into sudden spaces filled with what I had been. I knew, without logic or rational consideration, that as I was prisoner to these creatures, so that which lay below me was captive, contained. It was a darkness which welled with an icy fury, awoken by its chance encounter with the world of Man.

I pitied us all, then—myself, the men who had trusted in me, and the Germans who had first become its thralls. Pity did not interest this presence. It drove into my mind as callously as it had formed the ones who held me. Why it did so, I cannot tell. A random insanity, or some failing in what it had achieved thus far—the discovery that its own actions had destroyed the minds from which it might have learnt.

It reached deep, clumsily. I saw my father, that slow, shovel-handed man who tried to be kind and so often failed; my mother's pale, oval face as she visited his grave in the Transvaal, a dusty hummock amongst dozens like it. Part of me was in the cavern mouth—part of me followed the presence's search within me.

If I had no understanding of what it was, it had little understanding of the human mind. I felt its incomprehension. More than once I thought that it recoiled from my memories. And then, just as I felt sure that I was soon to be discarded and consigned to that dreadful, blinded crew, it broke into a new place.

"Here, lad, close one eye and look through the other," said my father, the rough material of his uniform pressed against my bare arms. I should have been in bed, but he'd shared a beer with his mates, and we were in the back garden, his old telescope to hand. "The moon's easiest— craters and all—and then we can try some of the brighter stars."

I held onto his arm, a moment of warmth and security, of rare love, as we scanned the heavens together, father and son...

My Flanders body jerked, spasmed in the depths and almost tore itself from my captors' arms as the monstrous presence ran wild through my brain, scattering and confusing memories. Venus, low on the horizon, and my mother taking the brass telescope to the pawn shop. My first attempt to find the Pole Star. A picture I drew of the Man in the Moon, grinning like old Mr Clegg from down our street...

I swear that the bedrock moved. Around me, crystal columns shattered, razor-edged fragments striking the insensate men next to me, and a shard cut open my cheek. Their grip weakened as the presence in the depths recoiled from me.

It had seen. I had seen.

As much as it could read from me, I read from it, and would never be able to forget. That it was bound, it knew, and its fell malignity had fed upon that frustration for such spans of time as I could not grasp. But now...

My father had taught me the stars, and they were wrong. Not wrong for a man and his ten-year-old son, crouched in a Surrey garden— but for this terrible thing trapped within the depths of Flanders, to which I had brought a new madness.

This place was its prison, which fuelled hatred enough. What shuddered the earth at that moment was its sight of the heavens above our planet, excavated from my mind. Heavens where the stars which hung on cold velvet were so alien to the presence that it found no sense, not even the vaguest comprehension of their configuration.

It had thought itself held, confined in some corner of its own time and space, but now it knew.

It was lost.

Utterly lost.

The hands fell away from me, the presence withdrawn into a roiling fury greater than any before. Touched by its madness, those around me staggered blindly, and I ran. An overwhelming need for escape possessed me, nor do I think that the emotion came only from within myself.

Shoving a German aside, I blundered into and over shattered crystal; I fell and rose again, many times, until blood ran down my arms and legs. I cannot know what God or instinct took me to the original fissure by which we had entered the nightmare below, but there came a moment when I saw the most welcome of all sights, the discarded wrapper from a bar of British chocolate.

Weeping, I clambered up the clay slope formed by the camouflet, and found the safety of our own tunnel. Hearing no pursuit, I crawled towards the blockage in the main shaft, to claw at the wet earth with my bare hands ...

And I found physical salvation, if nothing else. Others from the 183rd must have been digging for hours. My broken nails reached into empty space, and there were men, men with eyes of blue and grey and brown, eyes which held nothing more than concern. They hauled me from there, roping me and lifting me as gently as they could to the head of the shaft.

It was night, but I could not look up.

"I need..." A sapper lifted his canteen to my lips. I drank until he took the canteen away. "I need... Major Cartwright."

The stiff-backed officer arrived in minutes, eyes dark at the bloody mess which lay upon the stretcher. At me. There was unsuspected humanity in the man, for he knelt and took one of my lacerated hands in his.

"It's alright, Allen. The doctor is coming." He pulled on his moustache, nervous. "The rest of your men..."

"Dead." It was as good as word as any.

"You've been lucky."

Lucky. I choked down laughter, hysteria.

"Major, for God's sake - you must blow the mines... as soon as you can."

"You need rest, Lieutenant. We'll send you back to Blighty, and..."

My grip might have been enough to crush granite. He winced as I hauled him closer.

"The German are in the depths! The Germans. I've seen them."

I described the insignia, any insignia, which I had seen upon the German tunnellers. I blocked out their faces, but babbled out every small detail I could remember. Another officer, one of the Royal Engineers, appeared, and was told the same fragmented story.

"A Saxon unit," he muttered. "They were reported east of here, a couple of months ago."

The Major frowned. "Then — "

"We can't risk waiting." The engineer was scribbling in a small notebook. "If they come up into our galleries and pull the fuses..."

I gabbled lies and truths, anything to convince them. Field telephones whirred; runners came and went. I was loaded onto a truck, and taken to a field hospital. I was waiting, waiting for what must surely be done, and I clutched my watch in bandaged fingers, possessed by the slow movement of the hands under the scratched glass. One o'clock, two o'clock...

At ten past three in the morning, while two nurses were trying to make me take a sedative, the face of Flanders changed.

I could not see it from the hospital hut, with its blanket-covered windows, but I was told that great columns of crimson flame burst from the torn earth, like Hell emerging for its due. I heard the remaining window-glass shatter, and instruments rattled in their trays. The man next to me, his face bandaged, fell from his bunk, and the nurses rushed to help him.

Explosion after explosion, in close succession, shaking the hut and driving strange, hot winds across the land. Surely, I thought, surely it would be enough. Whether or not our mines destroyed the German trenches, I did not care. My only thought was of tunnels, galleries and chambers, each of them flattened, crushed, and the blessed clay collapsing in its tens of thousands of tons to seal those terrible, crystalline depths.

A prison around a prison...

My father's eyes close, and his breathing slows. Hopefully he will sleep for a while. An old clock, left by the previous residents, ticks loud in the corner. I must see to it tomorrow, in case it keeps him awake at night. I arrange the blanket over his legs, and tuck the journal under my arm.

The words I have written must be nonsense. Better to believe that he is emerging from shell shock and madness, rather than accept what he recounted. Better to believe that my father, who has never lied to me, nor given credence to another's fancies, has been changed by war.

I step out into a blustery Scottish evening. The sky is leaden, much as the sea, and the breeze holds the iodine and salt tang of James McCallister's seaweed from across the isle. There are no stars to see, and beneath me is only solid rock.

I wonder if I should pray.

A SONG FOR
GRANITE KHRONOS

AARON BESSON

First Circle

Hey, Over here! You the F.N.G. Simmons sent over about the ops position? Alright, get your ass in here, you'll catch your death. There, much better. What's with the face? You're in a sewer an' a little smell surprises you? Oh, you're gonna to be a fun one, I can tell. Simmer down, just fuckin' with you. Simmons said you was good people, which is good enough for me. Here, have some coffee. Take a small sip, trust me on this. Yeah, warned you. Awful stuff, believe me I know. The wife makes it like tar even after forty-four years of me askin' her otherwise. Come this way. Alright, grab one of them flashlights there. The lighting here needs a helluva lot of work, but don't get it in your head to try. The lazy bastards in maintenance have been sitting' on their hands over it forever, but blow a lung if you so much as try to change a light bulb on your own. Bums, the lot of 'em. Almost enough to make you hate unions. C'mon, I'll show you the ropes.

Second Circle

Gotta be honest, when I first saw you walkin' up, I pegged you for lost. Most kids your age wouldn't think to be caught dead doin' work like this, too busy with their upstarts and their dotty coms and all that crap. I swear, whole generation with their head in the clouds, worse than the goddamn hippies, if such a thing was ever possible. "Do what you love." Heh, isn't that what you kids say? Watch your head steppin' down, that's a low pipe. Do what you love, that's precisely the type of woo-woo bullshit I'd expect from some snot nose little shit that thinks that civic infrastructure is created by goddamn unicorns.

 Smell that? That's the sewage system of a major metropolitan area. How many "sanitation engineers" do you think love rootin' around in there? Don't mean to yell at you, just bitchin'. It's not a job you're gonna love, but you gotta love how much it needs doin'. It's hilarious to think about sometimes. Get a load of this; Friend of mine, Eddie, been drivin' the garbage trucks on East Side for longer than I can remember. Anyways, Eddie's a big ol' bookworm. He was tellin' me how in India they got these things called castes. Imagine bein' born and bein' told as soon as you pop out "You're a prince, nothin' will ever change that." Fine and good, sounds like a sweet deal, right? Well, now imagine that as soon as you pop out they tell you "You're a poor piece of shit, nothin' will ever change that." That's what this caste thing is all about. Bum deal all around, I think, but what are you gonna do? Anyways, one of these castes is called untouchables. Not like that Al Capone movie from awhile back, fuckin' love that film. DeNiro is a national treasure. No, they're called that because every other caste can't stand them. They're considered filthy and low in a way we can't even begin to hate like. Here's the kicker; in Calcutta, that's in India, the richest man is the head of the garbage department! The guy's loaded. Now guess what caste he is? You got it! Ain't that a kick in the head? All these other hoighty-toighty types gotta go around knowin' that the man who could make their lives hygienically miserable and wipes his ass with more money than they could think of havin' is one of those poor bastards they look down on! How do you even begin to wrap your head around that? I bet that bastard is doing what he loves, makin' those snooty jagoffs mind their p's and q's around him. Makes me feel good, almost gives you hope, you know?

Third Circle

You'd think that stuff like that would make the really rich pricks over here piss in their punch bowls, but it ain't gonna happen. They know what I know; civilization and cities are two different things. Remember this, kid, you're never goin' to hear it admitted to elsewise: Civilization is what's shown, and cities are what's concealed. I'm not jokin', wipe that goddamn smirk off your face. Think about it; you live in this grand mix of all that is supposed to be great in the world, but you know and I know that every one of these bastards livin' here is a sandwich and a bad day away from being a complete goddamn savage. Does the city somehow magically attract the best humanity has to offer? Of course not! If nothin' else, this city is proof of how ready they are to fall back to some serious knuckle-draggin' ways.

Fourth Circle

Step down careful now, there's a bit of a slippery spot here. Whoa, you okay there? Yeah, I feel you. I got headaches when I first started down here. You do get used to it. So anyway...yeah, cities. No easy words for it. Easy, give me your hand. There you go. What you gotta remember is that all that's hidden in man is reflected in what's hidden in cities. Yeah, figured that wouldn't make much sense, still confuses the hell outta me sometimes. Such is mystery. Step down, watch your head. The city hides stuff, and odds are you'll find it down here. Believe you me, what winds up in the drainage filters is fuckin' nuts. Sure, there are good days where you find a nice watch or somethin' like that...you clean it, it's yours, by the way. Consider it a job perk...but then you find the other stuff that people really try to hide.

What was that? Yeah, you find a body or body part down here. It's a city, people think the sewer system is as good a place as any to hide a murder. We have a number for the PD when it happens, but it ain't needed often. That's not the worst you see down here. I remember a few years back, I'd been doing this job for near forever and a day and thought I'd seen it all. Then I found a backpack driftin' through the filters. Little kids bag, with Squarebob Spongeface or whatever the hell you call it. Anyway, I open it and there's a journal in it with *Bobby* written on the front in magic marker. I took a look at it, expectin' to read about how crappy school is and the like.

Nope, not even close. I ain't gonna go into it because it still makes me want to cry to think about. I don't know if Bobby threw the bag away or that bastard his mom hooked up with did, but I'd bet all the money I have that it didn't end well for the kid. They all hid it: Bobby, his journal, his mom's piece of shit boyfriend. They all hid a different, horrible part of what was goin' on, and that's why it came here. The city feeds on that concealment, it always has.

Fifth Circle

That's the problem with all of this, how people think it all works. Sure, you'll get people thinkin' they have at least a bit of a grasp on how bad it is, but once you listen to them for more than five minutes, you realize they don't have a clue. It's been the case since we fell outta the trees. We wrap ourselves up in the make-believe of being more than we are and bein' capable of more than we are, then forget that we did it. For instance, you never thought the sewers went down this far, didja? They have to, the filth just runs that deep. That's the important thing to remember; the filth runs that deep. That's how cities are, that's how people are, because there's a connection there. Consider that the first gospel.

Easy now. Here, lean over and breathe deep. There you go. You're goin' to be gettin' somethin' like a migraine halo. Ever have a migraine? Count your blessings, my aunt Tilly in Hoboken got them somethin' fierce and had to roll one of them damn oxygen tanks around with her just to make the pain a little tolerable. Anyway, after that you're goin' to be seeing some things. All I can say is go with it. This is an important step, and how you roll with it is gonna define a lot. If you've made it this far, that means you could be part of the rememberin'. Not gonna spoil it for you, you'll see.

Sixth Circle

C'mon, stay with me. You're doin' great. I know it's hard, but you need to work through this. I only sanctified the coffee enough to open the memory for you. You do as well as I think you're gonna do, you'll have full sacraments in no time. Anyway, you need to see the source of the memory, otherwise it's all gonna flow where it wants to, and that didn't work for them so well before. That's a poor choice of words, *them* is sort of a broad term. Has the memory sung the names to you yet? Don't try to talk if you can't, just nod yes or no. Okay, good, that saves some time. The Old Ones... they didn't exactly have a good turn of events, but still better than the young 'uns. We don't really say or think their names if it can be avoided, they're still pretty toxic. If all goes well you'll learn them in time, but I'm gettin' ahead of myself. Anyway, the young 'uns weren't too forward thinkin' when they came here from There, didn't respect their limits. They thought if they ran with their nature that it would be the purest expression of what they were and where they came from. They never expected here to be a sick spot for them, and it was too late when they figured it out, at least for awhile. You ever see *War of the Worlds*? H.G. Wells? Anyways, the Martians are kickin' ass and takin' names all over the place, then they get laid out flat with a flu, wipin' em' all out. That's what happened to the young uns', more or less. Sure, they were toxic to this place, but it goes both ways. Our cosm was toxic to them too. They were halfway gone before they even figured it out. Nobody's perfect, I guess.

The cities are a memory of them, you have to be seein' that now. Yeah, I know that look. Again, really sorry about this. Those things crawlin' over those giant carcasses you're seein'? That was us. It's unpleasant to think about, and try not to dwell on that too much, but accept it quick. With what time really is, that was practically yesterday when all that happened. The young 'uns were still rottin' when What We Were and Are came about, and what was left of their corpses fed us for millennia. What We Were and Are scrabbled over them like they were streets and buildings, never realizing they were corpses. What hadn't rotted away was the least poisonous of them, but dammit if it didn't taint us anyway, body and whatever else there is to us.

Yeah, that's why cities attract and repulse us. I see you're gettin' it now. That's good, that's real good.

Seventh Circle

Here, lemme help you up. Bend forward a bit, that'll keep the nausea down. Go ahead and let it out. It's okay to cry, I wept like a baby when I first did the rite of passage, everyone does. Well, almost everyone. Jim Whitaker, the guy who initiated me, he told me how every so often there's one who's just ready for it like they were born to it. They go through the memory with this smile on their faces and no pukin' at all and are just in the fuckin' moment of it. You'd think they'd be some sort of chosen one for the job, but nothin' could be further from the truth. Not only do they tend to wind up shootin' their mouths off to the wrong people, but the young uns' do not approve of it either. None of this works if we truly embrace it all the way. They need our inner revulsion along with our physical filth, plain and simple. The resistance, that sense of atrocity, it's something they feed on. They can never return any other way.

Raisin' the great cities of the world where the essence of where they lay dreamless isn't coincidence. They drew us here through what we ate of them eons ago, leading' us to build over and into where they wait. Civilization ain't nothin' more than a life support system for them, and we are both their nurses and their hospital food. Sure it's a shitty way to live, but you saw how we were? Crawling over their corpses like mad ants? Where we were once parasites, we are now...what's that word Eddie used? Oh yeah, symbiotes. The city is the black alchemy between us and them, their bones of granite and steel that we crawl over and feed from as they feed off of us. If you think about it, these sewers are the best thing we've ever done. That'd give those hoighty-toighty jagoffs in their art galleries a kick in the ass, huh?

Eighth Circle

Hey, don't puke there, come over to here. Right into that line there, there you go. Consider it like prayin'. Not that it'll bring you anythin', but it does make the memories mellow out some. No, they never truly go away. You learn to live with it, or at least I hope you do. I'm gettin' way too old for this shit, and need to pass a lot on to you if this all works out.

We're almost there, lemme help you down. Shhh, don't scream, that's just them getting' to know you. Just like shakin' hands. Shhhh, just like shakin' hands.

Okay, here we are. Got your flashlight? Excellent. I need you to go in and look down there. You need to see. I'll wait right here for you, there you go.

Ninth Circle

Okay, I got you. Here, take a drink of water. Don't go rubbin' your eyes now, let the blood stop on its own. Trust me here, you're doin' great. Just let it stop on its own.

You did fantastic. You can start Monday.

UNDR

SARAH PEPLOE

Her first time in this city and barely five minutes out of the train station, but already Rosie liked it; the architecture, the way everyone carried themselves, like they were all madly in love with themselves and had damn good reason to be, but their self-love would not scrape up against yours. It could encompass you too. Affable. That was the word. It was not a soft or rarefied place, but it had a great affability blowing through it with the summer breeze of roadworks and knock-off market perfume. A woman with a parakeet and half a bottle of Frosty Jack soaked her feet in a fountain beneath a statue of some dignitary or other. People were leaving work, in heels and suits, in polo shirts with name tags on, striding free. Plenty of kids in uniform tearing about too, though the schools would have kicked out a couple of hours ago.

A gang of hard-looking teenage girls filled up the pavement ahead, the kind of girls Rosie would have been scared of when she was a teenager. She would have been steeling herself for their hate as she approached, hoping it would only be verbal. But they moved to let her pass and one of them said to her friends, in tones of apparently sincere approval, "Ey, look at that lady's bag." It was her laptop bag, which had the fluffy face of a monster, with fang-shaped clasps and bulging plastic eyes. Presumably. Rosie couldn't imagine the kid getting excited about her little wheelie.

Good omen, Rosie told herself. She had been in two minds about bringing the laptop. She didn't want Cal to kick off at the sight of it. She honestly didn't plan to use it this weekend, except on the train. It had been good to get some writing done, on the way here. Thought seemed to flow better when she was on the move.

Her phone chirruped in her hand. She'd texted Cal when she'd gotten off the train, now he was replying:

Cool :) checked in a bit ago :) am in the foyer x

She swept into Maps with a finger, and made her way towards where he was waiting.

Rosie almost walked past the entrance. It looked like another upmarket office block, all glass and steel. Just one storey high, though, unlike its neighbours. And unlike its neighbours, it had an A-board standing in front of it, which was what made her stop and take notice. The board had the hotel's name, its TripAdvisor rating, and some of the programmes, websites and listicles it had featured in, all written in metallic markers.

She looked to her left. There was the name again, above the automatic doors. Thick block letters in burnished metal, with a jagged line running halfway through them like a horizon: UNDR. She went in.

Cal had said foyer; it was more like an anteroom. Small and sleek, with two sets of lifts at the back wall. Whites, greys and silvers abounded. She thought of spaceships, airlocks. It looked like the future.

There was a receptionist with a curly moustache and a bow tie, and a long-sleeved shirt with some kind of pattern on it that Rosie couldn't recognise. He smiled at her from behind a stand-up desk like a lectern. There were some lost-weekend-looking boys in backpacks, scratching necks and elbows, just leaving. And there was Cal. He hopped out of the hanging egg chair and they met and kissed. Cal broke off first and said "She's with me," to the receptionist.

The things he came out with sometimes, in utter straight-faced guilelessness! The things he thought needed clarifying! It was plain funny, but there was also a deep-seated relief there behind Rosie's giggle. That they could not see each other in the flesh sometimes for weeks and weeks, but when they reunited, they would both be the same as they ever were. The receptionist laughed too.

"Enjoy, guys," he said and busied himself with the tablet on the front of the lectern thing.

Rosie and Cal walked hand in hand to the lifts at the back of the room.

"Tiny, isn't it?" Rosie said.

"No." Cal was grinning. "It's huge. You didn't look it up?" He'd offered no details about the place, only that it was central, and cheap, and unusual. He pressed the button for the lift. A little down-pointing triangle.

They descended six floors. There were eleven in total.

"So, we're really...subterranean?" Of course, Rosie had been in underground car parks and clubs before, but there, you took the stairs or a ramp, you were eased under on a gradient, gradually. This was different. She felt like it should feel different, shuttling right down into the earth. More...profound.

"Welcome to my secret underground lair," he Dr Evil-ed in her ear. They snogged like teenagers, as was their way when they were alone together in lifts, even if nowadays it was more habit than passion.

▼▼▼

The sixth floor (or minus-sixth, Rosie thought) was almost painfully bright, but no windows. A window would have been a cool touch, a viewing panel, like a worm farm. But there were none. Just jointed grey walls, and the occasional poster showing various millennial professionals having fun, tinted silver. And white-grey doors either side with numbers written on the key panels, the numbers glowing, phosphorescent-looking. It smelt very recently cleaned.

They were in room 624. The room was small. It was the same colour as the rest of the building and had the same scrubbed, sanitised smell. She thought again of spaceships, of hurtling deeper and deeper into space in a white-grey plastic cell. There was the soft, constant whirr of aircon all about them; it didn't seem to have a single source.

On closer inspection, the room had oddly the look of having been slotted together, like a plastic puzzle you might get in a cracker. Rosie saw that a lot of these corners and folds were chairs, tables, bits of the room that could be folded out. There were also screens, sockets and keypads here and there. A phone-sized flatscreen with an image of a dial on it, above the bed.

The plastic pieces had stickers on them, densely symbolled written instructions for Getting The Most Out Of Your Stay. Too much information; her brain rebelled and she turned away. There was a stencil of a city skyline—not the city they were in, just a city, a non-specific jag of skyscrapers—on the wall.

She slid her bags under the bed. Cal hadn't said anything about the laptop, for which she was thankful. She sat on the edge of the mattress and slipped her flip-flops off, feeling odd. Boxed in, that was it. So completely enclosed. Even a public toilet, a fraction of the size of this room, would've had just a little square of frosted glass to let the world in. Unless it was a Portaloo, but she avoided those where possible.

"I really feel weird not having a window," Rosie said.

"There's a picture of a window," Cal said, pointing to the stencil.

"Yay?"

"And you can have all different lights. The same kind of light as you'd get through a window, any time of day." His thumb circled the dial above the bed and the room filled with a mild, purplish light. "This one's supposed to be calming."

"It's like living in a bruise."

"Well, there's other options." He thumbed again and the light changed to a pink glow. "Hay clarse brothel." Cold blue. "Anti-junkie toilet." Another swipe and it cycled rapidly between all three, violet, blue, pink. "Bisexual disco. Sky's the limit."

"What sky?"

He clicked his tongue. "Are you gonna be a mardarse all weekend?"

"Depends." She laid back on the bed and drew him close to her with a leg.

▼▼▼

It wasn't that bad really, Rosie decided afterwards, while they lay together in a sprawl of bedding and clothes. It was only a room, and only a base, and only for the weekend. It was cheap as chips, and five minutes from everything they might want to do or see. It was what they made of it.

Cal was lying with his head on her breasts. She twiddled his longish, straw hair absentmindedly. She always lost track of time when sex was involved, but she thought it must be about seven o'clock. She was starting to get hungry. Beside the bed, one of the cracker-puzzle plastic slabs of the wall bore the legend ROOM SERVICE! in fun, chunky silver letters. There was a laminated menu hanging to one side, and a phone to the other. Below ROOM and above SERVICE! were handles—she realised it was a dumbwaiter. There must be one in every room; you wouldn't even need to throw a T-shirt on and open your door. She laughed softly. This is like how they thought the future would be in the sixties, she was about to say to Cal, when she realised he was asleep. She thought to reach for the menu, which was attached to the wall by a chain at the perfect length to read in bed, but she didn't want to disturb him so she laid back. Soon her breath slowed to match Cal's. Her head fell to one side and her fingers dropped from his hair.

Hours later, Rosie woke, briefly but completely, with an acute jab of fear. The lights were still on. Mundane reality clearly lit all about her. It didn't help. She still had the distinct feeling that her and Cal were one and the same, and what they were was something small in a forest, tilting its head and waiting. Knowing, as a standing truth of the world, that it is being snuck up on, but not knowing how or from which direction.

But if they had been in a forest, it would have been their home too. It would have supported their life as well as the things that preyed on them. Their senses would have guided them, given them a head start at least. Here, they could have been anywhere. No light but the internal electrics, no sounds but the aircon, nothing human, nothing organic—

But then she thought she heard feet, shuffling, and the rattle-click-thud of an old suitcase, dragged complainingly down the hall. This calmed her. She reached up to the dial on the wall and turned the lights off completely, then laid back down to sleep. The aircon sighed and hissed above them.

Rosie and Cal woke together some hours hence, confused and hungry in the dark, feeling fundamentally out of sync. Both their phones had died at some point in the night. They put them to charge and turned on the TV. The blue sky behind the cheery presenters anchored them. Saturday morning. Cal worked out that the room had pre-programmed settings, so you could set it to slowly brighten as day broke, then darken as night fell. He dialled the room to a morning sort of light to match the TV.

There was a different receptionist on the front desk, a chirpy, lilac-haired girl this time, wearing the same sort of long-sleeved, obscurely patterned shirt as yesterday's incumbent. Must be part of the uniform. Rosie couldn't imagine anyone choosing to wear that on a day this sunny. At Rosie's request, she recommended a café round the corner.

"We do dumbwaiter room service too," she said, "I don't know if you were aware? Full English, eggs benedict, bircher muesli, whatever you like, *pshu*" —she gestured with ring-tattooed, neon-nailed fingers— "straight down to you."

"We saw," said Rosie. "Cool."

"So extra, innit," the girl said. "It's like how they thought the future would be in the sixties."

▼▼▼

They had breakfast and explored. A couple of art galleries, a hipster barbeque lunch, then shirt shopping for Cal. It was good being together, not thinking about the weird room and what the girl had said. I must just have an unoriginal mind, Rosie thought.

Doing stuff—Rosie had never been fond of the way people talked about "doing" a city or a country—started to get wearing. They went and sat together in the sun, near where Rosie had seen the parakeet woman the day before. The spray of the fountain took the edge off the heat. It was still the bright, airy, affable city she'd first arrived in.

"This is nice, isn't it?"

"Yeah," Cal said. "You know, it could always be like this."

"Mm." She laid her head on his shoulder.

"Serious," he went on. "Why don't we move here?"

"What about uni? What about your work?"

"I could find a job here. And you could commute. It's not that far. Anyway, you barely have to be there for a PhD, right?"

"It's not that—"

"Simple, yeah yeah, nothing's that simple. Always got to think everything into mince, haven't you."

His shoulder turned to gravestone granite under her cheek. She didn't say anything. She didn't want to make it worse. They sat in silence for a while, then Cal sighed and said "Let's just go back."

Their hands crept into each other's on the short walk to the hotel. That was something, Rosie thought, right? She snuck glances at him, trying to read his face. He did the same to her, but they never seemed to time it right, so they were looking at each other, until they got to the minus-sixth floor. He was skull-shadowed by the lights, he looked lost. He wrapped her in a hug.

"Baby," she said. "It's alright."

"I feel like it's leaking away," he moaned faintly.

"What?"

"This weekend. All of it."

"It's not. It's not. I love you," she whispered into his chest, his chin, his ear, she was on tiptoes now, feeling like she was about to trip and fall but not caring. He held on to her and told her he loved her too. She thought she heard people's luggage again. Coming from the fifth floor. Or fourth.

Reconciled, later, they walked back out into a half-dangerous Saturday night. The streets were thronged with young-seeming gangs of girls and boys, one with blood down his shirt already, but they were all headed for the bigger clubs and Rosie and Cal, these days, preferred interesting little places. Somewhere you could find a seat and have a conversation and the drinks weren't just there for getting you pissed enough to dance till you got thirsty enough to buy more drinks.

There was a fun-looking cellar bar, enticing you down its stairs with Bowie B-sides and walls painted pink as a throat, but they agreed they were more in the mood for the place with the rooftop terrace. It turned out to be a good choice, surprisingly quiet and with an offer on mojitos.

"Am photosynthesising," Rosie said, leaning her head back into the night sky, pleasingly tipsy. It had only just gone completely dark.

"Don't you need sunlight for that?" Cal was stroking her arm. She looked back at him across her shoulder, noticing as she did so that she had a little sideways diamond-shaped mark there. It might have been from the strap of the laptop bag rubbing against her. More likely it was a hickey.

"You are my sunlight," she sang inaccurately.

"Evening. Or morning," the receptionist smiled. A different receptionist again. They exchanged waves, Rosie and Cal gregarious in their drunkenness. The receptionist's shirt was rolled up to his elbows.

"Are you hungry?" Cal asked Rosie at the lift.

"We can do room service," the receptionist piped up. "All by dumbwaiter." When they looked back at him he was buttoning the cuffs at his wrists.

"Maybe just get some chips," Rosie murmured to Cal. "There was a van up the road."

"Sure. If you want to go back out there. So hard to go back out when you're in, isn't it? And round here it can get a bit, like, lairy. I'm sure you noticed. But we can do you chips, or whatever you like. Fully licensed, too." He gave them a thumbs-up.

"Cheers. We'll give it a think."

In the lift, Rosie whispered "I don't think they want us to leave. Like, see how him on the desk was? And all the stuff written round our room. It's so...nice, but under the surface it's saying, look at all the things we can give you, right here. Stay here. Stop in till morning. Or stop out till morning, if you like, just don't go leaving once you're in..."

Cal put an arm round her as they stepped out into the corridor. "That's called convenience, love. Most people like it."

They had almost reached their room when Rosie halted suddenly, in front of a poster.

"What's that, Cal?"

"How many have you had?"

"That." The poster showed three women sitting around a table, laughing uproariously over an unopened bottle of wine. The wall-slabs behind it weren't fully flush with each other so the poster frame was pushed out slightly. And from behind it, a long trail of something thick and yellow-green was seeping.

Rosie reached to touch it, then stopped herself. It smelled like the strongest, most astringent cleaning material imaginable, but also profoundly dirty.

"Are we—off?" she asked.

"What?" He looked hurt.

"I don't mean us! I mean this place. It's off centre, sort of. Don't you think? The door, for one. It wasn't like this." She pointed, not to their door, but to room 623. The door was six inches or so down the corridor from their own. "It was dead on, before."

"I...no, hotels don't make it so opposite doors are directly opposite. 'Cos it feels awkward if you come out of your room and you're staring dead into the eyes of some rando. I read that somewhere."

She looked back at the poster. The liquid crawling out towards the floor ever so slowly. It had a lustre to it, like an ugly jewel. Just some forgotten chemical. It'd be wiped away in the morning.

But in the room Rosie was unsure again. Hadn't those pieces by the toilet door been differently tessellated? Hadn't they looked more like a neat grid?

Unseen, things could be shifting. Anything could happen under here, it was—it was liminal space, the phrase of countless seminars and tutorials. But they weren't, were they. Hotels, under ground, underground hotels—all were very definite places unto themselves. She only thought of them as liminal because *she* did not belong.

Cal flopped happily onto the bed. Rosie went into the bathroom to take her makeup off and drink some water. The combination of the toilet to her left and the plastic surroundings were disquietingly reminiscent of a Portaloo. She hated them because of a story she'd been told once. Probably apocryphal, but still. A friend-of-a-friend-of-a-friend using one at a festival and someone else tipping it over. The filth of thousands washing over them like a nightmare snow globe.

▼▼▼

They slept till noon, heedless of the settings Cal had programmed the previous morning, and ordered massive hangover breakfasts from the dumbwaiter. It was the quickest room service Rosie had ever had. When the lights by the metal lettering lit up and Rosie reached in to take the plates out she smelt that clean-dirty smell again, roaring like a wind through the shaft. But the food was delicious.

After breakfast, they went out and looked round museums. Rosie hoped desperately that they wouldn't run out of things to do. They needed a good stock of reasons to be out of the room, above ground, not locked underneath in that hateful little wipe-clean cave. Organic matter in the earth. Either it's thrusting to the surface as quick as it can, or it's rotting there.

But they probably wouldn't. Run out of things to do. This was their last night after all. The last time they would sleep together for a month or two, maybe longer. Was it leaking away, like Cal said? she wondered. Whatever *it* was? Time, their time, everything?

They were standing in front of an Irish Elk fossil together. "Room service again tonight?" Cal said.

Rosie tilted her head, considering. The room service food was cheap and tasty. Staying in meant more time in the room, but going out meant having to come back to it. All the weird things they might see and feel on the way back down and in. And she wanted, most importantly of all, to be happy with him.

She nodded. He kissed the top of her head. They took a selfie with the elk, its antlers outspread above them, a canopy of bones.

Rosie lay on the bed, typing and imagining sky. It was getting late, but was probably still light outside, she decided. She was working on the laptop. Unformed notes poured out under her fingers. Just a few brief ideas on the intersection of gender and class which she thought would pull her chapters on moral panics together. Cal was having a shower. He wouldn't hear. She meant to be quick, but ideas kept growing on ideas and she had to get them down. This room was the mirror opposite of the places she usually liked to sit and write in. So it was odd, her thoughts being so fertile under here. Like a weird little sunless hothouse—

"Shit," Cal said, with real rancour. He was standing in the bathroom doorway, dripping.

She felt caught, but hot on the heels of her guilt was defiance. Was she supposed to sneak around him, learning and thinking only discreetly?

"I'm finished now, look." She was shutting the laptop down, strapping it back in to the monster's face.

"I thought you weren't going to, this weekend. You said you wouldn't."

"It's *only some notes.*" She reached for the menu and passed it to him. "What're we having for tea?"

He sighed through his nose like a bull. "It's not only some notes though. It's me asking you to not do something totally reasonable for just two days and you have to try and do it in a sneaky way—"

"I don't think I should have to do it in a sneaky way," she started to say, but he was ploughing on—

"—because you know—"

"*What* do I know?" Rosie asked. Cal did that bull-sigh again.

"It's...just...wasting. Everything. You know you can't stay curled up in university forever, you've got to go into the real world—"

"Like you, you mean?" Nasty, but she felt too riled to feel bad about it.

"Yeah, like me, the fate worse than death." He looked so hurt and tired, like they'd been locked in some miserable impasse for hours. They'd had a nice day. It bewildered her.

"Why are we fighting about nothing?" she asked. He cracked out a bitter laugh.

"Oh right, because you're always so nice and innocent and I'm the stupid bastard picking a fight, well maybe I *am* innocent and you're the—" he half-said *clever*. It withered away into a sigh. Then seconds on seconds of quiet.

"Clever bitch?" said Rosie.

"I didn't say th—"

She was out of the room, down the corridor, back towards the lift.

She didn't have her purse, phone, key card, anything with her. It was a silly, drama-queenish thing to do, storm out like that. But she couldn't endure it, being with him in this sunless clench of a building. She was compelled upwards, like a shoot. She had to move through the air, get into the light—even if it was sodium-grubby dusk light by now—breathe some air that didn't taste recycled and think, think. She had to get out of the bowels of the fucking earth.

She realised, with a snarl of frustration, that she was going the wrong way. Stupid. She'd turned right instead of left and was further than ever away from the lifts.

Or—no. She *had* turned left. Hadn't she? She had.

There had to be stairs, for fire safety, she reasoned. Not just the poxy lifts. So she'd come to a flight of stairs at some point if she kept walking. She turned one more corner, then another.

Then Rosie came to an impossible turn, not something that belonged in a sensible corridor. It was too tight. Almost a curl. She thought at first of things like donuts, Cumberland sausages. How could such architecture accommodate the rooms along here? Then she noticed it didn't. There were the walls, which seemed for all their plastic newness to warp and bulge like centuries-old buildings, but no doors. The weird smell that had leaked from behind the poster yesterday, it was stronger here. Overpowering.

There were emergency exit signs, lit up, overhead. With the arrow and the picture of the little running person. She had been following them. She was sure had already passed five or six of the things. Where were the stairs? Or if she'd turned as many corners as she thought, shouldn't she have come back on herself by now? Shouldn't there be at least a clue to the way up, the way out? Panic started to yammer in her head, *I can't be under, can't be so far under so much earth, packed tight as stone, can't breathe—*

Ground yourself, she told herself, but the word *ground* in her head made her moan out loud with fear. Come on. Five things you can see. Wall. Sign. Hand. Other hand—

Something like a chicken fillet the size of a Labrador scuttled round the corner towards her. Its eight pointy feet clicking on the floor, its lumpen tail thudding behind it. A scream flew out between Rosie's fingers. The thing didn't seem to notice.

"Don't be afraid," someone said.

"It's flora, of a kind." Someone else. Both voices familiar, but indistinct, mucoid.

"It does good works. Breaks things down."

"Helps keep things moving. That's important."

It was the receptionists. The first two. There was a corridor ahead, that hadn't been there before. They were standing side by side in it. The light was dimmer, down here. Rosie had left the hotel's surgical brightness far behind.

"Why would you leave?" the male one asked.

"You didn't need to leave your room," said the female one. "You had everything you needed in there. We could reach you if we needed to."

"Foolish."

Rosie's feet were moving, spreading apart of their own accord.

"What is this?" She asked. The floor was splitting like orderly ice floes under her feet, and under that—flesh. Red-grey-green and slick as the inside of an eyelid. She turned her head. Already the corner she had come round was invisible to her, twisted and swollen shut.

"Why did you choose to stay here?" said the woman, not unkindly.

"I didn't. M-my boyfriend—"

"Why did *he* choose to stay here?"

"Unusual," she managed. "Central."

Rosie saw the gleam of teeth under the moustache, then. "Yeah. You don't get much more central than this."

"It's alive," Rosie whispered. "The whole earth?"

"No. It lives in the earth."

"It shall inherit the earth," the male receptionist laughed softly. Rosie hopped to a larger slab of floor. This only brought her closer to the receptionists. She tried to support herself on the fragmenting walls. The slime she had seen behind the poster, yesterday, was here again, glossy, inches thick on every meaty surface.

"You thought—futuristic, no? No. Quite the opposite. We crawled from the seas and from the trees at its sufferance and walked above it, likewise, at its sufferance. Slipped down through its pores, by its sufferance."

The space around her undulated. She stumbled—if she threw out a hand to break her fall, would that stinking goo burn her to the bones? She dropped to a crouch, to her knees. It was easier.

"That is the arrangement. For its part, it...acquires. Feeds. Mostly a little, sometimes a lot. It can consume, at every part of its self. Their organs aren't quite like ours. That's why we're so *temporary*, in comparison."

Rosie was finding it harder now to tell which of the receptionists was speaking. Sometimes it seemed the voice of one came from the mouth of the other.

"You like to wonder at things," they said. "Well, isn't that wondrous? And these are only the guts." The receptionists were so joyous, wedding joyous, childbirth joyous. "Imagine the heart. Imagine the head."

They moved still closer to Rosie, treading blithely on the flesh of the floor. Both were shirtless, and wore nothing else on top. Even as Rosie hated them, she felt a twist inside for their sheer humanness, the slight paunch, the different-sized breasts. They were covered in little sideways sores like diamond mouths.

"And it bides. Hibernating, I suppose is the closest you could get, in our language. When it is strong enough, it will stir."

"It won't be long now. Not for they who have waited so long."

A breeze rushed past so foul and toxic, it seemed to poison Rosie at every cell. She was retching. The stench was a solid presence like a forearm shoved down her throat. Her head ached with the effort of breathing, or not breathing. The girl with lilac hair tutted.

"To me, it smells beautiful," she said. "What's perfume anyway? Whale sick. Bee bait." She reached out and pressed her inner wrist to the wall, not the false plastic but the truth behind it. There was a bubbling, and cutting through the general reek, the smell of flesh, rendered. "This is the smell of home."

"I have to get out," Rosie croaked.

"No life *has* to do anything. Only serve. Only feed. That is the lesson of down here."

"Please." The hopelessness of trying to beg or bargain hit her like a killing fist, working its way up through her insides to meet the stench working its way down. "I wouldn't say anything, about under here. Who would believe me? Please. Just let us go."

"Us?" Their heads tilted in unison, dog-like.

"Callum," she said, so quietly. Sour spittle gathered at the edges of her mouth. "If—if you can't let me, then...but Callum, he hasn't seen any of this, so you could let him—"

"Oh. The boy. He thought you thought too much. Worried too much. But then he became worried. He came looking for you."

"So that," one or other or both of the receptionists said, "we can help with."

Callum rose out of the solid flesh walls like something bobbing from a river. There were holes sizzled through the flesh above his cheekbones. His teeth glowed through, blank and white like his rolled-back eyes.

There was enough time, just, to scream. Then the insides of the creature, the whatever-it-was that Rosie would die not understanding, rose and fell again, pressing Cal's remains into her living body. It took her, through him, for what sustenance it could. They sunk together, entirely, into the old under-here, and then they were one and the same. They were what it made of them.

TELLURIAN FACADE

CHRISTOPHER SLATSKY

Ian remembered the mossy cow skulls floating outside his window. The thought came to him like a vague dream, so distant yet intrusive he felt like a ghost invading the privacy of his own childhood.

But that was a lifetime ago. These days the only phantoms puttering around on the ranch took the shape of his father attired in the bones of a ruined past.

Josh and Lindsay's bedrooms remained just as he remembered. As each of them flew the coop their parents simply shut the doors and ignored the empty rooms—out of sight out of mind time capsules. He touched Josh's door, suppressed the memories that ran through his fingertips like a current. He wasn't looking forward to his siblings flying out, but their father's funeral meant a reunion could no longer be avoided. Even inside the house he smelled the sweet smoke of someone burning leaves on the other side of the mountain.

He still had dreams about swinging that hay hook into his dad's neck. All these years later he regretted that he never had the balls to wake up, sneak into his parent's bedroom, and sink that steel point into the fucker's throat. But no matter how many times he'd pulled the hook slit open, or how much blood he spilled onto the barn floor, he'd always wake up just as empty as he'd been before.

He wandered down the old familiar hall with its scratched wood paneling pocked by holes where 4-H ribbon awards had once been prominently displayed. An aggressive wind forced drizzle against the windows with a clatter. It sounded like an animal trying to get inside. Ian walked into the dining room.

The landline had been cut shortly after his father's illness. Ian didn't remember if he'd ever even seen him make a phone call. He was uncomfortable exploring his old home, anxious at the realization he was as isolated as anyone could be in this day and age.

He pressed a thumb against the tabletop, print perfectly captured in the dust as if he'd been booked.

It was early morning but the birch trees had grown so close to the house the only light came from the unobstructed window. A flipped switch gave no response.

Ian was grateful he'd held onto his dad's Vietnam Zippo. He wrangled up some candles. Their dim incandescence allowed him to read something engraved on the lighter.

NON GRATUM ANUS RODENTUM.

The autumn air made him feel like a kid again. The woods out back beckoned. He blew out the candles. Their waxy odor drowned out the scent of the distant blazing leaf pile.

Ian hiked further up the mountain, intoxicated by the scent of Douglas fir trees. Tangerine and scarlet and purple leaves tumbled over each other so he couldn't tell what was alive or animated by a breeze. Animals screamed, not quite chirps or yips. He wondered what had riled them up. His boots slipped in the mud. Every step forward was an accomplishment.

He hiked until he'd traveled deep enough to find his old underground fort. He'd spent an entire summer digging the pit and the passages branching off. Planned on reinforcing the walls, but couldn't lug cinder blocks this far. Adolescent dreams of miles of tunnels in his own underground empire, but all he'd managed was a shallow den and a few short crawlspaces. The whole system had caved in after a heavy rain, then brimmed with water that turned larvae infested.

A gnarled blackberry bush grew from the banks of the depression. Ian realized with a touch of sadness that his secret stash of *Devil Dinosaur* comics and Mack Bolan novels buried down there for over three decades had to be nothing but pulp now.

He gingerly pushed the thorny vines aside and found a stone wall, shin high, running alongside a tunnel split off from the foliage choked hole. It was a dark mossy green, slick from the condensation glittering like jewels on its surface. He was surprised to discover this was the natural color—no lichens grew on the marble smooth stone so tightly stacked he couldn't tell if there was any mortar. Had no idea how he could've missed the wall in all the years he'd roamed these parts.

The unusual mineral color made him think of his projectile point collection. His elementary school library had a guide that helped him become adept at differentiating a dart from an arrow tip—though his father had always insisted the ones he found on the property were thunderstones. Ian laughed at the thought; his father had also believed that animal burrows were entrances to abandoned cities.

But there'd been a knapped arrowhead he'd never managed to locate in any reference book. Made from a deep jade colored stone similar to this wall. The July he'd found it was the summer someone broke through the sliding glass door at the side of the house. Plenty of accessible rifles and trapping gear to steal, but all the bastards had taken was his projectile collection.

He pressed an ear against the wall and heard things below—watery tinkle of small stones rolling down an embankment, maybe an underground stream or lake. There were lots of subterranean reservoirs in these parts. Nez Perce had probably built this. Maybe a scrapped try at a well and geological activity had recently exposed the stones.

So much history in the forest, all kinds of wonders bound to come to the surface eventually. As his dad used to say, *Worlds buried beneath worlds.*

▼▼▼

Terminar antes de la puesta del sol, Ambrose said as if failing to finish his chores quickly would attract the attention of something he wanted to avoid. The ranch hand had shown up later than usual. Ian was glad to see him. He'd forgotten what an integral presence he'd been growing up.

The barn had fallen into disrepair. Walls sagged, marked by cavities where horses had chewed the wood raw like poorly healed wounds. The reek of mildew and manure and a stronger odor emanated from cracks in the cement floor. Ian didn't understand how sewage had managed to leak uphill from the septic tank into the barn. He said this out loud.

Pasajes secretos. Here long before the Indios, Ambrose explained.

Passages? Ian was slightly embarrassed; his mother had been born and raised in Guanajuato, but he'd only managed to pick up a smattering of Spanish. And most of that was learned from Ambrose himself.

Abandonado burrows, conectados por lo México cuevas. Indios explore, things found down there, no le gustaba.

What'd they find? Encontrar?

Oh, ancient ceremonias. Ambrose frowned.

Cómo?

Practicante de la Vias Verdes, Tlaloc fanáticos.

Ian wasn't sure what to make of this. He rolled his thumb across the wheel of his dad's Zippo, held it next to a fracture in the floor. The flame tip wavered towards the opening.

Ambrose's Mesoamerican fables were familiar, reminiscent of Ian's father whisking the family away to this ranch 35-plus years ago under the pretense he was saving them from conflicts in the Middle East, gas crises, and nuclear threats. Filled his kid's heads with tales about tribes that prospered in the Americas long before humans crossed the Bering Strait, of all manner of flesh and blood spirits slipping out of their intangible worlds to haunt this tangible soil.

As he'd told it, certain clans used to banish their strongest braves because they were just too damned good at fighting to fit into polite society. That's how he'd seen himself—didn't belong with the nine-to-fives; returned from a war tour then moved his family far away from the entropy of civilization.

A real goddamn warrior.

Fanáticos, Ian agreed.

The rift in the barn floor brought to mind cenotes, sinkholes where ancient Mayans had lowered sacrificial victims into the watery depths. Ian half expected his old man to pop up from behind a rotting hay bale like a mossy jack-in-the-box.

Ambrose didn't go to the second floor. Ian was grateful for not having to make up an excuse to avoid treading up those ominous stairs where his dad had ruined everything.

▼▼▼

Talk of tunnels inspired Ian to hike to his underground fort again. Sunlight shimmered between gaps in the cloudy sky, softly warmed the forest floor a burgundy hue.

The stone wall had ascended in the brief time he was away. He could now see petroglyphs etched into its surface. Ian estimated it was thirty feet lengthwise now. Yellow tamarack needles and alder cones were bunched around the perimeter.

Someone had started to stack stones here long ago and the lakes underfoot had moved the earth, swallowed everything, held it in its gut for ages, and now the waters were forcing the wall through the forest floor.

In a matter of hours.

This was the only scenario that made sense.

Ian placed his hands on the wall and felt something reverberating against it again and again deep below. Frenetic pummeling, rushing waters, roaring streams.

Or drumming.

That made no sense. It was water. That must be it. Subterranean rivers.

He'd come out first thing in the morning. Get some gloves. Do some measuring. Clear away those blackberry vines.

Ian began the hike back to the house. He thought the strange green sky was some weird optical illusion due to the full moon having not yet fully set. He couldn't come up with any other explanation.

Josh and Lindsay waved to get Ian's attention as he approached the luggage turnstile. His sister looked great, his brother paunchy—a barrel shaped torso gave him a bovine appearance. He'd once overheard their father say that at fourteen Josh was the mental equivalent of an eight year old. Ian wondered what mental age his forty-something brother had finally achieved.

This had stayed with him all these years, fueled his hatred of Josh as his relatives coddled and made excuses for his big brother's failures.

He'd struggled for what little he had, borne the full brunt of the bankruptcy and subsequent divorce while his parents hadn't chipped in a dime. But when Josh needed help after one of his many hare-brained schemes, there'd always been a spare room or funds to help him get back on his feet.

Ian helped them gather their luggage. They stopped at the airport restaurant before hitting the road.

His brother and sister ordered food. Ian sipped his beer at a deliberately slow pace to show how much self-discipline he'd mustered. He was on his fourth by the time the food arrived.

You two ok sleeping in your old rooms? Not much has changed. Ian spun his coaster around in a puddle of beer glass sweat.

Not much? Albino kids still tappin' at your window? Josh snorted in amusement.

Not even a goddamn Bigfoot, though I'm expectin' one'll smell your filthy ass and come a callin'.

Hah hah. Remember when you saw kids runnin' in the woods one night? Heads all weird?

Sounds like something dad made up.

Dad didn't make things up. He knew the land.

Only reason we moved to the boonies was it made it easier for him to beat the shit outta his wife and kids without any neighbors complaining.

C'mon. He knew what was what.

Yeah, knew all about cities built before the Pleistocene. He ever tell you about the Chiricahua riding pterodactyls outta tunnels in Arizona? Bullshit. Old fool knew fuck all.

Lindsay interceded, Ian please don't use big words just so you can make yourself feel smarter than your brother. And keep it down. People are looking.

Not my words. Dad's. Remember? Hollow planet, worlds beneath worlds, all that shit? A tellurian façade?

No. I don't remember. And I don't know why you feel the need to embarrass us in public. We're going to bury our father tomorrow and this is no way to honor his memory.

Ian found it difficult to restrain an outburst with the accumulation of alcohol and anger in his belly. He almost brought up what their dad had done in the barn right then and there.

Thought better of it.

Not much was said on the long drive back to the house, though Lindsay stared out her window and remarked on how wan the setting sun looked and was that the moon up already?

Ian gripped the steering wheel, stared at the gnats swirling above the rutted road in the half-light.

Nothin' but a goddamn tellurian façade, he mumbled through clenched teeth.

▼▼▼

Desangrado. Enfermedad nueva. Cuatro head of cattle, Ambrose said.

Head of cattle. It sounded weird to Ian, like the cows were missing their heads, while their round clumsy bodies still roamed around in the pasture.

You said they'd bled out?

Si. El Hombre Verde visito.

Cascar. Their back legs are broken. Ian made a snapping gesture.

Ambrose nodded, waved away a fat greenbottle fly.

Reses muertas, bring wrong animales down.

Bobcats did this?

No bobcats with luces en la montaña.

Lights?

Ambrose nodded emphatically, his battered cowboy hat slipped over his eyes. Linterna.

Poachers with lanterns. Ian was only half-joking.

Demasiado pequeños.

Mind taking care of it? I mean like con fuego? Torch 'em. Let the realtor and the next poor bastard worry about this shithole.

A horse whinnied long and loud. Ian helped Ambrose drag the cattle behind the barn. Flies swirled in the air, settled on the carcasses in black twitching blankets.

It was time to enter the barn's second floor. Ian's hands shook. He'd put it off too long. Couldn't stop thinking about his dad, sweat streaming off his angry face.

Ian, Lindsay and Josh had been building hay forts when their father stomped up the barn stairs.

He'd grabbed Josh by the throat, lifted him off the floor, backhanded repeatedly with a free hand. The boy had dangled there at the end of his dad's arm, oddly calm during the whole ordeal. Walleyed and accepting as if everyone had a father who disciplined with his knuckles.

Kids done messed up my bales!

Punched Josh in the chest so hard he flopped around like a mobile above an epileptic baby's crib.

Ian and Lindsay could only watch as their brother bawled, drool slick on a wet chin like a newborn calf.

Dad spun Josh to the wood floor, grabbed the belt loop on the back of his jeans. Pressed a knee into his son's spine, one hand around his throat, other holding onto the denim slipping over the boy's hips as Josh screamed for mom but they all knew she was in town grocery shopping and Ian could tell by his voice that this had happened so many times before and mom had never shown up then either.

Yanked the head back so he was staring directly at his brother and sister. All Ian could think of was how dad would put calves in a headlock and force feed them from a bottle.

He'd laughed at the sight of his brother sprawled there, jeans pulled down bare-ass for all to see, hay clinging to his snot sticky face like one of those magnetic toys with the iron filings beard.

This is funny? Their father's voice sustained rage.

No sir, Ian and Lindsay had replied in unison.

They'd left Josh behind and ran into the forest to swordfight each other with broken broom handles.

Ancient history, Ian said quietly. Water under bridges. The walls seemed to absorb his words, spat them back. He grabbed a tape measure, shovel and gloves. Hurried downstairs to the barn floor.

He wandered outside and found himself in the corral, in the precise spot he'd held the dog's legs down while his dad castrated it with nothing but a buck knife and rags soaked in hot water. He'd refused to allow Ian to name the animal; its sole purpose was to scare off whatever had been sneaking down from the mountain to steal chickens.

He'd mutilated the dog, left it to recuperate in the dirt, panting and whining in the muddy blood, testicles unceremoniously tossed nearby. The dog had survived the ordeal. Lived long enough to die years later when a spooked horse kicked him in the head.

Ian wasn't sure what he would've called the dog.

He waved to Ambrose, asked if he needed any help. He waved back and shook his head in the negative. Josh and Lindsay were probably still asleep. Ian had time to waste.

He trekked up the hill. Ran dog names through his head until he found himself at his fort again. He extended the tape measure along the stone wall to find it had risen even more. He removed the gloves, slid his hand across the sleek surface, fingertips dipping into the petroglyphs' grooves.

The bottom of the pit had fallen into a deep hole. The blackberry bushes were gone, presumably into the opening. He couldn't see the bottom. Three more knee-high wall sections had pierced the ground, surrounding the maw like rising antigorite towers.

Maybe there was a whole village beneath his feet.

He threw some branches into the gaping entrance, but felt wary as if standing before the chasm made him vulnerable. Josh and Lindsay were probably awake by now and wondering where he'd gone off to. He needed a shower.

He headed back down the mountain. The shovel, tape measure and gloves were left behind.

Ambrose had started to burn the cattle. Ian walked towards the plume of smoke darkening the sky like an appeasement blotting out the heavens.

▼▼▼

Ian imagined his father's skin had been so weakened by age he could press his thumbprint into it. The funeral home's deep avocado walls and tobacco stain yellow curtains accentuated the room's dinginess. It seemed fitting—there was no romance to be found in death, nothing beautiful or profound. Death was as mundane as bad breath, as glamorous as clogged pores or greasy hair.

Josh and Lindsay spoke solemnly with yet another war vet he had yet to meet. Lindsay's put upon expression let Ian know how she felt about him not participating in the conversation.

He didn't care. His father had degenerated into inert particles that represented something torn down from a former glory, tarnished by what he'd become later in life. Fucking waste matter.

The veteran noticed Ian standing alone.

I'm Donald. 1st Infantry Division. What a great man we've lost.

Thanks for paying your respects.

Least I could do. A great man.

Yeah, a real warrior, Ian said.

Lindsay glanced across the funeral home in reaction to his sarcastic tone. Ian wondered if she resented anything, if she harbored the past's poisons in a secret place. He looked away from his sister and watched Josh touch the casket as if to confirm its solidity.

Ian was impatient for the service to end, even though he was dreading following through on their father's request to bury the Vietnam Zippo in the forest where they'd dispersed their mother's ashes. But it had been one of the few requests in the will. That and passing the ranch on to his daughter and sons. He was obligated.

He was all for selling the war memento online to a collector. When he'd mentioned this to Lindsay she'd accused him of being intentionally hurtful. He hadn't told her she should be used to intentional harm.

▼▼▼

Josh scooped a shallow grave in the soft dirt. Lindsay reverently placed the Zippo in the hole, pushed soil back over it, stamped it down.

She said a prayer.

Josh's head nodded like a child doing their best to appear respectful as he wiped his muddy palms against his slacks. Ian kept glancing into the woods, wanting this all to end so he could get back to the house and the alcohol.

As they turned to head back he glimpsed a diminutive figure up on the hill moving its arms as if to catch his eye, or maybe warn him away. It was too blurry to make anything out at this distance, so he may have been waving back to a small shrub in the wind when his gaze shifted to movement in a copse of golden aspen their leaves blazing in the sunlight.

He looked back. There was no figure or foliage or anything there at all.

Ian poured Lindsay and Josh each a scotch. He was on his fifth. The dining room window gave a beautiful view of the pasture.

Went into the barn this morning, he said.

Everyone makes mistakes. Lindsay was infuriatingly calm.

Mom having kids with that sumbitch was a mistake.

Still our father, Josh said.

Ian was frustrated by his sister's refusal to back him up, infuriated by Josh's dim witted complacency. His temper flared.

Josh. He put you in the fucking hospital.

No business bein' in the barn. Josh whispered as if afraid their father was listening behind one of the bedroom doors.

Did things to us. Not just talkin' the barn here.

Still our father, Josh spoke lovingly, as if their agony had been of necessity.

That tone. That oblivious grin.

Ian loathed his brother more than anything at that moment. He was repulsed by Josh's weakness. Sickened by his degradation.

Still our father. Josh repeated.

Rage suffused Ian's body, triggered him to react without thought. He swung at his big brother's moronic face, fist landing on the left temple punch after punch.

The louder Josh shrieked the more Ian hoped that helpless child suffered terribly at the hands of their father. Thick ropes of phlegmy blood gushed across Josh's cheeks.

Lindsay pulled Ian away.

His fury made everything grainy and momentarily sapped his memory. He stormed out of the house.

He found himself standing on the second floor of the barn.

Ian sat upright at the sensation of moist breath on his face. He'd fallen asleep on a pile of damp horse blankets. It'd only been a short time; there was still daylight.

He looked around, but the barn was empty.

He walked back to the house. Josh and Lindsay were gone. Ambrose must have given them a ride into town to book a hotel. The remains of a broken bottle of scotch on the kitchen floor suggested the drama had continued without him. Ian wondered why they'd left their luggage behind. Someone had tracked clumps of sopping moss all over the house.

He sat down at the table, looked out the dining room window at the pasture's borders defined by clusters of dogwood trees truncated by a shallow crick just beginning to swell dangerously high as winter encroached, narrow one-lane blacktop road interrupted by a rickety bridge county taxes had long neglected, light and air performed their alchemy, transformed the creek water and bronzed the leaves and the driveway's wet gravel into gleaming metals, the landscape coppery from a sun that was taking its sweet time to set.

He cried, sticky tears and mucous running down his chin. Just like Josh.

Jasper. My dog's name is Jasper.

Solitude gave him free reign to continue drinking, so he did just that.

▼▼▼

Ian woke beneath a green sky. He was on the forest floor next to the pit. The shovel and gloves and tape measure were near. He threw his empty bottle of scotch into the hole. It took far too long before it struck a surface. He was startled to hear a splash as it sank into deep waters.

His legs wouldn't work.

Several malachite buildings now stood.

Monoliths risen from their graves, the original walls nearly attaining their former glory in witness to the birth pangs of an ancient city. This made so little sense to Ian he could only focus on what he assumed was a decayed stump that looked like a warrior crouching. The spear resting on the misshapen shoulder must have been an errant branch. A slab of moss covered bark peeling away gave it a cow-skull profile.

The moon was massive, the morning sun effete compared to its companion's illumination. The lunar mass moved far too quickly, like a theatrical prop pushed over the crest, sailing into the sky, hovering, a giant's idiot face projecting a magnificent verdigris glow over everything as it swelled to such a size it revealed the dark areas as mossy patches.

The moon's surface was covered in petroglyphs.

Ian's legs wouldn't respond.

He pulled himself hand over fist across the ground's crust as fragile as his dead father's skin, over unseen realms connected by hidden arteries deep beneath. The weird moon's light revealed stone stairs leading down into the pit, narrow and steep, chiseled for something much smaller than himself.

A bird called somewhere in that viridian-stone city. It sounded an awful lot like Josh screaming, then Lindsay, sometimes far away, sometimes close. Sometimes as if it were emanating from within the pit but the clatter of loose dirt falling into the opening was probably just an animal scrabbling down there. The hole groaned with the rumble of fast moving water.

I hurt my legs Lindsay! Please help me! I'm so sorry Josh! Ian shouted with no reason to think anyone was within earshot. Even so, he found the exhalation of profound silence far more disconcerting than if an ominous voice had responded.

His gaze was caught by a metallic gleam on the step, just above the point a rising tide of darkness swallowed the stairs.

He stretched his arm out to the shining object.

It was the only thing that mattered to him at that very moment. Memories of cenotes and ritual victims sacrificed to the planet's dank seeping depths trickled through his brain. But this was his. He leaned in so close his head passed the edge of the hole.

Something way down deep was running up the stairs.

Ian extended his fingers as far as he could. The pounding footfalls grew louder.

This was all he had left, the only evidence he could hold that proved his father had once been worthy of his mother's love.

He reached into the dark dribbling up his wrist until he could no longer see his hand just a hair's breadth away from the glinting artifact.

Several more footsteps joined in. The ground quaked with a proliferation of activity.

Ian's fingers closed over the cold surface of his father's Zippo lighter just as the first shape detached itself from the darkness below.

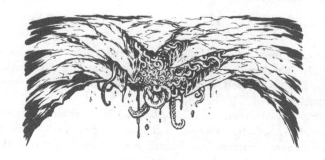

THE END OF A SUMMER'S DAY

RAMSEY CAMPBELL

Don't sit there, missus," the guide shouted, "you'll get your knickers wet!"

Maria leapt from the stone at the entrance to the cave. She felt degraded; she saw the others laugh at her and follow the guide – the boisterous couple whose laughter she'd heard the length of the bus, the weak pale spinster led by the bearded woman who'd scoffed at the faltering Chinese in front, the others anonymous as the murmur bouncing from the bus roof like bees. She wouldn't follow; she'd preserve her dignity, hold herself apart from them. Then Tony gripped her hand, strengthening her. She glanced back once at the sunlight on the vast hillside tufted with trees, the birds cast down like leaves by the wind above the hamburger stall, and let him lead her.

Into blindness. The guide's flashlight was cut off around a corner. Below the railed walk they could sense the river rushing from the sunlight. Tony pulled her blouse aside and kissed her shoulder. Maria Thornton, she whispered as an invocation, Maria Thornton. Goodbye, Maria West, goodbye forever. The river thrust into blind tunnels.

They hurried towards the echoing laughter. In a dark niche between two ridged stalactites they saw a couple: the girl's head was back, gulping as at water, their heads rotated on the axis of their mouths like planets in the darkness. For a moment Maria

was chilled; it took her back to the coach – the pane through which she'd sometimes stared had been bleared by hair cream from some past kiss. She touched what for a long time she couldn't bring herself to name: they'd finally decided on Tony's "manhood".

On the bus she'd caressed him for reassurance as the bearded woman's taunts at the Chinese grew in her ears; nobody had noticed. "Tony Thornton," she intoned as a charm.

A light fanned out from the tunnel ahead; the tallow stalactites gleamed. "Come on, missus," the guide called, "slap him down!"

The party had gathered in a vault; someone lit a cigarette and threw the match into the river, where it hissed and died among hamburger papers. "I am come here to holiday," the Chinese told anyone who'd listen.

"Isn't it marvellous?" the bearded woman chortled, ignoring the spinster pulling at her hand. "Listen, Chinky, you've come here *on* holiday, right? *On* holiday. You'd think English wasn't good enough for him," she shouted.

"Oh, Tony, I hate this," Maria whispered, hanging back.

"No need to, darling. She's compensating for fear of ridicule and he's temporarily rootless. He'll be back home soon," he said, squeezing her hand, strong as stone but not hard or cold.

"Come on, you lot," the guide urged them on, holding his flashlight high. "I don't want to lose you all. I brought up last week's party only yesterday."

"Oh, God! Oh, hoo hoo hoo!" shrieked the boisterous couple, spilling mirth. "Hey, mate, don't leave me alone with him!" screamed the wife.

The party was drawn forward by a shifting ring of light, torn by stalactites like tusks. Behind her Maria heard the couple from the niche whisper and embrace. She kissed Tony hungrily. One night they'd eaten in a dingy cafe: dog-eared tablecloths,

congealed ketchup, waitresses wiping plates on napkins. At another table she'd watched a couple eat, legs touching. "She's probably his mistress," Tony had said in her ear; gently he showed her such things, which previously she'd wanted to ignore. "Do you want me to be your mistress, Tony?" she'd said, half laughing, half yearning, instantly ashamed – but his face had opened. "No, Maria, I want you to be my wife."

Deep in shade a blind face with drooping lips of tallow mouthed. Peering upwards, Maria saw them everywhere: the cave walls were like those childhood puzzle pictures which once had frightened her, forests from whose trees faces formed like dryads. She clung to Tony's arm. When they were engaged she'd agreed to holiday with him; they'd settled for coach trips, memories to which they had returned for their honeymoon. One day, nine months ago, they'd left the coach and found a tower above the sea; they'd run through the hot sand and climbed. At the top they'd gazed out on the sea on which gulls floated like leaves, and Tony had said "I like the perfume." "It's lavender water," she'd replied, and suddenly burst into tears. "Oh, Tony, lavender water, like a spinster! I can't cook, I take ages to get ready, I'll be no good in bed – I'm meant to be a spinster!" But he'd raised her face and met her eyes; above them pigeons were shaken out from the tower like handkerchiefs. "Let me prove you're not a spinster," he said.

The guide carried his flashlight across a subterranean bridge; beneath in the black water, he strode like an inverted Christ. The faces of the party peered from the river and were swept glittering away. "Now, all of you just listen for a moment," the guide said on the other side. "I

77

don't advise anyone to come down here without me. If it rains this river rises as far as that roof." He pointed. But now, when he should be grave, his voice still grinned. "I don't like him," Maria whispered. "You couldn't rely on him if anything happened. I'm glad you're here, Tony." His hand closed on hers. "It can't last forever," he told her. She knew he was thinking of the hotel, and laid her head against his shoulder.

"So long as the roof doesn't cave in!" yelled the boisterous man.

"Cave in!" the guide shouted, resonating from the walls; the faces above gave no sign that they'd heard. "Ha ha, very good! Must remember that one." He poured his flashlight beam into a low tunnel and ushered them onwards. Behind her on the bridge Maria heard the couple from the niche. She lifted her head from Tony's shoulder. Thinking of the hotel – the first pain had faded, but in the darkness of their bedroom Tony seemed to leave her; the weight on her body, the thrust inside her, the hands exploring blindly, were no longer Tony. Yet she wasn't ready to leave the light on. Even afterwards, as they lay quiet, bodies touching trustingly, she never felt that peace which releases the tongue, enabling her to tell him what she felt. Often she dreamed of the tower above the sea; one day they'd return there and she'd be wholly his at last.

The vault was vast. The walls curved up like ribs, fanged with dislocated teeth about to salivate and close. Behind her, emerging from the tunnel, the other couple gasped. Stalactites thrust from the roof like inverted Oriental turrets or hung like giant candles ready to drip. The walls held back from the flashlight beam; Maria sensed the faces. In the depths dripped laughter. The party clustered like moths around the exploring flashlight. "Come on, lovebirds, come closer," the guide echoed. "I've brought thirty of you down and I don't want to have to fiddle my inventory." Maria thrust her fingers between Tony's and moved forward, staying at the edge of light.

"Now before we go on I want to warn you all," the guide said sinisterly. "Was anybody in the blackout? Not you, missus, I don't believe it! That's your father you're with, isn't it, not your husband!" The boisterous woman spluttered. "Even if you were," the guide continued, "you've never seen complete darkness. There's no such thing on God's earth. Of course that doesn't apply down here. You see?" He switched off the flashlight.

Darkness caved in on them. Maria lost Tony's hand and, groping, found it. "Oh God! Where was Moses!" yelled the boisterous couple. The young girl from the niche giggled. Somewhere, it seemed across a universe, a cigarette glowed. Whispers settled through the blackness. Maria's hand clenched on Tony's; she was back in the bedroom, blind, yearning for the tower above the sea.

"I hope we haven't lost anyone," the guide's face said, lit from below like a waxwork. "That's it for today. I hope someone knows the way out, that's all." He waved the flashlight to draw the procession. Laughing silhouettes made for the tunnel. Maria still felt afraid of the figure in the dark; she pulled Tony towards the flashlight. Suddenly she was ashamed, and turned to kiss him. The man whose hand she was holding was not Tony.

Maria fell back. As the light's edge drew away, the face went out. "Tony!" she cried, and ran towards the tunnel.

"Wait," the man called. "Don't leave me. I can't see."

The guide returned; figures crawled from the tunnel like insects, drawn by the light. "Don't be too long, lovebirds," he complained. "I've got another party in an hour."

"My husband," Maria said unevenly. "I've lost him. Please find him for me."

"Don't tell me he's run out on you!" Behind the guide the party had reformed within the vault; Maria searched the faces shaken by the roving flashlight beam, but none of them was Tony's. "There he is, missus!" the guide said, pointing. "Were you going to leave him behind?"

Maria turned joyfully; he was pointing at the man behind her. The man was moving back and forth in shadow, arms outstretched. The flashlight beam touched his face, and she saw why. He was blind.

"That's not my husband," Maria said, holding her voice in check.

"Looks like him to me, love. That your wife, mate?" Then he saw the man's eyes. His voice hardened. "Come on," he told Maria, "you'd better look after him."

"Is husband?" the Chinese said. "Is not husband? No."

"What's that, mate?" asked the guide – but the bearded woman shouted "Don't listen to the Chink, he can't even speak our language! You saw them together, didn't you?" she prompted, gripping her companion's arm.

"I can't say I did," the spinster said.

"Of course you did! They were sitting right behind us!"

"Well, maybe I did," the spinster admitted.

"Just fancy," the boisterous woman said, "bringing a blind man on a trip like this! Cruel, I call it."

Maria was surrounded by stone faces, mouthing words that her blood swept from her ears. She turned desperately to the vault, the man stumbling in a circle, the darkness beyond which anything might lie. "Please," she pleaded, £someone must have seen my husband? My Tony?" Faces gaped from the walls and ceiling, lines leading off into the depths. "You were behind us," she cried to the girl from the niche. "Didn't you see?"

"I don't know," the girl mused. "He doesn't look the right build to me."

"You know he isn't!" Maria cried, her hands grasping darkness. "His clothes are wrong! Please help me look for Tony!"

"Don't get involved," the girl's escort hissed. "You can see how she is."

"I think we've all had enough," the guide said. "Are you going to take care of him or not?"

"Just let me have your flashlight for a minute," Maria sobbed.

"Now I couldn't do that, could I? Suppose you dropped it?"

Maria stretched her hand towards the flashlight, still torn by hope, and a hand fumbled into hers. It was the blind man. "I don't like all this noise," he said. "Whoever you are, please help me."

"There you are," the guide rebuked, "now you've upset him. Show's over. Everybody out." And he lit up the gaping tunnel.

"Wonder what she'd have done with the flashlight?" "The blind leading the blind, if you ask me," voices chattered in the passage. The guide helped the blind man through the mouth. Maria, left inside the vault, began to walk into the darkness, arms outstretched to Tony, but immediately the dark was rent and the guide had caught her arm. "Now then, none of that," he threatened. "Listen, I brought thirty down and thirty's what I've got. Be a good girl and think about that."

He shoved her out of the tunnel. The blind man was surrounded. "Here she is," said someone. "Now you'll be all right." Maria shuddered. "I'll take him if you don't feel well," the guide said, suddenly solicitous. But they'd led the blind man forward and closed his hand on hers. The guide moved to the head of the party; the tunnel mouth darkened, was swallowed. "Tony!" Maria screamed, hearing only her own echo. "Don't," the blind man pleaded piteously.

She heard the river sweep beneath the bridge, choked with darkness, erasing Tony Thornton. For a moment she could have thrust the blind man into the gulf and run back to the vault. But his hand gripped hers with the ruthlessness of need. Around her faces laughed and melted as the flashlight passed. They'd conspired, she told herself, to make away with Tony and to bring this other forth. She must fall in with them; they could leave her dead in some side tunnel. She looked down into the river and saw the sightless eyes beside her, unaware of her.

The guide's flashlight failed. Daylight flooded down the hillside just beyond. Anonymous figures chewed and waited at the hamburger stall. "All right, let's make sure everybody's here," the guide said. "I don't like the look of that sky." He counted; faces turned to her; the guide's gaze passed over her and hurried onwards. At her back the cave opene, inviting, protective. "Where are we?" the blind man asked feebly. "It feels like summer."

Maria thought of the coach trip ahead: the Chinese and the girl unsure but unwilling to speak, the bearded woman looking back to disapprove of her, the boisterous couple discussing her audibly – and deep in the caves Tony, perhaps unconscious, perhaps crawling over stone, calling out to her in darkness. She thought she heard him cry her name; it might have been a bird on the hill. The guide was waiting; the party shuffled, impatient. Suddenly she pushed the blind man forward; he stumbled out into the summer day. The others muttered protests; the guide called out – but she was running headlong into darkness, the last glint of sunlight broken by her tears like the sea beneath the tower, the river rushing by beneath. As the light vanished, she heard the first faint patter of the rain.

THE HARROW

GEMMA FILES

The earth is old and full of holes, Lydie Massenet's mother used to say, at least once a day, back when she was still Lydie Pell. *Its crust is thin, and underneath there's nothing but darkness. A rind, that's all we live on; just thin ice, waiting for it to thaw and crack. No need to dig, really—if they want to find you, they will. Never trust anything that comes out of a hole.*

And: *Okay, Mom,* Lydie would say, the way her father had taught her to. *That's good. That's fine.* Then just smile and nod, all the time staring off at nothing much, something invisible—contemplating Mars, he called it—until her mother finally stopped talking.

You have to know this, Lydie, if nothing else, her mother told her. *Darkness shifts, darkness conceals; it's impossible to know what's hiding inside it, no matter how hard you try. But if history teaches anything, it's that what we don't understand, we fear... and what we fear, eventually, we come to worship, if only to keep it in its rightful place. To make sure it doesn't come after us.*

Yes, Mom. Okay. Sure.

'Till, one day: *Stop saying that, goddamnit!* her mother yelled, and slapped Lydie across the face, so hard her glasses cracked in half. That was the day her father brought Doctor Russ home, the day before her mother went somewhere else—first for a rest, and then, after everything they did to her while she was there had utterly failed to make her well enough to come home again, to stay.

What's wrong with her, Daddy? Lydie asked her father, at last, to which he only shook his head and sniffed, trying to pretend he hadn't been crying.

Honey, I wish to God I knew, was all he said, in return. And hugged her a little too long, a little too tight.

By April, Lydie couldn't stand it anymore. "I have to learn how to drive," she said to her husband, Ethan.

"Told you," he replied.

Thing was, in Toronto proper, you just didn't need to have a car, let alone a license—*she* certainly hadn't, her first twenty-one years of life. Lydie had vague memories of having passed the Young Drivers of Canada exam's written portion, once upon a time, but more as a personal challenge; to go further required money she was loath to spare, at the time, and after that there was always the subway, or streetcars, buses, even taxis. Living in the downtown core, where she and Ethan first met, meant you could speed-walk almost anywhere you needed to in an hour or less.

Five anniversaries in, however, the powers that be decided Toronto proper was too expensive a place to rent offices, relocating wholesale to Mississauga. No big deal for Ethan, who'd grown up there. But to Lydie, it was the ends of the earth—"suburbs" squared, with no sidewalks, no easy-access stores. For a few seconds, the day they'd arrived, she'd fantasized about dragging her shopping cart the equivalent of five blocks to the local GO Train station, then investing in a four-hour/ twelve-dollar return trip just to pick up enough food for the week from her previous neighbourhood's supermarket.

"Oh, no need," her mother-in-law had offered, helpfully, when she voiced this idea. "There's a mall, just twenty minutes northeast."

"Can I walk it?"

An odd look. "I...really wouldn't, dear."

In the morning, she saw for herself just why: the sole connecting road was a highway turned freeway, overpass after overpass looping sharply up, around and down, like J. G. Ballard porn brought to life. Standing there in shock, she couldn't keep from asking Ethan: "People *live* like this?"

"Well, yeah, Lyd, apparently so. And most of them manage just fine."

"How?"

He shot her a pitying look. "They have *cars*."

That morning, she woke with a headache-seed lodged right between her brows, hard and sharp as Bosch's Stone of Folly. Google gave her a list of numbers to call, trying to line up an appointment with an Adult Drivers instructor. By noon she was still on her cellphone, out in the back yard—another unfamiliar Mississauga oddity, weird combination of luxurious and annoying—when she came across what she'd eventually call the artifact: felt something uneven shift under her foot as she stepped back, almost tripping her, then squatted to squint at the ground, regardless of how high her skirt might hike.

There, just protruding out of the earth with its uppermost portion wreathed in grass (a tiny crown, promise-green and fertile), a rough-carved, triangular little face peeped up at her, framed by a pair of short horns or antennae—one broken off jaggedly, almost at the root.

Black rock, lighter than it looked, and warm to the touch once she'd scratched it free, ruining Monday's manicure. Her fingers curled 'round it instinctively, an almost sensual grip, to find it fit the hollow shaped between thumb, forefinger and palm, as if made for it.

Some sort of insect on top, yes, carapaced and six-limbed. But in the centre, where its thorax should be, something else sat instead: the sketch of a human skull, empty-socketed and noseless, grinning wide. With a neat little hole placed just where its brow-ridge should be, for no apparently obvious reason.

"What's that?" Ethan asked when he came home to find her sitting at the kitchen table, dinner not even slightly started, still staring at it. And: "I don't know," Lydie answered, barely looking up; just kept on studying the bug-skull-thing in her hand, 'til at last he sighed, and called out for pizza.

Later, she took pictures with her phone and ran the result through Google Images. A trail of links (*insect totems, catal huyuk, gobekli tepe, lbk culture, tallheim death-pit, herxheim*) led her to something recognizable: prehistoric trepanning, the procedure of cutting a hole in the skull to relieve cranial pressure, as of a subdural haematoma. Sometimes done for ritual purposes, or so various archaeologists claimed...but in Mesoamerica, at least, those waters had been muddied by the fact that prisoners' and sacrificial victims' skulls were often routinely pierced to facilitate the creation of skull-racks: rows on rows of severed heads, hung up on pegs, or hooks.

The hole goes at the back, usually, she thought, tapping a finger against her teeth. *Or on top. Never in front.*

Between the brows, though, or slightly higher—there was a symbolism there, right? The pineal gland. The third eye.

Around two, she lay down next to Ethan with her eyes open, contemplating the ceiling while he snored. Thinking: *I wonder if there's more.*

When she and Lydie's father were kids, there'd been a girl, Lydie's mother used to tell her. And one day, when they were all out in the woods playing, this girl had somehow stepped...wrong, laid her foot on the one place she shouldn't have, and broke through, opening up a hole. Had tumbled down into what later proved to be a cave that went straight down, too deep to see the bottom, and with no earthly way of ever getting back up out, once you were in.

A story grew up amongst the group of children Lydie's mother ran with, afterwards, that if you were to go to that hole, that cave, and hang your head out over the edge—if you did that, and whispered your greatest fear or wish or dream down into the black pit below, while clinging on for dear life with both hands—then if you only waited long enough, a voice would answer. And that voice would tell you if your dream, or wish, or fear would...if it *should*...come true.

Whose voice, Mom?

No one knows.

Didn't anyone ever ask?

Oh, no. No. That would be...

Here Lydie's mother had trailed away into silence, one so long Lydie had thought at the time it might signify the conversation was over, before finally adding, minutes later—

...never, no, never. No one would dare.

Lydie studied her hands for another few beats of her pulse, letting the moment stretch on. Then asked: *Did* you *ever do that?*

Lydie's mother swallowed.

Once, yes, she said, reluctantly. *Only once. And that was a mistake.*

Why? No reply. *But...did it answer you, Mom?*

And: *No,* her mother replied, with a sad, angry sort of hunger. *But that's just as well, isn't it? Because you can't trust such things, I've told you that already...those sorts of places, the earth's open holes. The dark, and the ones who live there.*

Why not?

Because...they lie.

▼▼▼

"What is it you're digging, dear, exactly?" her mother-in-law asked, on Friday, when she turned up to take Lydie shopping. Lydie smiled and drew her gardening gloves off, pausing to thwack them clean against the stake she'd sunk to mark her initial excavation; dirt fell in clumps, dusting her boots. "Flowerbed," she replied, without blinking.

"Ah. Eh—isn't that one already, over there?"

"Sure. I just...wanted more."

"A little project, to keep you busy 'til driving school?"

"You got it."

Ethan never even bothered to ask what she was doing out there, all day, every day—not after that first night. Not so long as she got her cooking done in the morning, and made sure there was something for him to eat when he came home.

"Boss might want to come for dinner," he told her, skimming headlines on his iPad, as she catalogued her latest finds: more insects, some mammals, even a figure or two. Through the window, the tarp she'd thrown over the hole caught her eye, dun and dull, flat as a cataract. Without prompting, her mind went to those other things she'd uncovered, the ones she'd never bring inside: some locked in the shed, others still underground, concealed by the dig's lip. Down in the

90

dark with the worms, where no one would see, unless—one day soon, perhaps—she decided she wanted them to.

"Better to take her out, don't you think?" she suggested, smoothly. "That place with the steak, maybe—the Korean banquet-house. You remember."

"Oh yeah, that's right. Where we took Mom and Dad, for their fiftieth."

"That's the one."

"Mmm, good call, hon. She'd like that."

"There you go."

▼▼▼

Some people say God turned the world upside down, once, Lydie's mother whispered, into the close, hot air of her small, dim hospital room. *Just for fun. And many strange things came up out of the earth, then, things trapped down there for a hundred thousand years, ever since the world was made...just like the Flood, but different. And many bad people joined with these things, and flourished, and many good people died screaming. Until finally, when he didn't find it quite as funny anymore, God flipped it all back over again, and made everything the way it was. Like when you lift up a rock to see the bugs crawling underneath, and when you're bored, you just drop it again, and squash them; you don't have to care what happens, because they're just bugs, after all. And better yet, it's not like you have to see it.*

But some people say he never did flip it back again at all, God, Lydie's mother whispered, later. *That's why things are so bad up here, even though God made us, and everything around us. Because this world, all we see, was never meant to be on top at all. It was meant to be hidden, kept down, trapped. Because where we live, right now...we live in hell. What* was *meant to be hell.*

Shush, Irma. For Christ's sake, shush.

91

(But: Where did the people who were meant to be in hell live, then? Lydie used to wonder. And the things down there in the dark, the people who weren't people, the ones her mother kept on warning her about...who were they? Was that meant to be *heaven*, down there?)

What happened to that girl, anyways? Lydie was finally unable to keep from asking her father, one night, as he stroked her mother's hair back from her rigid, sweating face. *The one from the story. The one who fell into the hole.*

Oh, well...they never did find her, honey, though they looked a good long time, all the time your Mom and me were at school together. And that's why you should stay away from places like that—in the woods, under the ground. To stay safe.

But: *Karl, why would you lie to her that way, our own daughter?* Her mother broke in, suddenly. *You know as well as I do that she did come back, eventually...all cold and wet and naked, knocking on her family's door and crying, in the middle of the night. But they knew they shouldn't let her in, because they were old now, and she—she was the same, just a kid. Just like the last time they saw her.*

Irma, please, be quiet. My God, why won't you ever keep quiet? You'll frighten her to death.

At this, Lydie's mother's lips drew back; you couldn't call it a smile, not quite, for all it involved lips turning upwards. Not after you'd spent some time alone with it.

Oh no, she said. *No, she's not frightened—are you, darling? Don't listen to him, Lydie; go where you want, do what you want. Go dig. Go whisper in every hole you see, for all anybody cares.*

See what you get, then.

▼▼▼

In agriculture, a harrow (often called a set of harrows, in a plurale tantum sense) is an implement for breaking up and smoothing out the surface of the soil, distinct from the plough, which is used for deeper tillage. Harrowing is often carried out on fields to follow the rougher finish left by ploughing operations. The purpose of harrowing is to break up clods of soil and provide a finer finish, a good tilth or soil structure, suitable for seedbed use.

In Christian mythology we speak of "the harrowing of hell," Jesus's descent into the underworld during his three days of death. In this case, the word "harrow" derives from the Old English hergian, meaning to harry or despoil—the idea that Christ invaded and triumphed over hell, releasing all those kept captive there, including redeeming Adam and Eve, the fount of all original sin.

"Excuse me," a voice said, from behind the back fence.

Lydie bookmarked her page and set the iPad aside. Someone was looking in at her through the narrow mesh of the gate next to the shed, so dense it barely suggested their eyes, like the facial grille of an Afghan *chadri*—female by the voice, Lydie could only assume, which was husky, flute-y. Though the level of the shadow "she" threw did suggest a fairly unusual height.

"I'm sorry," Lydie said, automatically. "Can I help you?"

"I hope so, yes," the voice said. "Could I come in and talk to you, just for a minute?" Quickly adding, a moment later, as Lydie hesitated: "Boy, that *does* sound sinister, doesn't it? Better to come back later, maybe, when you're not all alone. I'll bring pamphlets."

"Oh, no, no, no," Lydie found herself protesting, hand already on the latch. "I'm—it's fine, really. I just...wasn't expecting anybody."

As she opened the gate, the woman—it *was* a woman, now Lydie saw her up close; she was almost sure—smiled, lips canting sidelong like a slow-typed emoticon (back-slash, then semi-colon plus an apostrophe, to mark where that dimple formed closed-quotes punctuation), and stepped inside. Her skin was aggressively tanned, hair bleached at the top and brown at the tips as though she'd been out in the sun for weeks somewhere far hotter than here, let alone today, and held back with a tight-wound bandana so low it brushed the tops of her equally-pale eyebrows.

"Paula Neath," she announced. "From the Society for Ecological Rebalance."

While: *1. in or to a lower position*; Lydie's brain filled in, automatically. *Below. 2. underneath, prep. 3. under. 4. farther down than. 5. lower...*

She shook her head, scattering words, and held out her hand, smiling too. "Lydie Massenet. I don't think I've ever heard of you."

"Well, we're a fairly recently-formed project. Most of us were doing other things before we got the call... I was in Turkey, for example, tracking genetic variation in honeybees, locust migration patterns, that sort of thing. But actually, what I'm here to talk about is bats."

"That's an interesting subject-shift."

"Not really. All part of the same eco-system." Paula jogged her head towards the yard's back left corner. "Now, the reason I wanted a word is that as it so happens, your property corners onto this block's drainage ditch—do you know where that is?"

Lydie nodded. "Runs under the mouths of all the driveways on the south side, then dips down under the street. Tell you the truth, I hate that thing: when it rains, it's a stream; the rest of the time, it's a sump, stagnant. It stinks."

"Exactly—perfect for breeding mosquitos, which spread West Nile disease. Previously, the city's plan to deal with that involved spraying, but we're seeing some very alarming fallout from that... denuded bee population, for one, which affects pollination, which cuts down on new growth generally. So we'd like to put up a grouping of bat-houses in various areas, including right here."

"Like a birdhouse, but for bats."

"Exactly." That smile again. "I'll be honest, Mrs Massenet—"

"Lydie."

"—a lot of people seem to think the idea of opening their arms to flying mice is a bit of a deal-breaker. One lady was convinced they spread rabies, for example; that sort of stereotype. Old wives' tales, to put it frankly."

"Didn't want guano in their hair?"

"Didn't want *bats* in their hair." They both chuckled. "Foolish, I know. Bats are nocturnal, far more interested in insects and nectar than anybody's follicles. You'd barely see them, except at dusk."

"Sounds sort of nice, to me. Do they make noise?"

"Not within the hearing-range of most humans."

Lydie shrugged. "Okay, then. I'm sold."

"Wonderful! You won't regret it—we'll be in and out, no muss, no fuss. And the public health benefits will be striking, once the bats have had a bit of time to do their work."

"I don't doubt it. So...you must be from the university, right? Did they bus you in?"

"Most of us, yes; some of us live here, in the area."

"Nice to work where you live."

"Yes." Paula's sharp eyes—an odd non-colour, neither grey nor blue, almost clear when glimpsed straight-on—shifted from Lydie's, focusing instead on the tarp, as well as the earth piled neatly next to it. "You've been doing some work of your own, by the look of it."

"Oh, uh...not officially. I mean—"

"May I see?"

"Well..."

...why not?

Surprising, in its way, the idea that she would *want* to show Paula, a complete stranger, what she'd so carefully managed to keep from everyone else—her loved ones, supposedly. The people who loved her. And yet, that did seem to be what that usually-silent voice deep inside her was suggesting...that midnight whisper, sexless and dark, ambiguous as Paula's own throaty purr.

(*Don't listen, Lydie. They lie.*)

So—

"Yes," Lydie replied, and moved the tarp aside, allowing Paula to see: the hole, and what it concealed. A gaping, sod-lipped mouth which never quite promised answers, for everything else it delivered; oddities, rarities, the strange, the unique. Something you could hold in your hand and study, but never fully understand, except perhaps in dreams.

The dig went ten feet in, these days, much of it almost straight down—a ladder she'd found in the shed providing access, tall enough to reach the roof when unfurled—and with an odd little trailing twist at the bottom, brief sloping sketch of further possibilities. Ethan would be horrified; Lydie couldn't even venture a guess at what her mother-in-law would think. They were such sweet people, really, it seemed only *right* to hide the truth where it couldn't hurt them...kinder, in its way, than the alternative.

If Mom'd only done that, she found herself thinking, sometimes, as she hadn't let herself for years, *then things would've—might've been —very different.*

Paula took in everything Lydie'd spent the last two months doing, then hiding—the open wound of her craziness, at long last laid bare— with one swift, shrewd, searching glance. Then turned her back, stepping down into darkness, sinking 'til all Lydie could see of her was the top of her head; her voice seeped back up, dirt-magnified, made hollow at the bone. "Fascinating," she said. "This is...Neolithic, would you say?"

"Older, maybe. I think it got folded under when the glaciers shifted."

"Yes, very likely. You're extremely perceptive, Mrs Massenet."

Lydie shrugged, embarrassed. "Hardly. I mean—it's weird to think about, something like *this* under our feet, just hidden away... still so perfect after so many years, with all this suburban crap slapped on top. But there you go."

"It is odd," Paula agreed, words deepening further as she bent to rummage through the slick bottom of the shaft, picking and choosing. "But no more so than anything, really. The earth is older than any of us care to acknowledge, and *everywhere* was somewhere else, once. Most people simply don't bother to look any closer than they have to at what they already think they know, unless..."

"...unless something *makes* them."

"Exactly."

(*Old, and full of holes. But do not put your hand down to see, because*)

Lydie took a small, shallow breath. There was something—she wasn't sure what. A kind of wobble, at the corner of her eyes; black spots hovering, blinking. Was she going to pass out?

A few moments later, however, Paula had made back up the ladder in two massive steps, and was standing once more on the lip's moustache-like rut of trodden grass. Extending one huge, muck-filled hand, she scoured an entirely new type of totem free between her thumb and forefingers, with swift, almost brutal strokes: a squat, oval thing, bulgy at both ends like a toad, and small enough even she might've mistaken it for a mere clot of mud-wrapped rock... except for the fact that she knew where to look, and what for.

"Beautiful," Paula named it, reverently. "How many have you found, so far?"

"Oh, more and more, usually five, eight a day...sometimes ten, if I can dig uninterrupted 'till my husband comes home. They don't ever seem to stop. I'm thinking votive objects, a whole cache of them, brought here on pilgrimage and buried, as some sort of—prayer, or sacrifice. Some sort of payment."

"You've done your research." As Lydie shook her head: "No? Then your instincts are *very* good, considering. Nice work, either way."

"I took archaeology in university," Lydie offered. "Just one course a year, but I kept it up all the way through my degree; I'd've liked to go back, to specialize, but..."

"Things happen, yes—sadly, almost always. We move away from our dreams, or they move away from us; seem to, at any rate. But sometimes, the universe provides a second chance." Here Paula closed her hand, tucking the totem away, and watching as Lydie couldn't stop herself from flinching. "May I keep this? Not forever, believe me... just for a few days. I'd like to show it to my supervisor."

"Um...all right, sure, okay. You do that."

"I promise I'll bring it back soon, after the bathouse goes up. Would that be acceptable?"

"...yes."

That smile again, a little wider. "Then it's a deal."

Gone, moments later, as though she'd never been. Only the tarp, peeled back like a lid, gave any evidence of her passage. Lydie stood there looking at it for a few more breaths, thinking: *You need a break, food, a minute. Go inside. No more today.*

But the sun was hot and bright, the cool, dark hole inviting. A minute more, therefore, and she was already halfway down—far enough inside to glance back up, just for a second, and almost think she saw the hole itself blink shut, grass-fringed rim knitting like eyelashes, to shutter away her from the harsh surface world forever.

So nice, she thought, happily, going down on both knees to grub in the mud some more. *So very nice, always, to come home.*

The bathouse went up both fast and easy, as advertised. A week on, Lydie watched its inhabitants fly up at twilight, scattering like thoughts into the night as they chased their food, the next echo, each other. By bed-time, undressing in front of the window that looked down onto the back yard, she felt as though could still hear them twittering, even though she knew they probably weren't there. Beneath its tarp-lid, the hole gaped open, its presence always a slightly painful, slightly pleasurable ache; she lay there trying not to think about it, but enjoying when she failed.

"Today wasn't your first class, was it?" Ethan asked, sleepily, from beside her.

"What?"

"Well, you said six weeks..." No reply. "You missed it, didn't you? Oh, honey."

"I can make it up."

"Yeah, hope so."

Annoyed, Lydie turned over, scoffing. "C'mon, Ethan, they want our money, don't they—*your* money. Of course I can."

The next day, however, she was back down in the hole (cell phone still charging on the bedside table, blissfully forgotten) when Paula's long shadow fell over her, making her look up. And: "Hey!" Lydie called. "So you *did* come back, after all."

"I said I would."

"Uh huh. Your supervisor...he like the artifact?"

"Very much. I've got it, if you want it back."

"Just give me a sec."

More like thirty to finish up, thirty more to clamber free, wiping the sweat from her eyes. Paula stood there, toad-rock already extended, offered up; Lydie put out her hand as she dropped it, fisting the totem gratefully, as if reclaiming a lost piece of herself. She gave a cave-deep sigh.

"That feels good," she'd said out loud, before she could think to stop herself.

Paula smiled. "I thought it would. Now—if you don't mind me disturbing you just a *little* bit further, might I possibly be able to see what's in the shed?"

▼▼▼

No actual rack, just a long, low trio of shelves which had once held flowerpots, before Lydie relocated them. She'd cleaned the skulls off carefully, one by one—each so muddy they'd initially looked like they were sculpted from clay—by first letting them dry before going at them with a variety of unofficial find-cleaning tools, paring away dirt and grime with brushes meant for paints or makeup, scaling the eye-sockets with wire loops to remove as much detritus as possible before breaking out the sand, the bleach soaks, the polyurethane sprays. Now they grinned in welcome, display-organized left to right, until Paula gingerly picked up the first on the uppermost row, raising it towards the light.

Each came with a hole just above where the bridge of the nose would be, if there was a nose, mirroring the totems, and on each the hole at first seemed differently-shaped, though careful examination revealed another, more subtle pattern of variation. For in those holes, so seamlessly fitted they almost appeared to have been individually made *for* the space it now occupied, Lydie had laid each of the totems she'd dug up carefully to rest: insect, bird, snake, bat, toad, plus some sort of low, broad thing with long claws, squat legs and a blunt, blind head, like a mole or badger. A catalogue of every crawling and creeping thing which ever forced itself through some crack in the earth and hid itself inside, trading light for dark, at the urging of some hidden, hollow voice.

"Thought they were signs of trepanning, at first," Lydie heard herself explain, her own tone thinning, flattening, words tumbling out in a breathy, secretive rush, as though she feared being stopped before she could finish. "Even though they were in the wrong place. I didn't even think to match them up for...must've been weeks, a month. A happy accident."

"Often the way," Paula murmured. "And then what?"

"I started thinking about why. The point of the exercise." Lydie paused, feeling her way, waiting for the words to suggest themselves. "What you could hope to—extract, that way. From the same place people used to think visions came from, or dreams...the seat of enlightenment."

"The *ajna*, or brow chakra. Where things open up."

"Yeah, but not if something's blocking it—fear, maybe. Desire. Some kind of...lower instinct. Like an animal."

"And you think that's what they were removing."

"Metaphorically, it makes a certain kind of sense—I mean, no *sense* at all, really. But still...that *is* what it looks like, to me: like they were trying to create a completely new way of seeing. A totem for every hole, a congealed bit of nightmare, a filter that needs to be removed, before you can see clearly. The plug that keeps us all from letting something out—"

"—or in."

"Or in, yes. The light..."

(*the dark*)

Unable to keep from connecting the dots, now it'd finally been said—from seeing the hole, the place left empty for an answer, and being therefore driven to fill it. To keep from wondering whether that had perhaps been her mother's problem all along, solution inherent in its own equation: *could* she have been cured all along, and this easily? A single, fairly simple operation, just one; cut a hole, take out what you find there and throw it away, down into the dark. Just offer it up to whatever wants it, and find the courage to finally accept things *as they really goddamn are*, without having to be afraid. And then...

...and then.

Standing there wound down, sunk inside herself, no longer able to tell whether or not she was saying any of this out loud, or what.

Then something at the corner of her gaze again, a black flicker; she looked up. Just in time to see Paula put down the skull (carefully, gently, *reverently*) and reach up, behind her head, to flick open some sort of knot or clip, slackening her headband until it was loose enough to unwind. Which she began to do, one long fold at a time, without haste or worry—slow and careful, the very same way she told Lydie, still smiling—

"I *knew* we were right about you, Mrs Massenet...Lydie. Though of course, I haven't been as entirely honest, from the beginning, as I might have hoped to be; I knew you already, you see, that first day I came here. *Of* you, at any rate."

Lydie swallowed, dryly. "Oh?" she managed, eventually.

"Yes...as Lydie Pell, to be exact. Through your mother."

One twist, then another, then another—just one more, the final one. Leaving Paula's forehead bare at last, high and broad and smooth, yet pitted centrally with a perfect shell of scar tissue, cracked just a hint at its core: the very same place where Lydie could feel that intermittent migraine-seed of hers re-forming, bone-planted but pushing upwards and out, threatening to bloom. Because here she was at last, arrived, like she'd always somehow known she one day would be: this place, this very moment, teetering on the brink and wondering just what might be lurking under there, waiting, in the dark. A naked pineal bud, eyelid-furled, waiting to breach the scar's tissue-plated embrace, sip at the air, twitch and blink?

But: *does it matter, Lydie?* her mother replied, wearily, memory-locked. *The hole has its own reasons, always. Do you really want to know what they are?*

Inside the bathouse, the sleeping bats cooed and scrabbled, shrilling sleepily.

"I fell in a hole once, a long time ago," Paula went on, stroking down along the ridge that threatened to bisect her open, guileless gaze with one pinkie delicately lifted, as though she were about to serve tea. "Just like this one. And it was scary, at first: so dark, so deep. But after a while, once my eyes adjusted, I found that I didn't want to get out again at all, let alone go home. Because there were *so* many wonderful things down there, to see, and do, and be. Wouldn't you like to know what?"

"Do I have a choice?"

"Always. You always have a choice."

Which sounded plausible, and not, both at the same time—a truth, thinly disguised as a lie. Or vice versa.

Tongue leather, head swimming. Migraine between her eyes, turning in a tightening spiral, like a screw. Like the coin-shaped burr hole a trephine leaves behind, after the flesh has been cut away and the skull pierced, to show the sweet grey-pink beneath.

Thinking: *So the first harrowing was me breaking up the earth and sifting it for traces, exposing more and more of this buried ruin. But the second harrowing will be a descent into the underworld, a sort of anti-transfiguration...instead of rising into the sky, sinking into the earth and burrowing down, fertilizing it with yourself, a hole inside a hole. Become, at last, the mulch from which something new will grow.*

Lydie looked down, then up again, meeting Paula's gaze with her own. Felt herself nod.

"I thought so," Paula said, happily. "Now—hold still."

And Lydie did, drawing herself taut, rigid, eyes wide. Trying not to flinch as the wickedly curved black stone blade Paula pulled from behind her back made its necessarily painful mark, x-signing the spot where her Folly-stone hid, first one way, then the other. 'Til it radish-rosed a great peel of skin, parting the bloody petals key-into-lock smooth, to lay the slick white bone bare at last and open her up in one swift punch, digging the hole to set her final nightmare free.

Then down, always down, curve after curve, counter-clockwise—following the signs which marked her path 'til she could go no more: markings, so luminous and many-layered, on stone which had seemed empty under light, lit up like stars now darkness led the way. Until the surface disappeared. Until Ethan and the rest fell away. Until there was nothing left but one step and the next, over and over: the signs, the path, its eventual end.

(*Lydie, don't*)

The mouth of the cave, whispering in her blood. Her question, and its answer.

(*don't trust it*)

Like you never did, mother? Lydie thought, unsympathetic. Remembering Paula, whose family had cast her out instead of welcoming her back; Paula, who took the gifts they spurned, and grew to fit them. Paula, her three eyes shining, beckoning to her from the very, very bottom of the hole, the once-top of some inverted mountain huge enough to dwarf Chomolungma.

Here at the bottom, where she finally had worth, and truth, and purpose. Where in led out, and out back in. Where no one mattered more than she did, at least for the task at hand.

I walk the harrow, downwards-tending, Lydie Massenet Pell thought, wiping her own blood from her pitifully weak, light-dependent lower set of eyes, while concentrating hard enough to let the uppermost of all three show her the way. *Dragging my blades, ploughing 'til there is no more left to plow, waiting below 'til harvest comes, and we all ascend. 'Til the pale sun shrinks so far it becomes nothing more than just another star in a half-forgotten sky.*

Above her, the rock, like choirs. Below her, the dirt, like flesh, and blood, and food. The great, uprooted currents of the earth, pulling her towards its burning, pulsing, molten heart.

Home.

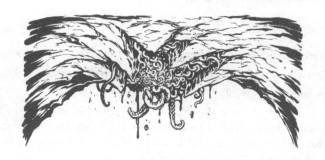

NIVEL DEL MAR

SCOTT SHANK

My brother was last seen in a park in San Francisco de Chiu Chiu, an oasis town in Chile's Atacama Desert that sits one-and-a-half miles above the sea and forty-five hundred from home. My Spanish isn't perfect, but I understood enough of what the old man who tended those rocks and cactuses told me. He remembered the gringo vividly, and he smiled when recounting how my brother had explained that he intended to set off on foot, out across the driest desert on Earth. My brother's destination was Cerro del Azufre, or Sulphur Mountain, out towards Bolivia.

"Estaba loco," the old man said.

I could only nod.

I climbed into my jeep and drove back to San Pedro where I'd been staying. I got drunk at one of the tourist joints and met a girl, an architecture student up from Valparaíso. The next day when I asked if she'd like to tag along, she agreed. Her name was Humberta, and she was something special.

I had need of her company. I knew Christopher must be dead. I knew I would never find his body. There was no way for me to know what route he had taken out of Chiu Chiu, let alone follow it, so I pretended he still lived and we drove north.

Humberta was very sympathetic about the whole thing, and with her smiling beside me I could almost believe I was just sightseeing during the drive up. Most of the Atacama was utter wasteland. Dust and rubble beneath a jewel-blue sky. In places the vistas took on greenish and mauve tones where plants somehow managed to take root. More impressive still were the volcanoes. The Cerro del Azufre was but one in a chain of snow-capped cones that rose like so many Mount Fujis on the horizon. We stopped once or twice to take pictures of llamas grazing at their feet.

As we approached Azufre, I grew more somber and Humberta's hand found mine on the stick shift. Christopher's was a sad story. He had been ill as long as I could remember, in and out of therapy and institutionalized for part of high school. By his early thirties he had become a perpetual student and we all thought he was a little better. We were wrong.

For years he'd been looking for his own cure, and he became convinced he had found it in the primary documents of his doctoral research. Christopher had been studying the history of the Canadian Pacific Railway Survey—Snoozeville, I know—when he came across accounts of suicides among the survey teams and workers in the high passes of the Rockies. These were recorded in the letters of one George Wallace McCharles, a Scottish geographer who worked on the Survey plotting routes through British Columbia. McCharles later headed down to South America to work for the Antofagasta (Chili) & Bolivia Railway

Company. In the altiplano, he again documented suicides among the engineers and work crews.

McCharles linked these suicides to the altitude, and in fact it seemed the geographer must have gone nuts himself during his time in the high Andes. In his last letter to the not-yet royal Scottish Geographic Society, he raved about the Pozo del Equilibrio, an apparently bottomless hole on the slope of the Cerro del Azufre that had certain curative properties for those suffering from 'nervous complaints.' In the Well of Equilibrium he had found a 'refuge from the baleful Æther.'

"So he came to find el Pozo for himself?" Humberta asked.

I nodded, my eyes fixed on the empty road. "That's right. Without warning he just picked up and left. I mean, I've been taking care of Christopher for years. He's been sleeping on my couch for so long I actually bought a dresser for the living room. I don't know what else I could have done. Then after a decade of never paying a dime in rent, he spends the last of his inheritance to come down here. Halfway around the world, to find his sanity at the bottom of a frigging hole."

Humberta looked out her side window. "Probably he was scared for years."

I glanced at the beautiful, ridiculously young woman beside me, and wondered if she had ever had to carry someone like Christopher, too.

When we were close to the GPS coordinates I had found in my brother's notes, I turned the 4x4 from the road and set off across the hinterland. It was rough in places but we made it to within a mile of the site. We left the truck and began our hike up the slope, ignoring the signs that declared ¡ADVERTENCIA! and ¡PROHIBIDO! along the way.

Humberta wagged her finger at me, which made me laugh. She had used the same you-naughty-boy gesture the night before. It seemed like the first sign in the secret code we were destined to teach each other.

A short time later we arrived.

I guess I expected some kind of grotto, like something a hermit would crawl into above the Dead Sea. What we found was a tin shed covered in camouflage mesh. I guess I expected the place to be abandoned. What we found was a man smiling at the door.

"Bienvenidos. Welcome," he said.

He was an older guy, a little weather-beaten, a fraying pony tail poking out from beneath one of those beige world-traveler hats geriatrics wear to pick up milk. But the striking thing about this guy was that he was covered with dust. I mean *covered*. His every wrinkle and neck crease were packed with grit, just as every flap of his cargo vest spilled sand. He looked as if he had just stepped out of a dust storm. Or, the thought came to me, as if he had been standing outside that shed for months, waiting for someone to come along.

"Buenas tardes, Señor," I said. "We are looking for the Pozo del Equilibrio."

"My favorite place on Earth."

"Is this it?"

"Of course. Come inside and I'll show you."

The man opened the shed's door and disappeared inside. I glanced at Humberta to see how she was doing. I had come all this way to find the Pozo, but the stranger gave me such a weird vibe that at that moment I almost wished she would give me an excuse to turn back.

She looked a little grim, but when she spoke she said, "Let's enter."

"It's kind of sketchy. I mean..."

"Vámonos, huevón."

A few dirty windows let in enough light to see, but after the desert sun the shed's interior seemed very dim. I was surprised to find shelves around the room's circumference, all fully stocked with supplies, as if this little shed truly were an outpost: tubs of dry goods, lanterns, batteries, rope, and lots of water.

The stranger sat on the only stool in the far corner. In the center of the floor gaped a black hole, maybe six feet across.

I peered over the edge. Nothing about that hole looked inviting. Metal rungs had been fixed to the inner wall, descending into the pit.

"This is the Pozo?" I asked.

"Of course."

"How deep does it go?"

"Sufficiently deep," the man said. "Tell me, did you walk far?"

"Only a mile or so. We parked down the slope."

"A pity," the man said.

"A pity? How is that?"

"You cannot be properly wearied. The Well's effects are appreciated best by those who are truly fatigued." He flashed a smile. It was an effort to return it in kind.

"I don't plan to go down the Pozo, Señor. I've come looking for my brother."

"Is that so?"

"Yes," I said. "But he set out to walk all the way from Chiu Chiu, so he could not possibly have made it."

The man nodded thoughtfully. "And before that he had come from far to the north."

"That's right."

"I remember him. He arrived not two months ago."

"He arrived?" I had given up all hope. The thought that Christopher might still live was more surreal than the idea that he had dropped dead walking across the Atacama, and it took a moment for me to regain myself. "Did he say where he was going next?"

"Down the Well. You should speak with him."

"He's down there?"

"Of course. And in wonderful company. Men and women come from every land to descend the Well. You really must experience it yourself."

I was reeling. Humberta took my hand and forced me to look at her. "I think I have to go down there," I said.

"Está claro," she said. "But it is not necessary that you go alone."

The man gave us carabiners and lanterns to hang from our belts. He gave us water, jam and bags of preservative-rich mini-croissants for us to deliver to those living in the dark.

Before we began to descend he resumed his position on the stool. My last view of him made me wonder whether we were making a mistake. The stranger's expression was not particularly encouraging, as you might expect. Rather, I would describe it as determined, or maybe even wilful. That is, he appeared to be willing us to go down the Well.

And so we did, and it was creepy as hell. Though the Pozo's sides were out of arm's reach, our echoing steps and breath brought them closer. If I were alone I would have quit after the first minute, but Humberta, who had gone first, continued downward, rung after rung, and so I followed.

After about twenty yards the ladder ended and the passage turned from a straight drop to a forty-degree angle. We continued down this slope for ten minutes before we came to another drop and another ladder. This one must have gone down fifty yards.

By this point I was getting a little freaked out. I closed my eyes as I climbed, imagining the open vistas above, the wide expanse of sky and the sense of boundlessness I had only ever half-perceived up on the surface. I couldn't handle much more of this. I was about to tell Humberta that we should turn back when she screamed.

The drop had again become a slope, and Humberta cowered before a scraggly figure who shielded his eyes from the lamp's light.

"Get away from her!" I yelled. I jumped the last few feet and stood between Humberta and the troglodyte as menacingly as I could. Though he was taller, the guy was scrawny, his belt cinched tight to keep up filthy jeans. His polo shirt hung from bony shoulders.

"I apologize if I frightened you," the man said, his cadence precise and German. "I am very thirsty. Can I have a sip of water?"

"Who are you?" I asked.

"I am Reinhold. I was thirstiest and so I volunteered to visit Herr Wind."

Humberta had regained her composure, and I figured the guy was no threat so I passed him some water. Though his lips were cracked and his eyeballs had sunk grotesquely from dehydration, he practiced incredible restraint, downing only half the bottle.

"Sometimes I doubt I will ever be ready," he said. "But look at me, talking about myself. Welcome, friends! It is always good to have someone new." I accepted Reinhold's hand and tried to ignore his stink. He smelt as if he had not bathed or changed his clothes in weeks. "Follow me," he said.

We followed. The German wasn't too talkative. As he walked he weaved unsteadily ahead of us and I began to worry about what shape I might find Christopher in.

Reinhold led us for maybe an hour, down slopes and ladders until finally he said, "We are close."

He didn't need to tell us. We were nearing the cave dwellers' latrine. Apparently, there were no facilities in the Pozo del Equilibrio, because soon we were slipping through human filth. Reinhold didn't seem to mind.

Then many voices bellowed from the tunnel ahead. It took me a moment to recognize the cacophony as a greeting, yelled in unison, like we were entering a sushi restaurant. There was much cheer in it.

111

Our lanterns lit our hosts. A dozen amateur anchorites held up palms to block the invading light, squatting along the sides of the tunnel in their rags. Christopher was among them and he looked like shit.

We embraced. I shed a few tears.

"I thought you were dead," I said.

"Me? No way."

"But how could you have survived the desert?"

"I had the wind at my back."

"I'm getting you out of here," I said. "I'm going to take you home."

Christopher parted from me and smiled. It was a wry smile, with a little too much condescension, the kind I always wanted to punch as a kid. Over his shoulder I saw his new compadres avert their gaze.

"Listen," my brother said. "I love you and I totally appreciate you coming all the way down here to check on me, but really, it wasn't necessary. I'm doing fine."

"Christopher," I said. "You can't possibly—."

"I'm telling you. I've never been better in my whole life. It's awesome down here. We're all doing great!"

"You aren't doing great," I said. "You look like you've got scurvy. Are you guys really living off of jam?"

"Hey everybody, they brought jam!"

A half dozen of the starving bastards stood and pressed towards us. Humberta and I distributed the food, and the recluses sat about happily chatting like picnickers.

There was nowhere to go, so I sat there brooding as they ate. "Don't be too hard," Humberta whispered to me. She was right of course. Yelling never helped, but after a lifetime of putting up with my brother's manic swings, it was hard to keep levelheaded.

I waited until I had cooled off before I scuttled over beside him. "Christopher," I said. "Why are you down here?"

"You must have gone through my notes," he said. "You know why."

"You're looking for a cure."

"I'm not looking, I found one! And it's not just my illness, the Pozo del Equilibrio offers shelter from what plagues the entire human race."

"Christopher..."

"It's not just me. McCharles' discovery has never been forgotten. There are hundreds around the world who are planning to join us here."

"We have our own wiki," Reinhold piped in.

I looked to Humberta for support. She stood a few yards along the passage, peering down another drop. She displayed neither the fear nor the exasperation that were overcoming me, and once again I was thankful for her calmness.

"You see this," Christopher said, as he picked crumbs from his grimy shirt. "We can't even pass up mini-croissants. This is how you know we aren't ready." Several of the others nodded.

"Ready for what?" I asked.

"For the final stretch." He waved to the drop where Humberta stood. "McCharles called that The Last Scamp."

My curiosity was sufficiently aroused that I joined Humberta. I don't know how I could tell such a thing, but I knew the next descent was frighteningly deep. I backed away fast. "How far down does it go?"

"Down to sea level," my brother said.

"That's impossible. Sea level must be another six thousand feet down."

"Yeah, about that."

"If you try to climb that, you'll fall. You're too weak."

"I won't go until I'm ready."

"But what do you even suppose is down there?"

"Equilibrium, of course."

I dearly wished at that moment Humberta would step away from the edge and back me up. It was hard to be the lone voice of sanity. I had never been much good at talking sense into my brother. "This is daft, Christopher. If sea level is your cure, it would have been easier to go to the beach."

"Ah, but for this cure to work one must first consume a fatal dose of the poison."

"And what poison would that be? Mountain air? The 'baleful Æther'?"

"Yes, exactly. The sky, and more particularly, the wind."

"The wind's not poison!" My voice boomed. It sounded ugly even to my own ears.

Humberta came back and slipped a warm arm around my waist. "Querido," she said, her even contralto pacifying me with one word. "It is not good to disdain."

"Thank you," Christopher said. "It might seem hard to credit, but if you have studied the matter as closely as I have, it wouldn't seem so outrageous. Mr. Wind has resented us since our ancestors first crawled out of the sea. He wants us to leave his domain." Several others mumbled agreement.

"Mr. Wind?"

"You've met him," my brother said.

"He will provide for us until we are ready," Reinhold chipped in. "But, you know, he really quite hates us. Ja."

I rubbed my temples. Despite Humberta's soothing touch, I was ready to toss these idiots down The Last Scamp myself. "Christopher," I said. "You won't make it down six thousand feet in your condition. And even if you did, you will never have the strength to come back up."

"That's all right by me."

We were falling into our old pattern. Him talking crazy and me getting mad, so we took a break. I sat with my back to the rock wall and ignored the petering conversation. I yawned and checked my watch and was depressed to find that it was 10 p.m. The prospect of emerging into starlight was a powerful draw, but I was too exhausted to climb all the way back up to the surface. Somebody turned off the lantern. I did not object because I was already half asleep.

I had not really imagined how my brother and his new friends lived until I sat there drowsing in the pitch black. I could sense their bodies nearby, their warmth and their tranquility. Humberta sat next to me and for a while I buried my head in her neck. She smelled vaguely like licorice and I couldn't get enough of it. She really knew how to ground me. By the time Christopher found a place on my other side, I was ready to make up. We didn't talk, but we sat for a while with our arms around each other's shoulders for the first time in thirty years. Soon I was asleep.

I had a dream of wayfaring. The world was all horizon, all peaks and plains. I knew I should feel free, yet wherever I wandered I was haunted by a distant howl. It was very troubling, because it was the sound of the wind and I could not escape it. Wherever I went, it followed, somewhere high above, hounding me forward.

Finally I managed to force myself awake. I lay there, panting in the dark. I was sure my eyes were open, but still I heard it. Somewhere high up, seeking me out.

It wasn't possible—we were hundreds of yards down, past who knew how many twists and turns, and yet it was so clear, and it was getting stronger.

By the others' breathing, I could tell they listened too. I tried to keep calm, but once the sound of the tin shed shuddering started to echo through the tunnel I began to tremble myself. There is something about wind-rattled walls that grabs you by the throat. Some primal knowledge that all our houses are doomed to fall down on our heads, that nothing we build will stand up to the world when it decides to do its worst.

"This can't be," I whimpered.

Christopher put his arm around me and said, "Shh. You're in the best place now."

I could not believe I was in the best place. Some perverse aspect of the Pozo's geometry magnified the wind a thousandfold, if not more, because soon it truly began to roar. I had never lived through a tornado, but I had seen footage, and now I felt like one of those Oklahomans hunkering down in his basement. I could no longer hear my own breathing, let alone my own thoughts.

And it only got worse. My heart was beating so hard I thought I was going to have a coronary. I covered my head. Believe it or not, I prayed. I was sure the world had ended because the only reason I could imagine for the wind to roar like that was if the atmosphere had been peeled from the Earth.

"Don't be scared," Christopher whispered, and this time his words were so clear that they sank in like fishhooks and I followed them up. "You're in the right place."

After that, the sound seemed to recede and I could hear the others again, as if the whole thing had been some passing hallucination. I knew it wasn't. Some of the others fidgeted, but most were still and I became profoundly grateful for the peace of our little abyss.

"What's happening up there?" I whispered.

"Mr. Wind's telling us to go all the way down." Christopher said.

"What if we don't go?"

"Then we'll all stay crazy."

"But I'm not crazy!" I cried.

"Sure you are."

Don't ask me how I slept after that, but I did. This time there were no dreams, and when I awoke there was no wind. I got up and tripped on the lantern. I checked my watch. It was 6:30 a.m. Time to go.

"Humberta?"

She didn't answer.

I turned on the lantern. She wasn't among the sleepers. I walked to the latrine, trying not to lose it, but she wasn't there either. By the time I got back I was so knotted up inside I felt like puking. The others were all awake.

"Where is she?"

The hermits made conciliatory faces.

"She was ready," Christopher said. "It was obvious from the moment she got here. Man, she had such a great aura. I really liked her."

"Shut your mouth." I edged towards The Last Scamp and looked down. I tried to rationalize, to tell myself that overnight she had gotten so scared that she had fled back up the Pozo, but I knew that was wrong. "I'm going after her," I said.

Christopher put his hand on my shoulder. "No you're not."

I stood there staring down the fathomless drop. Somewhere, in that black, the coolest girl I had ever met was climbing down to live out her days beneath a volcano. I just stood there, wishing she would look up and see the light.

"How long could she possibly last?" I asked.

"Don't worry about her," Christopher said. "She's beyond us now."

And he was right. There was no way I was going to follow her down.

I slumped against the wall, and though I was the only one not dying of hunger or thirst, they filled me with jam and water as I blubbered. Finally, Christopher squatted beside me and said, "Hey. Hey, little brother. Maybe it's time for you to go."

I didn't argue. I was just glad they weren't begging me to stay. I got up and let each one pat me on the back.

"It's going to be all right," Christopher said. "If you're at peace with things up there, that's wonderful, good for you. But if you ever feel like you're ready, you know where we'll be."

I couldn't wait any longer, so I left, and I was the one I felt sorry for.

I tried to walk without the light, but the dark was too much to bear. Though my backpack was empty, the climb wore me out and I had to stop four or five times along the way. When I finally made it to the bottom of the last ascent, I paused for a long while, staring up into the daylit shed above.

Eventually I got moving and a few minutes later I emerged. Mr. Wind was still sitting in the same spot.

I wanted to act normal, as if he were just some old guy who served as custodian to this hole. It was no use. As soon as I got out of the Pozo I scrambled away as if he were a barrel of toxic waste. He didn't move a hair. Only his eyes followed me.

He was exactly as I had left him, but now I read more than determination in the ancient lines of his face. I read his hatred. I was the worm in his apple, and he wanted nothing more than to smear me against the rocks.

I ran down Azufre's slope and got the hell out of Chile.

My perspective started to shift on the flight home. I sat by the window and watched how the sunlight splashed across the pillow-top clouds, and I realized it was all wrong. The view was beautiful, like a pint of amber on a hot day, but if Christopher was to be believed, it was one laced with arsenic.

What if he was right? I can't deny what I experienced in the Well. Maybe I was delirious in the dark, but now I can't help but think of the wind as my enemy. Ever since I got home, I've been spending more time indoors.

More than that, I just can't reconcile how a girl like Humberta would descend the Last Scamp. In our short time together, I couldn't find a single flaw in her. But in the end, she turned out to be more like Christopher than myself.

Maybe there is something wrong with me. Maybe the world, the sky—whatever—should make me more mental and fearful. My problem is that I just don't feel it, no matter how hard I try. And even if my brother was right, that we must all return to sea level and there's a right way to get there, how fed up would you have to be to embrace the Pozo's cure?

So I just lead my life. Punching the clock. Stretching out on my empty couch. Saving money on groceries, now that there's just me.

I'm not happy. I'm not ready for the Well, but I've got a plan.

I'm leaving tomorrow. My destination is forty-five hundred miles from here and the walk will take one thousand days. I will pass through the rust belt and Bible belt and border provinces abandoned to cartels. I will hack through jungles, wade piranha-infested waters and sprint through cocaine plantations, dodging the rebels' fire.

Maybe I'll fall along the way, but I think I'll get there, properly fatigued and ready to welcome the Pozo's cure. In fact, I'm confident I will, as long as the wind's at my back.

THE RATS IN
THE WALLS

H. P. LOVECRAFT

On July 16, 1923, I moved into Exham Priory after the last workman had finished his labours. The restoration had been a stupendous task, for little had remained of the deserted pile but a shell-like ruin; yet because it had been the seat of my ancestors I let no expense deter me. The place had not been inhabited since the reign of James the First, when a tragedy of intensely hideous, though largely unexplained, nature had struck down the master, five of his children, and several servants; and driven forth under a cloud of suspicion and terror the third son, my lineal progenitor and the only survivor of the abhorred line. With this sole heir denounced as a murderer, the estate had reverted to the crown, nor had the accused man made any attempt to exculpate himself or regain his property. Shaken by some horror greater than that of conscience or the law, and expressing only a frantic wish to exclude the ancient edifice from his sight and memory, Walter de la Poer, eleventh Baron Exham, fled to Virginia and there founded the family which by the next century had become known as Delapore.

Exham Priory had remained untenanted, though later allotted to the estates of the Norrys family and much studied because of its peculiarly composite architecture; an architecture involving Gothic towers resting on a Saxon or Romanesque substructure, whose foundation in turn was of a still earlier order or blend of orders—Roman, and even Druidic or native Cymric, if legends speak truly. This foundation was a very singular thing, being merged on one side with the solid limestone of the precipice from whose brink the priory overlooked a desolate valley three miles west of the village of Anchester. Architects and antiquarians loved to examine this strange relic of forgotten centuries, but the country folk hated it. They had hated it hundreds of years before, when my ancestors lived there, and they hated it now, with the moss and mould of abandonment on it. I had not been a day in Anchester before I knew I came of an accursed house. And this week workmen have blown up Exham Priory, and are busy obliterating the traces of its foundations.

The bare statistics of my ancestry I had always known, together with the fact that my first American forbear had come to the colonies under a strange cloud. Of details, however, I had been kept wholly ignorant through the policy of reticence always maintained by the Delapores. Unlike our planter neighbours, we seldom boasted of crusading ancestors or other mediaeval and Renaissance heroes; nor was any kind of tradition handed down except what may have been recorded in the sealed envelope left before the Civil War by every squire to his eldest son for posthumous opening. The glories we cherished were those achieved since the migration; the glories of a proud and honourable, if somewhat reserved and unsocial Virginia line.

During the war our fortunes were extinguished and our whole existence changed by the burning of Carfax, our home on the banks of the James. My grandfather, advanced in years, had perished in that incendiary outrage, and with him the envelope that bound us all to the past. I can recall that fire today as I saw it then at the age of seven, with the Federal soldiers shouting, the women screaming, and the negroes howling and praying. My father was in the army, defending Richmond, and after many formalities my mother and I were passed through the lines to join him. When the war ended we all moved north, whence my mother had come; and I grew to manhood, middle age, and ultimate wealth as a stolid Yankee. Neither my father nor I ever knew what our hereditary envelope had contained, and as I merged into the greyness of Massachusetts business life I lost all interest in the mysteries which evidently lurked far back in my family tree. Had I suspected their nature, how gladly I would have left Exham Priory to its moss, bats, and cobwebs!

My father died in 1904, but without any message to leave me, or to my only child, Alfred, a motherless boy of ten. It was this boy who reversed the order of family information; for although I could give him only jesting conjectures about the past, he wrote me of some very interesting ancestral legends when the late war took him to England in 1917 as an aviation officer. Apparently the Delapores had a colourful and perhaps sinister history, for a friend of my son's, Capt. Edward Norrys of the Royal Flying Corps, dwelt near the family seat at Anchester and related some peasant superstitions which few novelists could equal for wildness and incredibility. Norrys himself, of course, did not take them seriously; but they amused my son and made good material for his letters to me. It was this legendry which definitely turned my attention to my transatlantic heritage, and made me resolve to purchase and restore the family seat which Norrys shewed to Alfred in its picturesque desertion, and offered to get for him at a surprisingly reasonable figure, since his own uncle was the present owner.

I bought Exham Priory in 1918, but was almost immediately distracted from my plans of restoration by the return of my son as a maimed invalid. During the two years that he lived I thought of nothing but his care, having even placed my business under the direction of partners. In 1921, as I found myself bereaved and aimless, a retired manufacturer no longer young, I resolved to divert my remaining years with my new possession. Visiting Anchester in December, I was entertained by Capt. Norrys, a plump, amiable young man who had thought much of my son, and secured his assistance in gathering plans and anecdotes to guide in the coming restoration. Exham Priory itself I saw without emotion, a jumble of tottering mediaeval ruins covered with lichens and honeycombed with rooks' nests, perched perilously upon a precipice, and denuded of floors or other interior features save the stone walls of the separate towers.

As I gradually recovered the image of the edifice as it had been when my ancestor left it over three centuries before, I began to hire workmen for the reconstruction. In every case I was forced to go outside the immediate locality, for the Anchester villagers had an almost unbelievable fear and hatred of the place. This sentiment was so great that it was sometimes communicated to the outside labourers, causing numerous desertions; whilst its scope appeared to include both the priory and its ancient family.

My son had told me that he was somewhat avoided during his visits because he was a de la Poer, and I now found myself subtly ostracised for a like reason until I convinced the peasants how little I knew of my heritage. Even then they sullenly disliked me, so that I had to collect most of the village traditions through the mediation of Norrys. What the people could not forgive, perhaps, was that I had come to restore a symbol so abhorrent to them; for, rationally or not, they viewed Exham Priory as nothing less than a haunt of fiends and werewolves.

Piecing together the tales which Norrys collected for me, and supplementing them with the accounts of several savants who had studied the ruins, I deduced that Exham Priory stood on the site of a prehistoric temple; a Druidical or ante-Druidical thing which must have been contemporary with Stonehenge. That indescribable rites had been celebrated there, few doubted; and there were unpleasant tales of the transference of these rites into the Cybele-worship which the Romans had introduced. Inscriptions still visible in the sub-cellar bore such unmistakable letters as "DIV...OPS...MAGNA. MAT ..." sign of the Magna Mater whose dark worship was once vainly forbidden to Roman citizens. Anchester had been the camp of the third Augustan legion, as many remains attest, and it was said that the temple of Cybele was splendid and thronged with worshippers who performed nameless ceremonies at the bidding of a Phrygian priest. Tales added that the fall of the old religion did not end the orgies at the temple, but that the priests lived on in the new faith without real change. Likewise was it said that the rites did not vanish with the Roman power, and that certain among the Saxons added to what remained of the temple, and gave it the essential outline it subsequently preserved, making it the centre of a cult feared through half the heptarchy. About 1000 A.D. the place is mentioned in a chronicle as being a substantial stone priory housing a strange and powerful monastic order and surrounded by extensive gardens which needed no walls to exclude a frightened populace. It was never destroyed by the Danes, though after the Norman Conquest it must have declined tremendously; since there was no impediment when Henry the Third granted the site to my ancestor, Gilbert de la Poer, First Baron Exham, in 1261.

Of my family before this date there is no evil report, but something strange must have happened then. In one chronicle there is a reference to a de la Poer as "cursed of God" in 1307, whilst village legendry had nothing but evil and frantic fear to tell of the castle that went up on the foundations of the old temple and priory. The fireside tales were of the most grisly description, all the ghastlier because of their frightened reticence and cloudy evasiveness. They represented my ancestors as a race of hereditary daemons beside whom Gilles de Retz and the Marquis de Sade would seem the veriest tyros, and hinted whisperingly at their responsibility for the occasional disappearance of villagers through several generations.

The worst characters, apparently, were the barons and their direct heirs; at least, most was whispered about these. If of healthier inclinations, it was said, an heir would early and mysteriously die to make way for another more typical scion. There seemed to be an inner cult in the family, presided over by the head of the house, and sometimes closed except to a few members. Temperament rather than ancestry was evidently the basis of this cult, for it was entered by several who married into the family. Lady Margaret Trevor from Cornwall, wife of Godfrey, the second son of the fifth baron, became a favourite bane of children all over the countryside, and the daemon heroine of a particularly horrible old ballad not yet extinct near the Welsh border. Preserved in balladry, too, though not illustrating the same point, is the hideous tale of Lady Mary de la Poer, who shortly after her marriage to the Earl of Shrewsfield was killed by him and his mother, both of the slayers being absolved and blessed by the priest to whom they confessed what they dared not repeat to the world.

These myths and ballads, typical as they were of crude superstition, repelled me greatly. Their persistence, and their application to so long a line of my ancestors, were especially annoying; whilst the imputations of monstrous habits proved unpleasantly reminiscent of the one known scandal of my immediate forbears—the case of my cousin, young Randolph Delapore of Carfax, who went among the negroes and became a voodoo priest after he returned from the Mexican War.

I was much less disturbed by the vaguer tales of wails and howlings in the barren, windswept valley beneath the limestone cliff; of the graveyard stenches after the spring rains; of the floundering, squealing white thing on which Sir John Clave's horse had trod one night in a lonely field; and of the servant who had gone mad at what he saw in the priory in the full light of day. These things were hackneyed spectral lore, and I was at that time a pronounced sceptic. The accounts of vanished peasants were less to be dismissed, though not especially significant in view of mediaeval custom. Prying curiosity meant death, and more than one severed head had been publicly shewn on the bastions—now effaced—around Exham Priory.

A few of the tales were exceedingly picturesque, and made me wish I had learnt more of comparative mythology in my youth. There was, for instance, the belief that a legion of bat-winged devils kept Witches' Sabbath each night at the priory—a legion whose sustenance might explain the disproportionate abundance of coarse vegetables harvested in the vast gardens. And, most vivid of all, there was the dramatic epic of the rats—the scampering army of obscene vermin which had burst forth from the castle three months after the tragedy that doomed it to desertion—the lean, filthy, ravenous army which had swept all before it and devoured fowl, cats, dogs, hogs, sheep, and even two hapless human beings before its fury was spent. Around that unforgettable rodent army a whole separate cycle of myths revolves, for it scattered among the village homes and brought curses and horrors in its train.

Such was the lore that assailed me as I pushed to completion, with an elderly obstinacy, the work of restoring my ancestral home. It must not be imagined for a moment that these tales formed my principal psychological environment. On the other hand, I was constantly praised and encouraged by Capt. Norrys and the antiquarians who surrounded and aided me. When the task was done, over two years after its commencement, I viewed the great rooms, wainscotted walls, vaulted ceilings, mullioned windows, and broad staircases with a pride which fully compensated for the prodigious expense of the restoration. Every attribute of the Middle Ages was cunningly reproduced, and the new parts blended perfectly with the original walls and foundations. The seat of my fathers was complete, and I looked forward to redeeming at last the local fame of the line which ended in me. I would reside here permanently, and prove that a de la Poer (for I had adopted again the original spelling of the name) need not be a fiend. My comfort was perhaps augmented by the fact that, although Exham Priory was mediaevally fitted, its interior was in truth wholly new and free from old vermin and old ghosts alike.

As I have said, I moved in on July 16, 1923. My household consisted of seven servants and nine cats, of which latter species I am particularly fond. My eldest cat, "Nigger-Man", was seven years old and had come with me from my home in Bolton, Massachusetts; the others I had accumulated whilst living with Capt. Norrys' family during the restoration of the priory. For five days our routine proceeded with the utmost placidity, my time being spent mostly in the codification of old family data. I had now obtained some very circumstantial accounts of the final tragedy and flight of Walter de la Poer, which I conceived to be the probable contents of the hereditary paper lost in the fire at Carfax. It appeared that my ancestor was accused with much reason of having killed all the other members of his household, except four servant confederates, in their sleep, about two weeks after a shocking discovery which changed his whole demeanour, but which, except by implication, he disclosed to no one save perhaps the servants who assisted him and afterward fled beyond reach.

This deliberate slaughter, which included a father, three brothers, and two sisters, was largely condoned by the villagers, and so slackly treated by the law that its perpetrator escaped honoured, unharmed, and undisguised to Virginia; the general whispered sentiment being that he had purged the land of an immemorial curse. What discovery had prompted an act so terrible, I could scarcely even conjecture. Walter de la Poer must have known for years the sinister tales about his family, so that this material could have given him no fresh impulse. Had he, then, witnessed some appalling ancient rite, or stumbled upon some frightful and revealing symbol in the priory or its vicinity? He was reputed to have been a shy, gentle youth in England. In Virginia he seemed not so much hard or bitter as harassed and apprehensive. He was spoken of in the diary of another gentleman-adventurer, Francis Harley of Bellview, as a man of unexampled justice, honour, and delicacy.

On July 22 occurred the first incident which, though lightly dismissed at the time, takes on a preternatural significance in relation to later events. It was so simple as to be almost negligible, and could not possibly have been noticed under the circumstances; for it must be recalled that since I was in a building practically fresh and new except for the walls, and surrounded by a well-balanced staff of servitors, apprehension would have been absurd despite the locality. What I afterward remembered is merely this—that my old black cat, whose moods I know so well, was undoubtedly alert and anxious to an extent wholly out of keeping with his natural character. He roved from room to room, restless and disturbed, and sniffed constantly about the walls which formed part of the old Gothic structure. I realise how trite this sounds—like the inevitable dog in the ghost story, which always growls before his master sees the sheeted figure—yet I cannot consistently suppress it.

The following day a servant complained of restlessness among all the cats in the house. He came to me in my study, a lofty west room on the second story, with groined arches, black oak panelling, and a triple Gothic window overlooking the limestone cliff and desolate valley; and even as he spoke I saw the jetty form of Nigger-Man creeping along the west wall and scratching at the new panels which overlaid the ancient stone. I told the man that there must be some singular odour or emanation from the old stonework, imperceptible to human senses, but affecting the delicate organs of cats even through the new woodwork. This I truly believed, and when the fellow suggested the presence of mice or rats, I mentioned that there had been no rats there for three hundred years, and that even the field mice of the surrounding country could hardly be found in these high walls, where they had never been known to stray. That afternoon I called on Capt. Norrys, and he assured me that it would be quite incredible for field mice to infest the priory in such a sudden and unprecedented fashion.

That night, dispensing as usual with a valet, I retired in the west tower chamber which I had chosen as my own, reached from the study by a stone staircase and short gallery—the former partly ancient, the latter entirely restored. This room was circular, very high, and without wainscotting, being hung with arras which I had myself chosen in London. Seeing that Nigger-Man was with me, I shut the heavy Gothic door and retired by the light of the electric bulbs which so cleverly counterfeited candles, finally switching off the light and sinking on the carved and canopied four-poster, with the venerable cat in his accustomed place across my feet. I did not draw the curtains, but gazed out at the narrow north window which I faced. There was a suspicion of aurora in the sky, and the delicate traceries of the window were pleasantly silhouetted.

At some time I must have fallen quietly asleep, for I recall a distinct sense of leaving strange dreams, when the cat started violently from his placid position. I saw him in the faint auroral glow, head strained forward, fore feet on my ankles, and hind feet stretched behind. He was looking intensely at a point on the wall somewhat west of the window, a point which to my eye had nothing to mark it, but toward which all my attention was now directed. And as I watched, I knew that Nigger-Man was not vainly excited. Whether the arras actually moved I cannot say. I think it did, very slightly. But what I can swear to is that behind it I heard a low, distinct scurrying as of rats or mice. In a moment the cat had jumped bodily on the screening tapestry, bringing the affected section to the floor with his weight, and exposing a damp, ancient wall of stone; patched here and there by the restorers, and devoid of any trace of rodent prowlers. Nigger-Man raced up and down the floor by this part of the wall, clawing the fallen arras and seemingly trying at times to insert a paw between the wall and the oaken floor. He found nothing, and after a time returned wearily to his place across my feet. I had not moved, but I did not sleep again that night.

In the morning I questioned all the servants, and found that none of them had noticed anything unusual, save that the cook remembered the actions of a cat which had rested on her windowsill. This cat had howled at some unknown hour of the night, awaking the cook in time for her to see him dart purposefully out of the open door down the stairs. I drowsed away the noontime, and in the afternoon called again on Capt. Norrys, who became exceedingly interested in what I told him. The odd incidents—so slight yet so curious—appealed to his sense of the picturesque, and elicited from him a number of reminiscences of local ghostly lore. We were genuinely perplexed at the presence of rats, and Norrys lent me some traps and Paris green, which I had the servants place in strategic localities when I returned.

I retired early, being very sleepy, but was harassed by dreams of the most horrible sort. I seemed to be looking down from an immense height upon a twilit grotto, knee-deep with filth, where a white-bearded daemon swineherd drove about with his staff a flock of fungous, flabby beasts whose appearance filled me with unutterable loathing. Then, as the swineherd paused and nodded over his task, a mighty swarm of rats rained down on the stinking abyss and fell to devouring beasts and man alike.

From this terrific vision I was abruptly awaked by the motions of Nigger-Man, who had been sleeping as usual across my feet. This time I did not have to question the source of his snarls and hisses, and of the fear which made him sink his claws into my ankle, unconscious of their effect; for on every side of the chamber the walls were alive with nauseous sound—the verminous slithering of ravenous, gigantic rats. There was now no aurora to shew the state of the arras—the fallen section of which had been replaced—but I was not too frightened to switch on the light.

As the bulbs leapt into radiance I saw a hideous shaking all over the tapestry, causing the somewhat peculiar designs to execute a singular dance of death. This motion disappeared almost at once, and the sound with it. Springing out of bed, I poked at the arras with the long handle of a warming-pan that rested near, and lifted one section to see what lay beneath. There was nothing but the patched stone wall, and even the cat had lost his tense realisation of abnormal presences. When I examined the circular trap that had been placed in the room, I found all of the openings sprung, though no trace remained of what had been caught and had escaped.

Further sleep was out of the question, so, lighting a candle, I opened the door and went out in the gallery toward the stairs to my study, Nigger-Man following at my heels. Before we had reached the stone steps, however, the cat darted ahead of me and vanished down the ancient flight. As I descended the stairs myself, I became suddenly aware of sounds in the great room below; sounds of a nature which could not be mistaken. The oak-panelled walls were alive with rats, scampering and milling, whilst Nigger-Man was racing about with the fury of a baffled hunter. Reaching the bottom, I switched on the light, which did not this time cause the noise to subside. The rats continued their riot, stampeding with such force and distinctness that I could finally assign to their motions a definite direction. These creatures, in numbers apparently inexhaustible, were engaged in one stupendous migration from inconceivable heights to some depth conceivably, or inconceivably, below.

I now heard steps in the corridor, and in another moment two servants pushed open the massive door. They were searching the house for some unknown source of disturbance which had thrown all the cats into a snarling panic and caused them to plunge precipitately down several flights of stairs and squat, yowling, before the closed door to the sub-cellar. I asked them if they had heard the rats, but they replied in the negative. And when I turned to call their attention to the sounds in the panels, I realised that the noise had ceased. With the two men, I went down to the door of the sub-cellar, but found the cats already dispersed. Later I resolved to explore the crypt below, but for the present I merely made a round of the traps. All were sprung, yet all were tenantless. Satisfying myself that no one had heard the rats save the felines and me, I sat in my study till morning; thinking profoundly, and recalling every scrap of legend I had unearthed concerning the building I inhabited.

I slept some in the forenoon, leaning back in the one comfortable library chair which my mediaeval plan of furnishing could not banish. Later I telephoned to Capt. Norrys, who came over and helped me explore the sub-cellar. Absolutely nothing untoward was found, although we could not repress a thrill at the knowledge that this vault was built by Roman hands. Every low arch and massive pillar was Roman—not the debased Romanesque of the bungling Saxons, but the severe and harmonious classicism of the age of the Caesars; indeed, the walls abounded with inscriptions familiar to the antiquarians who had repeatedly explored the place—things like "P.GETAE. PROP...TEMP... DONA..." and "L. PRAEC...VS...PONTIFI...ATYS..."

The reference to Atys made me shiver, for I had read Catullus and knew something of the hideous rites of the Eastern god, whose worship was so mixed with that of Cybele. Norrys and I, by the light of lanterns, tried to interpret the odd and nearly effaced designs on certain irregularly rectangular blocks of stone generally held to be altars, but could make nothing of them. We remembered that one pattern, a sort of rayed sun, was held by students to imply a non-Roman origin, suggesting that these altars had merely been adopted by the Roman priests from some older and perhaps aboriginal temple on the same site. On one of these blocks were some brown stains which made me wonder. The largest, in the centre of the room, had certain features on the upper surface which indicated its connexion with fire—probably burnt offerings.

Such were the sights in that crypt before whose door the cats had howled, and where Norrys and I now determined to pass the night. Couches were brought down by the servants, who were told not to mind any nocturnal actions of the cats, and Nigger-Man was admitted as much for help as for companionship. We decided to keep the great oak door—a modern replica with slits for ventilation—tightly closed; and, with this attended to, we retired with lanterns still burning to await whatever might occur.

The vault was very deep in the foundations of the priory, and undoubtedly far down on the face of the beetling limestone cliff overlooking the waste valley. That it had been the goal of the scuffling and unexplainable rats I could not doubt, though why, I could not tell. As we lay there expectantly, I found my vigil occasionally mixed with half-formed dreams from which the uneasy motions of the cat across my feet would rouse me. These dreams were not wholesome, but horribly like the one I had had the night before. I saw again the twilit grotto, and the swineherd with his unmentionable fungous beasts wallowing in filth, and as I looked at these things they seemed nearer and more distinct—so distinct that I could almost observe their features. Then I did observe the flabby features of one of them —and awaked with such a scream that Nigger-Man started up, whilst Capt. Norrys, who had not slept, laughed considerably. Norrys might have laughed more—or perhaps less—had he known what it was that made me scream. But I did not remember myself till later. Ultimate horror often paralyses memory in a merciful way.

Norrys waked me when the phenomena began. Out of the same frightful dream I was called by his gentle shaking and his urging to listen to the cats. Indeed, there was much to listen to, for beyond the closed door at the head of the stone steps was a veritable nightmare of feline yelling and clawing, whilst Nigger-Man, unmindful of his kindred outside, was running excitedly around the bare stone walls, in which I heard the same babel of scurrying rats that had troubled me the night before.

An acute terror now rose within me, for here were anomalies which nothing normal could well explain. These rats, if not the creatures of a madness which I shared with the cats alone, must be burrowing and sliding in Roman walls I had thought to be of solid limestone blocks...

unless perhaps the action of water through more than seventeen centuries had eaten winding tunnels which rodent bodies had worn clear and ample... But even so, the spectral horror was no less; for if these were living vermin why did not Norrys hear their disgusting commotion? Why did he urge me to watch Nigger-Man and listen to the cats outside, and why did he guess wildly and vaguely at what could have aroused them?

By the time I had managed to tell him, as rationally as I could, what I thought I was hearing, my ears gave me the last fading impression of the scurrying; which had retreated *still downward*, far underneath this deepest of sub-cellars till it seemed as if the whole cliff below were riddled with questing rats. Norrys was not as sceptical as I had anticipated, but instead seemed profoundly moved. He motioned to me to notice that the cats at the door had ceased their clamour, as if giving up the rats for lost; whilst Nigger-Man had a burst of renewed restlessness, and was clawing frantically around the bottom of the large stone altar in the centre of the room, which was nearer Norrys' couch than mine.

My fear of the unknown was at this point very great. Something astounding had occurred, and I saw that Capt. Norrys, a younger, stouter, and presumably more naturally materialistic man, was affected fully as much as myself—perhaps because of his lifelong and intimate familiarity with local legend. We could for the moment do nothing but watch the old black cat as he pawed with decreasing fervour at the base of the altar, occasionally looking up and mewing to me in that persuasive manner which he used when he wished me to perform some favour for him.

Norrys now took a lantern close to the altar and examined the place where Nigger-Man was pawing; silently kneeling and scraping away the lichens of centuries which joined the massive pre-Roman block to the tessellated floor. He did not find anything, and was about to abandon his effort when I noticed a trivial circumstance which made me shudder, even though it implied nothing more than I had already imagined. I told him of it, and we both looked at its almost imperceptible manifestation with the fixedness of fascinated discovery and acknowledgment. It was only this—that the flame of the lantern set down near the altar was slightly but certainly flickering from a draught of air which it had not before received, and which came indubitably from the crevice between floor and altar where Norrys was scraping away the lichens.

We spent the rest of the night in the brilliantly lighted study, nervously discussing what we should do next. The discovery that some vault deeper than the deepest known masonry of the Romans underlay this accursed pile—some vault unsuspected by the curious antiquarians of three centuries—would have been sufficient to excite us without any background of the sinister. As it was, the fascination became twofold; and we paused in doubt whether to abandon our search and quit the priory forever in superstitious caution, or to gratify our sense of adventure and brave whatever horrors might await us in the unknown depths. By morning we had compromised, and decided to go to London to gather a group of archaeologists and scientific men fit to cope with the mystery. It should be mentioned that before leaving the sub-cellar we had vainly tried to move the central altar which we now recognised as the gate to a new pit of nameless fear. What secret would open the gate, wiser men than we would have to find.

During many days in London Capt. Norrys and I presented our facts, conjectures, and legendary anecdotes to five eminent authorities, all men who could be trusted to respect any family disclosures which future explorations might develop. We found most of them little disposed to scoff, but instead intensely interested and sincerely sympathetic. It is hardly necessary to name them all, but I may say that they included Sir William Brinton, whose excavations in the Troad excited most of the world in their day. As we all took the train for Anchester I felt myself poised on the brink of frightful revelations, a sensation symbolised by the air of mourning among the many Americans at the unexpected death of the President on the other side of the world.

On the evening of August 7th we reached Exham Priory, where the servants assured me that nothing unusual had occurred. The cats, even old Nigger-Man, had been perfectly placid; and not a trap in the house had been sprung. We were to begin exploring on the following day, awaiting which I assigned well-appointed rooms to all my guests. I myself retired in my own tower chamber, with Nigger-Man across my feet. Sleep came quickly, but hideous dreams assailed me. There was a vision of a Roman feast like that of Trimalchio, with a horror in a covered platter. Then came that damnable, recurrent thing about the swineherd and his filthy drove in the twilit grotto. Yet when I awoke it was full daylight, with normal sounds in the house below. The rats, living or spectral, had not troubled me; and Nigger-Man was quietly asleep. On going down, I found that the same tranquillity had prevailed elsewhere; a condition which one of the assembled savants—a fellow named Thornton, devoted to the psychic—rather absurdly laid to the fact that I had now been shewn the thing which certain forces had wished to shew me.

All was now ready, and at 11 a.m. our entire group of seven men, bearing powerful electric searchlights and implements of excavation, went down to the sub-cellar and bolted the door behind us. Nigger-Man was with us, for the investigators found no occasion to despise his excitability, and were indeed anxious that he be present in case of obscure rodent manifestations. We noted the Roman inscriptions and unknown altar designs only briefly, for three of the savants had already seen them, and all knew their characteristics. Prime attention was paid to the momentous central altar, and within an hour Sir William Brinton had caused it to tilt backward, balanced by some unknown species of counterweight.

There now lay revealed such a horror as would have overwhelmed us had we not been prepared. Through a nearly square opening in the tiled floor, sprawling on a flight of stone steps so prodigiously worn that it was little more than an inclined plane at the centre, was a ghastly array of human or semi-human bones. Those which retained their collocation as skeletons shewed attitudes of panic fear, and over all were the marks of rodent gnawing. The skulls denoted nothing short of utter idiocy, cretinism, or primitive semi-apedom. Above the hellishly littered steps arched a descending passage seemingly chiselled from the solid rock, and conducting a current of air. This current was not a sudden and noxious rush as from a closed vault, but a cool breeze with something of freshness in it. We did not pause long, but shiveringly began to clear a passage down the steps. It was then that Sir William, examining the hewn walls, made the odd observation that the passage, according to the direction of the strokes, must have been chiseled *from beneath*.

I must be very deliberate now, and choose my words.

After ploughing down a few steps amidst the gnawed bones we saw that there was light ahead; not any mystic phosphorescence, but a filtered daylight which could not come except from unknown fissures in the cliff that overlooked the waste valley. That such fissures had escaped notice from outside was hardly remarkable, for not only is the valley wholly uninhabited, but the cliff is so high and beetling that only an aëronaut could study its face in detail. A few steps more, and our breaths were literally snatched from us by what we saw; so literally that Thornton, the psychic investigator, actually fainted in the arms of the dazed man who stood behind him. Norrys, his plump face utterly white and flabby, simply cried out inarticulately; whilst I think that what I did was to gasp or hiss, and cover my eyes. The man behind me—the only one of the party older than I—croaked the hackneyed "My God!" in the most cracked voice I ever heard. Of seven cultivated men, only Sir William Brinton retained his composure; a thing more to his credit because he led the party and must have seen the sight first.

It was a twilit grotto of enormous height, stretching away farther than any eye could see; a subterraneous world of limitless mystery and horrible suggestion. There were buildings and other architectural remains—in one terrified glance I saw a weird pattern of tumuli, a savage circle of monoliths, a low-domed Roman ruin, a sprawling Saxon pile, and an early English edifice of wood—but all these were dwarfed by the ghoulish spectacle presented by the general surface of the ground. For yards about the steps extended an insane tangle of human bones, or bones at least as human as those on the steps. Like a foamy sea they stretched, some fallen apart, but others wholly or partly articulated as skeletons; these latter invariably in postures of daemoniac frenzy, either fighting off some menace or clutching other forms with cannibal intent.

When Dr. Trask, the anthropologist, stooped to classify the skulls, he found a degraded mixture which utterly baffled him. They were mostly lower than the Piltdown man in the scale of evolution, but in every case definitely human. Many were of higher grade, and a very few were the skulls of supremely and sensitively developed types. All the bones were gnawed, mostly by rats, but somewhat by others of the half-human drove. Mixed with them were many tiny bones of rats—fallen members of the lethal army which closed the ancient epic.

I wonder that any man among us lived and kept his sanity through that hideous day of discovery. Not Hoffmann or Huysmans could conceive a scene more wildly incredible, more frenetically repellent, or more Gothically grotesque than the twilit grotto through which we seven staggered; each stumbling on revelation after revelation, and trying to keep for the nonce from thinking of the events which must have taken place there three hundred years, or a thousand, or two thousand, or ten thousand years ago. It was the antechamber of hell, and poor Thornton fainted again when Trask told him that some of the skeleton things must have descended as quadrupeds through the last twenty or more generations.

Horror piled on horror as we began to interpret the architectural remains. The quadruped things—with their occasional recruits from the biped class—had been kept in stone pens, out of which they must have broken in their last delirium of hunger or rat-fear. There had been great herds of them, evidently fattened on the coarse vegetables whose remains could be found as a sort of poisonous ensilage at the bottom of huge stone bins older than Rome. I knew now why my ancestors had had such excessive gardens—would to heaven I could forget! The purpose of the herds I did not have to ask.

Sir William, standing with his searchlight in the Roman ruin, translated aloud the most shocking ritual I have ever known; and told of the diet of the antediluvian cult which the priests of Cybele found and mingled with their own. Norrys, used as he was to the trenches, could not walk straight when he came out of the English building. It was a butcher shop and kitchen—he had expected that—but it was too much to see familiar English implements in such a place, and to read familiar English *graffiti* there, some as recent as 1610. I could not go in that building—that building whose daemon activities were stopped only by the dagger of my ancestor Walter de la Poer.

What I did venture to enter was the low Saxon building, whose oaken door had fallen, and there I found a terrible row of ten stone cells with rusty bars. Three had tenants, all skeletons of high grade, and on the bony forefinger of one I found a seal ring with my own coat-of-arms. Sir William found a vault with far older cells below the Roman chapel, but these cells were empty. Below them was a low crypt with cases of formally arranged bones, some of them bearing terrible parallel inscriptions carved in Latin, Greek, and the tongue of Phrygia. Meanwhile, Dr. Trask had opened one of the prehistoric tumuli, and brought to light skulls which were slightly more human than a gorilla's, and which bore indescribable ideographic carvings. Through all this horror my cat stalked unperturbed. Once I saw him monstrously perched atop a mountain of bones, and wondered at the secrets that might lie behind his yellow eyes.

Having grasped to some slight degree the frightful revelations of this twilit area—an area so hideously foreshadowed by my recurrent dream—we turned to that apparently boundless depth of midnight cavern where no ray of light from the cliff could penetrate. We shall never know what sightless Stygian worlds yawn beyond the little distance we went, for it was decided that such secrets are not good for mankind. But there was plenty to engross us close at hand, for we had not gone far before the searchlights shewed that accursed infinity of pits in which the rats had feasted, and whose sudden lack of replenishment had driven the ravenous rodent army first to turn on the living herds of starving things, and then to burst forth from the priory in that historic orgy of devastation which the peasants will never forget.

God! those carrion black pits of sawed, picked bones and opened skulls! Those nightmare chasms choked with the pithecanthropoid, Celtic, Roman, and English bones of countless unhallowed centuries! Some of them were full, and none can say how deep they had once been. Others were still bottomless to our searchlights, and peopled by unnamable fancies. What, I thought, of the hapless rats that stumbled into such traps amidst the blackness of their quests in this grisly Tartarus?

Once my foot slipped near a horribly yawning brink, and I had a moment of ecstatic fear. I must have been musing a long time, for I could not see any of the party but the plump Capt. Norrys. Then there came a sound from that inky, boundless, farther distance that I thought I knew; and I saw my old black cat dart past me like a winged Egyptian god, straight into the illimitable gulf of the unknown. But I was not far behind, for there was no doubt after another second. It was the eldritch scurrying of those fiend-born rats, always questing for new horrors, and determined to lead me on even unto those grinning caverns of earth's centre where Nyarlathotep, the mad faceless god, howls blindly to the piping of two amorphous idiot flute-players.

My searchlight expired, but still I ran. I heard voices, and yowls, and echoes, but above all there gently rose that impious, insidious scurrying; gently rising, rising, as a stiff bloated corpse gently rises above an oily river that flows under endless onyx bridges to a black, putrid sea. Something bumped into me—something soft and plump. It must have been the rats; the viscous, gelatinous, ravenous army that feast on the dead and the living... Why shouldn't rats eat a de la Poer as a de la Poer eats forbidden things?...The war ate my boy, damn them all...and the Yanks ate Carfax with flames and burnt Grandsire Delapore and the secret...No, no, I tell you, I am *not* that daemon swineherd in the twilit grotto! It was *not* Edward Norrys' fat face on that flabby, fungous thing! Who says I am a de la Poer? He lived, but my boy died!... Shall a Norrys hold the lands of a de la Poer?...It's voodoo, I tell you... that spotted snake...Curse you, Thornton, I'll teach you to faint at what my family do!...'Sblood, thou stinkard, I'll learn ye how to gust... wolde ye swynke me thilke wys?...*Magna Mater! Magna Mater!...Atys... Dia ad aghaidh 's ad aodann...agus bas dunach ort! Dhonas 's dholas ort, agus leat-sa!...Ungl...ungl...rrrlh...chchch...*

That is what they say I said when they found me in the blackness after three hours; found me crouching in the blackness over the plump, half-eaten body of Capt. Norrys, with my own cat leaping and tearing at my throat. Now they have blown up Exham Priory, taken my Nigger-Man away from me, and shut me into this barred room at Hanwell with fearful whispers about my heredity and experiences. Thornton is in the next room, but they prevent me from talking to him. They are trying, too, to suppress most of the facts concerning the priory. When I speak of poor Norrys they accuse me of a hideous thing, but they must know that I did not do it. They must know it was the rats; the slithering, scurrying rats whose scampering will never let me sleep; the daemon rats that race behind the padding in this room and beckon me down to greater horrors than I have ever known; the rats they can never hear; the rats, the rats in the walls.

TENDING THE CORE

ADAM MILLARD

For billions of years they circle the core, four impervious titans riding upon colossal diamond bicycles. They know not why they ride, just that they must. Having never encountered each other—they remain equidistant at all times, therefore existing thousands of miles apart —each titan believes it is alone, a sole rider singlehandedly tending the core.

Never stopping.

An ethereal perpetual motion machine, clunking and wheezing and yet as robust as the day the riders set out.

Ka'al, the Great Black Rider, one day begins to consider its purpose as it completes rotation after rotation of the outer core. "There must be a reason!" it bellows into the abyssal tunnel ahead, still pedalling as quickly as its gargantuan legs will go. Its language is like none that has ever been spoken before, its voice a plangent lamentation which startles even Ka'al as it hits the mile-high tunnel walls on either side and returns, slightly altered in pitch and timbre.

All at once, hundreds of questions proceed to besiege Ka'al's previously vacant mind: *What am I? What have I been doing? Where did I come from? When did I start riding? What is this place, whose walls and darkness imprison me so? Why is it so important that I circle the core time after time?* One question follows another, and yet Ka'al cannot find the answer to any of them. It has come to accept its surroundings as infinitude; its unremitting cycling—around and around, a trillion times before resetting its internal counter to zero once again—a congenital defect for which there is no known cure.

For three whole circuits of the ceaseless tunnels, Ka'al considers its significance in the grand scheme of things, arriving at the conclusion that, somewhere out there, someone has the answer.

Whether subconsciously or unconsciously, the speed at which Ka'al rides through the abyss reduces. It has never happened before, but Ka'al feels the gradual change. Two-thousand-miles-per-hour becomes eighteen-hundred. Eighteen-hundred becomes fourteen-hundred. Ka'al knows it should not allow this to go on, for who knows what might happen should it stop altogether. The tunnels could collapse inward, burying the rider there beneath miles and miles of rubble for all eternity. The ground might open up beneath the smooth diamond wheels of Ka'al's bicycle, plunging him into a bottomless void.

But then again, *nothing* might happen.

And that is far too appealing to Ka'al for it to increase its velocity once again.

One-thousand-miles-per-hour.

Five-hundred.

It is barely moving now, and sees the walls around it clearly for the very first time. They're beautiful, peppered with things that glisten in the gloom, and it is almost too much for Ka'al to take.

Two-hundred.

One-hundred.

A silence has descended upon the tunnel. The Great Black Rider has grown so used to its own mechanical clamour that the sudden hush is almost twice as deafening.

Fifty.

Twenty.

No, you mustn't stop! You have to go on, lest something terrible happen!

But stop Ka'al does, and nothing terrible occurs, at least, not immediately. There is only silence and stillness, to which Ka'al does not know how to react. However, it is all at once aware of an existence wasted, for had it not been cycling relentlessly for the past four-and-a-half billion years, it might have discovered some better way to utilise its time.

The titan climbs down from its diamond bicycle and exhales deeply. It is a great relief to stop, and yet Ka'al is at a loss with itself, for what else is there to do down here in the darkness, rock and iron and nickel to its left and right and only darkness ahead?

It sits.

For an interminable amount of time it waits, pondering its existence, until an almighty roar appears in the distance and the tunnel walls begin to violently shake. Leaping to its feet, Ka'al is suddenly intrigued.

Even more so when, at two-thousand-miles-per-hour, a huge object slams into it, sending it sprawling into the darkness.

Rock and dust showers down from the tunnel walls, but Ka'al is not concerned, for it is only a small amount, not enough to displace the tunnel wholly. Gathering itself, Ka'al straightens up and sees, lying there next to a diamond bicycle, another being like itself, only it is the colour of alabaster.

"Who are you?" Ka'al asks as the new titan gets to its feet.

"I am Angoth, the Great White Rider," it says. "It is so strange to see another here in this place. For billions of years I believed myself to be alone."

Ka'al nods. "Why do you ride?" it asks.

"Why do you *not*?" comes the reply. "Is it not our purpose to ride? We must tend the core, must we not? Is that not our sole purpose?"

"Who knows what our purpose is?" Ka'al says as it drags Angoth's felled bicycle across the clearing. "Or what might happen should we falter."

They sit and talk, Angoth and Ka'al, failing to arrive at anything like a suitable conclusion. Once again, Ka'al can't help but feel as if he has been deprived of something. In this instance, billions of years of meaningful conversation with a compatible individual. A being who has only been a short distance behind all this time.

"Do you think there are others like us?" Ka'al asks as an exhalation, for it is relaxed and without a care in the world for the first time ever.

Angoth shrugs, and is about to answer in the affirmative when the tunnel walls begin to tremble and a thunderous roar fills up the darkness.

Ka'al helps Angoth to its feet and they stand at the centre of the tunnel, preparing for impact.

"Did it hurt when I ploughed into you earlier?" asks Angoth.

"I don't know," replies Ka'al with a frown.

Fortunately, as two titans standing in the middle of an oncoming third, they are visible. There comes, somewhere along the tunnel, the screeching of brakes, the plaintive howling of a flustered titan, followed by the unmistakable clatter as it is de-seated and hurtled forward into the darkness.

It comes to land at the feet of Ka'al, and Ka'al is unsurprised to find the third titan is identical to itself and to Angoth. "Do you require my help?" Ka'al asks of the fallen beast.

From the ground, the titan says, "That would be nice," and holds a giant hand out for Ka'al to grab.

Once on its feet, the newcomer introduces itself as Nomah, the Great Red Rider, before articulating its shock at discovering it has been cycling for all this time, unaware it was in such fine company.

"Yes, it is something of a puzzle," says Angoth. "It has always been about the core. Ride around the core, don't stop riding around the core, on and on we go. But that is no way in which to exist."

"But there is no other way for us, it seems," says Nomah. "I do believe this is our purpose, that to consider anything else is both irresponsible and naïve."

"It is no fun," says Ka'al. "Not like it was in the beginning. Do you think perhaps we could just take a little time off? To talk? To engage one another in stimulating dialogue?"

"That does sound riveting," says Angoth. "I, for one, would welcome a respite."

"Then we shall—"

But Ka'al does not get the chance to finish his sentence, for a fourth rider appears in the tunnel, accompanied by the conventional roar of its bicycle and the quaking of the walls.

"What's going on?" cries the newcomer as it disembarks from its diamond bicycle and wheels it toward the trio of obstacles in its path. "Who are you three, standing in the path of Sziba, the Great Blue Rider and solitary guardian of the core?"

"Actually," says Ka'al, calmly, "we are *all* tending the core."

"Well," says Angoth. "We *were*. Right now we're having a little breather

147

and a nice conversation. Would you care to join us?"

Sziba regards each of them warily before speaking. "I thought I'd *never* stop riding," it says. "I doubted I would ever see another like me down here, or up here, or wherever we are. Of *course* I would be delighted to pause, if only for a moment, so that we might palaver."

"It is odd how we can understand one another," says Nomah, "having never met before."

That is odd, Ka'al thinks, and yet nothing surprises him anymore.

And so they form a circle and natter for the longest of times. While the intention is to return to their bicycles once the conversation becomes vapid—it does not, not for many, many centuries—they soon forget about the diamond vehicles altogether.

"Do you think we are alone in the universe?" Ka'al asks one day.

"Perhaps," says Angoth.

"Don't be so *arrogant*," says Sziba. "Until recently we thought we were alone down here. Who *knows* what is out there in the great beyond!"

"We will never know," says Nomah with a shrug of indifference. "But I like to think there is life out there. Somewhere."

And as the conversation between the titans continues, the core grows slower and slower.

Until one day, it falls entirely still.

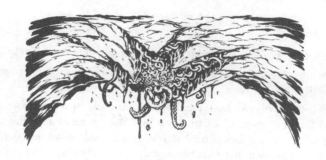

THE DRAGONS BENEATH

BELINDA LEWIS

Nhiriri was wedged tight in the tunnel's maw. She had slowly wormed her way down the narrowing stone gullet for most of the day. Now her hips were caught against rough granite and her bulky pack had twisted during the descent, trapping her arms and shoulders. The light of the setting sun was far above her head. Her breath was hot and brackish in the confined space.

Queens do not panic, she thought.

She picked at the rawhide knots lashing the pack to her body, wiggling her hips and bouncing on bare toes to create space between her body and the rock. Her painstaking efforts moved the pack up towards her neck until she could arch her body and force her sweat-slicked hips past the rock mouth. Tearing nails and skin, she pulled herself deeper into the earth. She landed lightly on the gravel cave floor. Her pack dropped beside her, the sound dull and muffled by the weight of the rocky sky.

Nhiriri's breathing was harsh but measured as she brushed dust from her tightly curled hair.

She sat down cross-legged and opened her pack. By feel she found her fire kit and a pouch of dried grasses. With movement made fluent by practice in the dark of her hut, she spun the rod against the board balanced between her feet. Her already abused shoulders and arms burned long before a coal began to form.

Queens do not give up, she thought.

She carefully coaxed a tiny flame into life. Her brown eyes danced in the light and she allowed herself a tight smile. She wrapped a large Wildebeest fur around her shoulders and bound smaller pieces of leather to her feet with thongs. She couldn't climb with the foot wrappings, but down here they were warm and would protect her stinging feet. She repacked her bag, lit a fat-soaked dung torch and walked down into the dark.

The tunnel was steep and narrow but soon opened onto a cavern. Its ceiling was studded with quartz, its walls wept moisture, and her breath made living shapes in the air. Nhiriri set up camp in a small raised alcove connected to the larger cave. She laid her sleeping furs on the ground and layered her precious supply of wood and charcoal between sleeping palette and furs to protect them from the damp. She dragged stones from around the chamber to create a raised fire pit at its entrance. She built a leather cowl over the pit and banked a burning coal for the night. Exhausted and stiff, but exhilarated, she went to sleep.

Nhiriri dreamed of dragons.

She watched them born sinuous in stars of unimaginable heat. They flew through the emptiness of space, ice crystals forming on corneas and talons. She watched them fight and mate in the skies above her Savannah. They hunted strange tusked-beasts with fire and with teeth. And she watched the Dragons die and turn to rock, their hot red blood cooling into shimmering metallic veins deep within the earth.

She awoke with the word swollen inside her mouth. "Copper," she whispered.

She began her search in earnest. Walking widening spirals from her camp, looking for glints of blood gold against the unending variations of rock, paying special attention to the layers of stone coloured with the blue and green of dragon scale.

It was luck that had lead her here, to these caverns. Outside the grass was dry and the trees were gaunt and the animals had moved far from her kingdom searching for water and sustenance. Each hunt Nhiriri and her hunters had to travel farther and farther. And each time they returned with shrinking portions of stringy meat, when they found game at all.

They had been hunting Elephant, following the skeletal dying herd East, when they came across a man and a woman resting beneath a lifeless thorn tree. The strangers had golden skin and sable almond eyes and ornaments of dragon's blood pierced their ears and were pinned to their furs. The strangers were reluctant, it took many hours, and it wasn't until she put out the woman's eyes that they finally told her the secrets of the metal. Of the finding and the waking and the shaping. Of the wealth and magic of dragon's blood. Of copper mirrors that let one see the future and own the past. Of the power she needed to save her tribe.

On her first day beneath the earth she discovered tunnels where fine silver threads contoured the walls in dendritic patterns. They looked like living rivers of fur, but when she brushed at them they were desiccated and sharp. Sometimes the dull needles drew the silhouettes of animals against the walls and floor; that one the undulation of a giant centipede, that one a drowning bird. She shivered when she passed a fibrous form that gave the appearance of suckered tentacles and a human face.

Queens are not afraid of the dark, she thought.

She measured distance by the rhythm of her heart and scored a map of her passage onto the ceiling of her stone cocoon each night.

On the fifth day she found a chamber whose entire surface was covered in indigo gems. Its ceiling was too high to see and the crystals glowed with a sickly white light that seared her eyes even as the rock cut her footwear, and then her feet, to ribbons. That way was impassable. She crawled back to camp, trailing blood and pain. In her wake drops of red turned iridescent as long parched spores drank in briny moisture.

She did not have enough food. Hunger dripped into her dreams and the dragons were sluggish shapes covered in coats of pearled furs.

She found the copper seam the day her dried meat ran out. She beat the rock with her stone hammer again and again and again and filled her pack with crushed stone flecked with ruddy gold and redder blood. She made the journey between seam and camp until her hands and feet were stiff and clumsy. The air was milky with dust and spores.

She sat in her furs pounding rocks until they surrendered bright specks of copper ore. The soles of her feet had cracked open, the exposed flesh pale and spongy and painful to the touch. She moved around her camp on hands and knees. She gathered wood and charcoal, her tools and her hopes, and set to smelting the rock.

The secret, the golden man had told her, when he still had a tongue to do so, was to make the dragon blood remember. Remember the heat and power of being alive and flowing through the heart and mind of so colossal an Ancient. Remember the taste of scales and claws and the wind and the sky. On remembering, the metal would become pliable in her hands.

She began to measure her time, not in heartbeats or in periods of waking and sleeping, but in how much of her precious wood she had fed to the fire. It burned hot and bright and it nourished her better than food.

▼▼▼

The golden woman's bare chest was pierced with a hundred spokes of glowing copper, her eyes sizzled on her cheeks. She rode a dragon against a wall of stars. Stalks of light flowed from the stars and grew around and through the woman and dragon. The dragon roared and its breath was not fire, but ice. Nhiriri turned away, trying to protect her face with her arms. A storm of stinging ice blistered Nhiriri's eyes, her nose, her lungs.

Nhiriri woke in darkness. Her throat burned and ice crackled in her joints as she escaped her furs.

Her fire had gone out.

Queens do not panic, she whispered.

Her fingers found her fire kit, but she fumbled rod and then board and then rod again until she screamed and threw her kit into the cave.

Queens are not afraid of the dark, she whispered over and over, clutching her knees against her chest. She rocked herself back and forth, but she did not cry. After a time in the quiet of her thoughts she realized that it was no longer dark, not truly. A luminescence followed her, spewing from the cracks of her feet and threading through her hands and arm and torso.

She could feel something move within her. A lattice that connected her to every creature who had become host to this fruiting-body from across the stars.

Soon, she thought.

She licked the walls of the cave to ease the pain in her throat and went back to sleep.

▼▼▼

Nhiriri did not dream. And when she woke she did so humming a song, an old song from the hunt. The cave was alight with living fungal threads and she the glowing pearl at its center. She remembered other caves. And other forests and other oceans and other planets. The cilia in her spine and mind a connection to other times. She smiled slowly, still humming. She remembered dragons.

She hawked saliva alive with thousands of glowing wiggling threads onto the cave floor. With hands made legion by tendrils of mycelium she drew ruins around the dead fire. Then she blew onto the ashes and gave them life with breath filled with spores and salt. The fire burned with the cold flame of things that have never seen the sun.

By the time she had finished her song the copper was molten. She channeled the flowing ruddy gold into a shallow clay bowl, swirling the dragon's blood around the vessel to coat the sides. It cooled quickly in the dampness of the cavern and she polished it with a leather scrap until it shone like the star. Until it shone like the birthplace of a dragon.

She looked into the mirror and saw her face, drawn and proud and writhing and shimmering with fungus.

And then she saw everything.

She saw Dragons born in exploding stars fly through the emptiness of space towards her tiny part of the cosmos. She understood time and distance and how small she really was. She tasted the strength of their blood—blood unhurt by heat or magic. Her people harnessed this strength, breaking stone to boil the corpses of dragons. They used their power and wealth to enslave other tribes, they built an empire on the death of Dragons and the death of Men. Pale men came from the north to subjugate her people and steal their power and strength. These vanquishers celebrated the slaughter of her people with dancing and feasting. They claimed the empire for their own. She saw their distant ancestors learn all the secrets of copper. Its alchemy and magic and science. They worked it into wires, like spiders they spun their copper webs across her Savannah and then across the world. Slowly, every living thing died beneath a web of heat and crackling magic current.

She saw her own death, her throat eventually too full of convoluted filaments to breath. And her people buried her, their Great Queen on the top of a hill. They buried her sitting, because even in death she was too revered to lie down. Letting her watch what her quest for power had wrought until the Earth died, and all dragon's blood was returned to the stars.

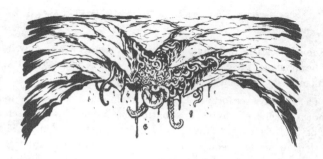

THE RE'EM

ADAM McOMBER

Upon the death of German monk Ulrich Gottard (drowned in the pale and churning waters of the River Lech) a manuscript is delivered to the Roman Curia for consideration by the Holy See. Lord Protector of Cromberg Cloister, Father Benedict, writes in his letter of submittal that he deems the document a distressing epistle due, in part, to its bizarre and heretical nature. "It is most certainly a *renunciation*," Benedict writes, "however unusual, however obscure." What is perhaps more troubling to the Lord Protector though is the reaction the manuscript incites among the younger initiates of his German cloister. Like the drowned monk himself, these youths are said to be delicate and romantic. "Troublesome searchers," Benedict calls them, "the sort that might wipe tears from their eyes at Matins." He notes that these "followers" of Gottard began to meet secretly in a dimly lit chamber beneath the cloister's chapter hall. It was there they attempted an interpretation of the manuscript, treating its passages as if they were some holy writ. The group began referring to itself as the

"Re'em." "These boys cling to one another," Father Benedict writes. "They hold each other in such dreadful high esteem. And together, they find meaning where meaning is not."

The narrative set forth in Ulrich Gottard's manuscript—now well known in higher echelons of the Roman Church—unfolds over a series of days during a visit to the Holy Land soon after his taking of First Orders. An amateur geologist as well as a man of God, Gottard begins his writings with a description of certain curious formations of volcanic alkaline rock in the arid landscape surrounding Mount Sinai in Egypt. Gottard notes that the rocks had, in places, fused together and formed what looked like the arches of a "black and imposing architecture, crumbling on the stony hillside—as if left there by some ancient and unknown race."

It was in one such glittering vault of blackish stone Gottard encountered the creature that would soon overwhelm his thoughts, as well as the thoughts of his future acolytes. "The animal stood upon its four legs," Gottard writes, "and was the size and approximate shape of a Calabrese stallion. Its coat was pale in color. The hair of its pelt was longish, matted. This was not a domesticated beast, and yet its state did not bespeak brutishness either."

Other attributes of the animal's appearance were entirely unique. For unlike a horse, the creature was possessed of a cloven hoof and a short leathery tail. It watched the monk's approach with a serene and thoughtful gaze, "as a sovereign might regard his subject." The creature's most striking feature was the single braided horn that protruded from the center of its head. "The horn," Gottard writes, "in certain light, appeared semi-translucent and at other times, looked as though it was made of stone. There were even moments it gleamed, as if forged of silver." The monk soon begins referring to the creature as a "re'em"— an animal mentioned in the Vulgate of St. Jerome (*Canst thou bind the horned re'em with his band in the furrow? Or will he harrow the valley after thee?*)

Upon returning to the village near the mountain, Gottard ascertained that such creatures, though uncommon, were at times sighted in the area. Their home—a valley some distance west of Mount Sinai—was accessible if accompanied by a suitable guide. Gottard, unable to banish the strange encounter from his thoughts, produced coins from his purse, and a guide was brought forth: a tall young man, dressed in white linen, introduced only as Chaths.

Gottard writes that, upon seeing the young man for the first time, he felt what might well be called an uncanny sense of recognition. It was not that Gottard had met the guide before, but in Chaths, he saw something of himself. "He did not resemble me in appearance. His eyes were dark. His brow, delicate and smooth. Yet all the while, I felt as though the villagers had produced, not a guide for me but a mirror. There was some evident tether stretched between the two of us. It bound us, as a man's reflection is fastened to him but is never precisely the same as him."

Early the following morning, Gottard and Chaths set out to locate the valley of the re'em. They made their way through the rocky landscape, with Gottard stealing sidelong glances at this curious "mirror." The guide remained a silent presence. Any given query from Gottard produced, at most, a few mumbled phrases in Chath's own language. The journey lasted longer than the monk expected, and soon the guide indicated they should make camp for the night. This would allow them to arrive at the valley by morning light. "It would be unwise to approach after nightfall," Chaths said in words finally plain enough for Gottard to comprehend.

"Are there dangers?" Gottard asked.

"We are in the desert," Chaths replied. "There are always dangers."

Despite a long day of travel, the monk found he could not sleep. A wind called from the distant hills. Small animals scuttled in the shadows just beyond the reach of the firelight. Gottard spent much of the night considering patterns in the flames. He imagined he saw within them the re'em, walking in circles. Wherever the re'em trod, black formations of stone appeared to rise—elegant horns that pierced the earth. The creature shifted and turned in the light. It drew nearer, then moved further away. The re'em no longer looked like a sovereign. Instead, it seemed to Gottard that he watched the dance of some ancient god.

After hours of this, the monk finally forced himself to turn from these visions. He regarded his sleeping guide and was surprised to find that the so-called mirror of the other man's face had changed during the night. There was now something in Chaths' features that reminded Gottard—not only of himself—but also of a boy called Aenor he'd known during his school days. Aenor had been a quiet sort, tall and thin, prone to exhaustion. He and Gottard often walked together along the stony banks of the River Lech. The boys skipped stones across the river's silt-white waters. They talked of the life of the soul. They would sometimes sit together beneath a crooked tree. Aenor would put his head on Gottard's shoulder, claiming he needed rest. Once, Aenor had taken Gottard's hand and said, "My mother says I am handsome. Do you think I am handsome as well, Ulrich?" Gottard did not know how to respond to such a question. He merely waited in silence, gazing out at the white River Lech. Finally, the silence itself became an answer.

The sun rose like a bronze seal above the desert. To Gottard, the white sky looked like the closed door of Heaven. The monk went to kneel at the edge of the firelight. He wanted to pray in order soothe himself. His memories of Aenor troubled him. The boy had been gentle and so kind. Gottard told Aenor that he could not love him. He loved only God.

"I bowed my head," he writes. "As I began my prayers, I felt a terrible sensation. It was as if an invisible hand had pressed itself against the very surface of my soul. For the first time, my prayers felt as though they would not rise. They would not ascend the heavenly ladder. Instead, they remained trapped inside my own flesh. Confined in that prison."

This disturbance caused Gottard to call out, waking Chaths. The guide blinked at him in the morning light.

"Can you hear my voice, brother?" Gottard asked the guide. His voice was pleading.

"I hear you plainly," Chaths replied.

Gottard crossed himself. "And when I make the cross, can you see it?"

"I can see your gesture," Chaths said. He stood and brought water in a wooden cup. "You must drink."

Gottard did drink. He found he wanted to take Chaths' hand. He wanted to feel the warmth of the guide, the life of him. "I recognize something in you," he said.

"You should drink more water," Chaths replied.

"Please," the monk said. "You hold some secret."

Chaths knelt beside Gottard at the edge of the camp. It was as if he too intended to pray. But instead, he only gazed out over the landscape that was covered in bluish rock. Finally, he said, "It's not an animal you seek, Brother Gottard. Not as you believe."

"What then?" Gottard asked.

The guide lowered his head.

"What else could it be?" Gottard asked again.

"The animal does not exist as other things do," the guide responded. "Sight of it is thought to be caused by a fissure that develops in the brain. A fever—"

Gottard remembered feeling ill a few nights before he encountered the re'em. He'd attributed the sickness merely to the sort of malaise that often came on during travel. "You're saying the creature is some kind of dream?" Gottard asked.

Chaths shook his head. "The fissure—it allows a man to see crossways. The animal walks there in that light."

"I don't understand. Crossways in the light?"

Chaths offered more water to the monk. "This will help. The water soothed me as well."

"You've been afflicted by the fever too?" Gottard asked.

Chaths nodded. "That is why I am to be your guide."

The idea that sickness had caused him to see the re'em troubled Gottard. Was it possible he chased some mirage? Was all of this a fool's errand? "If I am sick," he asked, "will I be cured?

Chaths looked at the monk solemnly. "There is no cure, Brother Gottard," he said. "There is only the valley."

Chaths indicated they should begin their journey before the sun rose too high above the mountains. Gottard did his best not to stumble upon the rocks as they walked. He felt ill from his sleeplessness. Perhaps, he thought, the fever might return. Soon, the two men came upon, not a valley, but a kind of tunnel in the low wall of a rocky outcropping. The same black volcanic stones that Gottard had seen upon his original encounter with the re'em surrounded the entrance to the tunnel. For a moment, the passage appeared to waver, fluctuating in shape and size. Gottard wondered if this anomaly was yet another symptom of the supposed fissure in the brain.

Chaths indicated that Gottard must be silent once they were inside the tunnel. The horned creatures were not easily disturbed, he said. *But* there were other things that lived in the valley beyond the tunnel. Things that did not appreciate the presence of men. The young guide seemed troubled as he spoke, as if he could perceive some future the monk could not. Gottard wanted to provide comfort to Chaths. He reached toward the guide. But the guide pulled away, indicating that Gottard was not to touch him once they were in the valley.

It is in Gottard's description of the valley that the sense of his manuscript begins to falter. For what he saw after emerging from the other side of the tunnel does not correlate to any known topography in the vicinity of Mount Sinai. "It was a landscape, verdant and lush," he writes. "Like a garden allowed to run wild. There were large bright flowers, maddening things with flesh-like petals as big as a man's hand, and springs that spilled forth miraculously from stone." Further along, the landscape began to change and the earth became covered with what Gottard describes as a new variety of rock. The monk posits that the pressure of ancient volcanic activity had caused crystals to form. The large crystals protruded from the earth and were of varying colors: deep vermillion, saffron and azure. Sunlight streamed into the valley at an odd angle (cross-wise, thought Gottard) striking the crystals and causing a prismatic effect.

The deeper Gottard and Chaths moved into the garden, the more it seemed as though they were walking on the floor of a strange inland sea. The waters of the sea were composed of wildly contrasting colors, so utterly immersive that Gottard soon began to feel as though he was drowning. He fell to his knees finally, and Chaths came to support him. Gathered in the guide's arms, Gottard forgot he'd been warned not to touch Chaths in the valley, and he put his hand on the young man's face and then on his neck. Chaths was beautiful in that moment. "Not like a mirror," Gottard writes. "He was entirely himself."

It was then that Gottard heard the sound of hoof on stone, and he turned to look out into the valley. Standing between two of the great crystalline formations that rose from the earth was the horse with the single horn. And yet, this was no horse. Gottard was now certain of that. The re'em approached the two men, lowering its head. Colors that rose from the surrounding crystals appeared to intensify. They shifted to paint the body of the pale beast. Gottard, in his delirium, believed that the horn itself began to bleed. He realized the protrusion was made of neither crystal nor bone. It was some form of condensed light.

It ran in streams down the creature's face, filling its black and thoughtful eyes with color.

Gottard reached out to touch the braided horn (for the re'em was now close enough for him to do just that). Yet before he could touch the horn, he sensed a second approach. Chaths had said the re'em were not alone in the valley, and Gottard realized with great and trembling fear that this was true. The monk writes: "The being—for it *was* a sort of being that approached—proved too large to actually be perceived by my eye. It seemed instead that the atmosphere, the very air of the valley, grew dense. And it also seemed that the being sang in a voice that was too loud to be heard by my ear. Yet I could sense the sound of it, nonetheless."

"What advances?" Gottard asked.

"I am sorry, Brother Gottard," Chaths replied.

"What do you mean you are sorry?" the monk asked, turning to look at his guide. The young man was alive with bleeding color. Light swam across his body. He stood with his palm against the neck of the re'em.

"You are not permitted," Chaths said.

Gottard felt a horror at this. For he wanted to understand this place, to understand the re'em. And even more, to understand Chaths himself. "Who grants such permission?" Gottard asked.

Chaths did not respond.

"It was then," Gottard writes, "that the approaching form—the great intelligence—enclosed me. I felt as if I was drawn up into the palm of a vast hand—a hand too large for me to see. Chaths watched from his place in the garden, as did the re'em. I was lifted high enough I could perceive the entirety of the valley. All of it was alive with maddening color. I saw the lush and flesh-like flowers shining. I saw a whole heard of re'em running—making rivers in the shifting light. I was drawn higher still, until I felt that I was being pulled out into the heavenly spheres. I could hear the spheres singing; they joined their voices with the voice of the great being. And still, I was drawn upward, toward the cold Empyrean itself. When finally I awoke, I found myself on the hillside where I'd first encountered the beast. I lay beneath the crumbling black architecture there, already forgetting the colors I'd seen. Such was the dullness of our world. I called out for Chaths. My call went unanswered. The guide had remained in the valley. Likely he'd known all along he would stay. Perhaps that was the fate of all guides. And there beneath the black rock, I fell into a new delirium. I dreamed that I too would one day guide someone to the valley. And then I would finally be permitted.

PUGELBONE

NADIA BULKIN

I was born in the Warren, and the Warren was all I knew. Both my mother and father were Meers. We go back to the founders. My father was very proud of our ancestry, but he was also very ill. He talked about forging tunnels and building walls and digging rooms for more families, more, when of course the Warren was already finished, and there was no more concrete to dig a new space out of. The rooms had been split as small as they could go without forcing adults to stoop, without making stretching out to sleep completely impossible. Babies were being suffocated, usually under older children, sometimes under their parents. The tunnels had become so narrow that we could only pass through one by one, and even then we had to dodge laundry from the overhead apartments, and falling garbage bags, and other things that people decided they just didn't have room for. I guess before Warrens get finished—get carved up into this Swiss cheese honeycomb as far and as dense as they can go—people have high expectations of how it will turn out. I've seen my father's sketches. There is an order there that is inhuman, it is so exacting. My mother used to say that in a Warren, you eventually lose control. I don't just mean the jealous lovers that beat each other's heads against the floor, or the men we kids used to call trenchcoat nasties. I mean you lose control of the Warren.

And I don't mean to say that everything is shit in a Warren, because there are reasons people join Warrens, and they are good reasons. You save resources, save money, you don't drive so you don't clog the air. You know your neighbors. You're always close to help, close to home. You share. You keep each other warm. Warrens have saved lives. I'm not just saying this because my parents taught me to; I really did see it, every now and then. Every now and then I'd get a hint of what was so great about living in a Warren.

But mostly I was miserable. Mostly there were Pugelbones.

"You mean the *Helix Warrencola*."

"God, no, I *don't* mean that. I mean ..." Dr. Roman's blue ballpoint pen and razor-thin eyebrow lifted in warning. "I mean yeah, okay, whatever."

"Unless we're talking about something else. I just want us to be careful about our terms."

"Well, that's what I mean, the *Helix Warrencola*, but that isn't what we called them, and you know we saw them first. You know because we told you, over and over, that there were these things in the Warren, and we didn't know what they were, and nobody ever came to check ..."

Dr. Roman twirled her pen toward the cavity in her neck. "Me? I didn't come to this office until last year, Lizbet, and besides, we have nothing to do with Civil Security."

"I don't mean *you* you, I mean ..." The ceiling light in her office was very smooth, very large, very creamy and eggy white. Like a giant flattened pearl. Like Dr. Roman. "Never mind. It's nothing."

"Because remember, I'm here to *help* people like you."

"Yeah, right. I know." There was no way out. "I'm sorry." There was no other way.

Dr. Roman blinked with slow, heavily lacquered eyelashes. She was a woman who had time and space to spare. "Then go ahead."

Everyone in the Warren called them Pugelbones. But I learned it from my sister—Katrin, two years older. She was a fiddler until our old man neighbor asked our father to smash the fiddle up. Our walls were thin, some no thicker than a hand, and Katrin wasn't a very good fiddler. But she was very good at telling stories, and after our parents sent us to bed so they could hiss at each other in private, Katrin would lean down from her hammock, her eyes all big and jaundiced, and say, "I want to tell a story. Listen to my story." And we had to, my brother and I. He'd reach up from his hammock and grab my hand, sometimes my hair. We were stuck beneath her; her words had nowhere to go but down.

She said that sometimes bones don't make it to the grave with the rest of the body—in the Warren, cemetery space closed up fast, and people had to be buried on top of other, older corpses. Hopefully blood relatives. People die the way they live, I guess. So sometimes a bone would get washed up to the surface in a rainstorm, or get left behind in a moldy apartment where some poor hermit died without anybody noticing. Anyway, loose bones were always turning up in the Warren. My uncle said he'd found a skull once, although he never showed us. I found a bone myself, once, a back bone, a—vertebra. It was lying all by its lonesome in the hall outside our apartment. I picked it up and buried it, because this is what my sister told me: bones that don't know they're dead, that don't feel that blanket of soil and realize "my time has come, the worms inherit me," they will act like they're still alive. And they go searching for clothes and trash to cover themselves with, because bones aren't accustomed to being naked in the world. The very first time this happened, the bone was a femur of a garbage man named Johan Pugel. So we called them Pugelbones.

Nobody really knew what it was that Pugelbones did, because many of us had never actually seen one. On first glance they look like any old heap of clutter and waste. There were a lot of sightings, but the Warren is filled with shadows, see—nothing is flat. Even the walls bulge like they're filled egg sacs, so you see these shapes everywhere. Our old man neighbor complained to you people about an invasive species but a lot of grown-ups only mentioned it when we were being bad, like, shut your mouth or I'll sit you outside with the Pugelbones. No more whining now, I bet. And then you spend the whole night with your hands over your mouth, listening for the sound of something shuffling in the hallway. It's not footsteps. It's too soft and slow and continuous, like the sound of pillows falling. Walls no thicker than your hand, remember.

"Did you fight with your parents often?" Dr. Roman tilted her head to the left as if on an axis, as if she could swivel it all the way around if she wanted to. "Did they hurt you when they punished you?"

"What does that matter?" But it mattered. Because Marget was still in the holding center with a wrist band and a change of clothes, it mattered. "I mean, not really, no. We didn't fight. Fight's not the right word."

"Because it sounds like a toxic relationship." Dr. Roman let the "x" in toxic linger on in all its crisp and nasty consonants; maybe it was her favorite word. "It doesn't sound like you had any positive role models in the Warren. It's not unusual…"

"I don't need one to raise Marget." And then, because the stench of the old apartment and its phlegm and germs were defiling this lovely egg-white office, "My father was very ill. He didn't even know what he was saying at the end."

"Why, what did he say then?" Goddamn, she could catch a scent.

"Something about population control. He talked about rabbits and foxes…" Dr. Roman had gone very stiff and bloodless. "Like I said, he was very ill."

"The *Helix Warrencola* were a newly discovered species. The idea that they were in any way created as a weapon of some pogrom against the Meer people is not only offensive, it's inaccurate." So that was offense showing in her face. "Grossly inaccurate."

They were fond of "grossly" too. Grossly unfit to care for a child. Grossly deluded. Gross conditions and gross behavior. Maybe that was why it took them so long to respond to the Warren's distress calls— hard to keep clean in the muck of a massacre. When Civil Security finally arrived the officers in their camouflage armor could not stop complaining about the Warren's smell and its soggy streets. It was true that the Warren hid nothing, that there was no space in the Warren to provide the illusion of disinfection.

"You asked me what my father said. So I told you."

"You need to let go of this anger you hold toward us. Really we've done a lot to try to help the Meer people."

Anger beats at the heart like a call, like a drum, like a march. It is quick and to the point—it is easy. It Gets Shit Done. It Makes Shit Happen. Guilt, on the other hand, is a worm that burrows. "I wish I was angry." Hooks into the heart, hooks of all kind: metal hooks, hooks of green glass, hooks like anchors and hooks like hands. Some worms just cannot be un-dug.

Dr. Roman opened the case file and flipped through sheets of multi-colored paper. "You had a lot of anger as a child. You threw… bricks off rooftops? You punched one boy's teeth out of his head?" She wanted a response, but what would be correct? An apology? An excuse?

More confessions? Tears? Would tears bring Marget home? "Why do you think you did that?"

▼▼▼

Because I liked to break things down. My father built, I broke. My sister crafted, I destroyed. When our old man neighbor asked my father to smash up Katrin's fiddle, you know, he didn't have the heart to. So I did it. Ripped out its strings and pulled its neck off. It isn't that I wanted to hurt Katrin. We may have lost touch since moving to the city but she is still my sister. I just liked to see things come apart. I liked to see things in their rawest form, reduced so far they can't be reduced any more. Fiddles, bread loaves, radios, socks. Didn't matter. I had loved peeling layers ever since my mother handed me an orange when I was a baby—but I didn't start breaking things that weren't meant to be broken until I got older.

I was breaking pieces off the ledge of the rooftop playground. You know if the smog's not too bad, you can see the city from up there. It always looked so open and flat and sparse, like God the Creator just scattered a bunch of boxes over the plain and strung them together with long gray roads. Sprawling herds, my father said. Overfed cows in their golden barns.

Anyway I took a break to watch geese flying south—I never got to see the sky from our apartment—when I saw the Pugelbone in the far corner of the roof, near the storage shed. It looked like a pile of abandoned shit: some kid's torn-up corduroy jacket, a garbage bag, doll skin, drain hair, curdled milk, dead rats. Stuff that would have ended up incinerated or washed down the sewer into the River Becquerel. Except this pile was alive. I could tell. It was *breathing*. Like all these dead things had been wound together and reanimated. It was beautiful, and I wanted to strip it to the bone.

It didn't scare me like I thought it would. Didn't scare me like it should have. It was staring right at me, even though it didn't have eyes, and there was this innocence about it, like it knew it was rude to stare. When my father stared it felt like rubber bullets. With my mother and Katrin, more like needles. And with my brother... well, my point is: when this thing stared at me, all I felt was a flutter of eyelashes.

I should probably say that I didn't have much in the way of friends. The other kids thought I was a waste of space and carbon and oxygen—it's why I went after that kid Benjin, punched his teeth out. But Benjin was right about what he said. I *was* a leech, I *was* citizen failure. I was only ever good at breaking things, and in a Warren you have to be useful or you'll get ground up into fodder, living in some lonely crawl-space, eating other people's garbage because you're a good-for-nothing, can't-contribute-nothing, burden on the community. And I couldn't wire electricity. I couldn't fix drains or people or food. I had dreams where I'd find this tiny crack in the wall that I could fit my finger into, and then my hand, and then my arm, until I'd mash my whole body inside the concrete like a wad of gum and hope the renovators wouldn't come in yelling, "We need this space! Move out!"

So when the Pugelbone looked at me in fondness, well, I guess I paid it back.

▼▼▼

"You wanted it to be your friend."

"I thought if I was nice to it, then it would be nice to me."

Dr. Roman's eyes appeared to be closed, but she was only looking down. She was writing something secret on her little scented pad of paper.

"Is this a common theme in your relationships with other people?"

Other people were bodies in traffic, plump and heart-shaped faces like the ones on billboards and commercials. Polished and empty as the great big boulevards with their seasonal garlands and deserted buses. Foreign people, foreign lives. It's all about keypads and time sheets now, little Meerkat. "I don't know."

"What about with Marget's father?"

"I don't want to talk about that."

"You need to be forthcoming with me during these sessions." She tapped her pad of paper with the ink end of her mighty pen. "It's very important that I make an accurate assessment of your capacity as a caretaker."

"I don't know who he was." Blue shirt, iron-on logo of a red-crown. He'd heard Meer bitches were little tigers in the sack. He came and left without warning, while something on the stovetop burned down to an unrecognizable lump of char. Give and Ye Shall Receive. "So I guess I can't say."

Dr. Roman raised her eyebrows again but this time, for once, the room was quiet.

The Pugelbone followed me home that day. I used to ask myself this but now I know: I invited it. Not with words, because I didn't think it would understand those—but when I opened the door to go down below, I looked over my shoulder. You know, to see if it was coming. When I went down the metal staircase I could hear it shuffling after me, dropping its mass step to step. I thought I heard a muffled sort of panting but for all I know it could have been me. That stairwell was very close quarters.

I had never been followed before. Not even my little brother followed me. Not even the tiny brown mice that the crawl-space people hunted followed me, and I had even left them bread crumbs. I said to the Pugelbone, "I'm glad you're here," and its smile was like the curve of a rusty spoon. I could see the two of us running out of the Warren, over the plain and away. Not to the city. Just away.

I thought I would lose it in the street—someone kicked it, thinking it couldn't feel pain, and I picked out a rock I had in my pocket and threw it at the bastard—but when I got to our building and opened the door, the Pugelbone was right behind me, brushing up against my legs.

My brother was the only one home. He was drawing spiders on the floor where our mother usually stood to serve us dinner. He always liked spiders—he used to let whole packs of them crawl on his face when he was a baby, I don't know why. He said, "Hi Lizzie," and then kept on drawing. I don't know if he saw the Pugelbone behind me, but Timot was always such a space cadet. When he was three he sat himself down in the middle of a street to pick up a marble and was nearly trampled by the passers-by. We found him wedged in the dirt, bruised and smiling. "Too stupid to live," people said.

In the Warren, people will walk right into a space and take what's inside. There is the assumption, if your door opens, that you are either generous or dead. So I stepped aside to lock the door. It was only for a second. Three seconds, at most. What none of us realized is that there are mouths everywhere, and they find their way around doors. You have no idea how many mouths there are in this world, and all of them are open. All of us are food.

I screamed, but Timot didn't. I tell myself now that it happened too quickly for him to feel pain, but then I remember that his arms and legs were shaking—no, convulsing, slapping the floor so hard that I could feel the vibrations under my feet all the way on the other side of the apartment. I hope that he was already gone by then, and those were just the… twitches of a dying body. I heard a sound like someone sucking milk through a straw and I realized that the Pugelbone was drinking my baby brother dry.

The Pugelbone went up into the air duct and I lay down. I held his hand—I thought he'd want me to—but it was so limp, like an empty glove. There was blood tracked all over the floor and the wall, and as I lay there I thought to myself that the pattern read like some kind of message. But I don't know what. I never figured out what.

"Lizbet."

The room shifted. Dr. Roman was calling.

"Was this really an accident?"

"Yes, it was a fucking accident! Don't even ask me that!"

"But you said that you liked to break things."

"No. No, no, no! That is not fair! I would never fucking hurt him! Look at the case file, it's in the case file!"

"The case file only says that your brother was killed by an unknown entity. Later determined to be a *Helix Warrencola*. It doesn't say anything about whether or not you manipulated the situation. And I don't hold you responsible for that, Lizbet. You were a child. You were living in terrible conditions..."

Mother and Father had believed in the Warren, and cried when it was fumigated. Afterwards they'd wandered in and out of bungalows and parking lots, too old to build another life. "I didn't know. I swear I didn't know."

"I'm going to recommend that the Department of Child Welfare wait a little longer before returning custody of your daughter to you."

A "little longer" is not a schedule. A "little longer" is a young snake. This particular "little longer" was already five months long. When the Warren told the city that there were monsters in their walls, the "little longer" had stretched into a full, bloody year. "Tell me. Is there anything in that damn file that says I've ever hurt Marget?"

"But that's the reason you're here, Lizbet. You took Marget out of pre-school. Forcibly. You pushed her teacher's head into a white board. That is not acceptable behavior for any parent." Dr. Roman prodded the air with her chin. "Even a Meer."

"There was a Pugelbone in that classroom. It was in a cubby hole, and it was looking straight at Marget. It was like the time I took her to the city zoo, to the cages where they keep the predators. Most of the animals are stoned off tranquilizers, but there was this long, skinny, yellow-black tiger that stared at Marget with a living hunger, you know? A mother knows."

Dr. Roman sighed and glanced at the large clock on the wall. "We've already talked about this. You were hallucinating. You were stressed and you were tired and you'd been drinking the night before. Lizbet, sometimes I wonder if we've made any progress at all."

Were there Pugelbones in the holding center? Government closets ran deep. "Okay, okay. Forget I said anything."

"The *Helix Warrencola* is extinct. Do you understand? That's already been confirmed. And even if there were a few surviving individuals, they'd be stuck in the landfill where the Warren used to be." She leaned forward and whispered, because she was only trying to help, "I really don't want to add paranoid personality disorder to this case file."

Let Marget not be running, let Marget not be screaming. Let Marget be sitting quiet, playing cat's cradle with herself. "Just tell me what I need to do. Please, if you just give me…"

"You aren't ready, Lizbet." The case file fluttered shut. "I'll see you next month, same time."

In dreams she had been consumed many times. On occasion it was an act of sacrifice, and she would see Timot and later Marget tottering away on little mushroom-stem legs. More often it was just an attack, sudden and meaningless. In grocery stores, in the factory break room. No safe place. She'd wake up slapping her stomach, trying to put herself back together.

From City Plaza, southbound traffic was non-existent. A raccoon-eyed woman in a coat of chinchilla got off the bus at St. Greta's Hospital, and a pale man in a long tan raincoat got on. A wool scarf was wrapped under his chin so thoroughly that his neck looked like a swollen goitre. The bus was lurching forward when he sat down in the middle of the back row and placed his briefcase on his lap. Then he closed his eyes and sighed.

The small mass under his scarf began to tremble. His fingers pulled the scarf down and revealed a faceless knot of matter cradled in the wool, like a baby in a sling. It was latched onto the man's neck, but it disengaged with a pop and turned its large red sucker toward Lizbet. Blood ran from the withered wound.

"What do you want," drawled the man, scratching at his skin. "Goddamn Meer."

Lizbet drew her knees up as fortresses and gnawed on her nails. The broad boulevard stretched through the half-empty city, blind and merciless, and on into the night.

HOLLOW EARTHS

ORRIN GREY

A single bat lands with a thud on a mountain of guano. Its wings beat at the mound, but they cannot carry it aloft again, for it is too weighted down by the mass of its own excretions. From out of the mountain come cockroaches—first one or two questing antennae, then dozens, hundreds, swarming up from the digested remains of the bat's former prey—they mass over the body of the bat, which thrashes and squeaks in its impotent rage and terror, and bit by bit they tear it apart. Pale crabs join them in their feasting, boxy bodies looming over the low carapaces of the roaches, pulling off bits of bat flesh with their pincers. Eventually, nothing remains but a skeleton and, over time, it too disappears into the mound. So, we see how a king may go a progress through the guts of a beggar.

▼▼▼

From the Deposition of Annabel Chambers

Q: When did you last see Miss Martin?

A: You mean Dom?

Q: Dominique Martin, yes. When was the last time you were in   contact?

A: I hadn't seen her in years. Before the other day, I mean. We used to be friends, back in small times…

Q: Small times?

A: Since we were both little kids. We lived in the same apartments. She was across the parking lot from me. So we were in different buildings, but our bedrooms were maybe a hundred feet apart. You just went out our door, down the steps, past the cars, across the parking lot, up the stairs, and you were knocking on Dom's door.

Q: And you were friends?

A: I mean, yeah. Best friends, I guess, back when we were kids and we believed in stuff like best friends, y'know?

Q: But you said you hadn't seen her in years.

A: Right. The apartments caught on fire when we were in junior high, I guess. Eighth grade. My building burned down completely, Dom's not all the way but enough, y'know? Sparks blew over from my side onto their roof. That's what the firemen told us. We lost everything in the fire, my mom and me. We moved after that. Changed towns, changed schools. Mom said she wanted to get away, get a new start. Which meant that I lost Dom, too.

Q: And you didn't try to stay in touch at all?

A: We were kids, and this was a few years ago. It wasn't all smartphones and Facebook and shit yet, though, I mean, that was right around the corner. I went to high school, I guess Dom did too, and we just…lost track, y'know?

Q: Until Miss Martin contacted you on…April 17th?

A: Sure, if that's what I said before. I don't remember for sure, but it was through Facebook, so there'd be a record, I guess.

Q: What'd she say?

A: She said she wanted to get together. We'd both graduated, were both out on our own now. She said she missed me, wanted to catch up. All the usual stuff. She said she was still in town, and my mom had moved back, so I had a good excuse to drive in, meet Dom.

Q: And you met her...four days ago, is that correct? On Thursday, April 30th?

A: If that's the date. But yeah, I guess it was four days ago. That's what they tell me.

Q: Where did you meet?

A: This coffee shop. By the community college. I forget the name of it now. Something with Leaf in the name, I think.

Q: The New Branch Coffee House, on Perimeter Drive.

A: Branch, yeah, that's it.

Q: So what did you talk about?

A: The usual stuff. Small times, the old days. Our jobs. Dom looked different, but then, the last time I'd seen her she'd been, what, fourteen?

Q: Different how?

A: She'd gained a little weight, I guess, and she'd put a purple streak in her hair. She dressed different now than when she was fourteen, who doesn't?

Q: Did she look like she was in trouble? Like she was on drugs?

A: The fuck does that mean? What does someone who's *in trouble* look like?

Q: All I'm asking is, did anything seem wrong?

A: Well, no, not at first. She seemed like maybe she wasn't sleeping a lot, but she said she was taking college classes on the side, so, y'know, that would account for it, right?

183

Q: You said, "not at first."

A: Right. I mean, obviously, something was wrong, wasn't it? I'm fucking sitting here now, aren't I?

Q: Did you realize something was wrong while you were at the coffee shop?

A: I…don't know, really. I mean, now, sitting here, I think I did, but did I think so then, or am I just making it up? Hindsight, and all that. I know I was happy to see Dom again, happier than I'd expected to be. And I felt guilty.

Q: Guilty?

A: For not, y'know, being there for her. Trying to get in touch sooner. It'd been, shit, another thirteen, fourteen years since the fire. I could've tried to look her up once the internet really became a thing, y'know? Found her once Facebook took off.

Q: The way she found you?

A: Yeah. So things fell right back into the old rhythms, we were making the same old jokes, talking about the same stuff, and it was like no time had passed at all, except that I was feeling guilty, and that's when she brought up the Game.

Q: The game?

A: Yeah. That's where it all went to shit, isn't it?

▼ ▼ ▼

When we were kids, we used to play this game. I mean, little kids have obsessions, right? Princesses, ponies, fire trucks, whatever movie they watch over and over again right that minute. (I suppose so. Go on.) Well, with Dom it was always the same thing, all the way from small times. She was really into Hollow Earth stuff.

(Hollow earth stuff?)

Right. So, I dunno, back in the 1800s or whenever, there were all these theories that the world was hollow, instead of solid. Like, you know how in school they teach you that the world is made up of layers of dirt and then rock and then lava or something, and at the center there's this really dense core spinning around, keeping all the electromagnetism flowing or whatever? There was that movie where they had to jumpstart it with a nuke. Did you ever see that?

(No, I can't say that I did.)

It was dumb as balls. Anyway, that's what you learn in school, but we didn't *always* know that, right? So before we figured all that shit out, there were guys who were convinced that the earth was hollow and filled with…other worlds, I guess, on the inside. Guys named Symmes and Haley and shit like that. They tried to raise money to organize expeditions to the North Pole cuz they thought that's where they'd find a way in. Some of them started churches. All sorts of crazy stuff.

(Crazy stuff?)

I just mean…these guys really believed in all this, y'know? And Dom was really into it all. She had books these guys had written, and maps and charts and stuff taped up on her bedroom wall. Drawings of what these guys thought the Hollow Earth looked like, because of course they didn't all agree. Some of them thought it was just like a big hollow globe, with a tiny sun in the center; and others thought that it was a bunch of globes within globes—what do they call that? concentric!—and that each, I dunno, *layer* I guess rotated separately from the others. Hell, some of them even thought we were *already* inside the Hollow Earth; that when we looked up at the sky and the stars we were actually just looking *in*. That's pretty dumb, but maybe it's also a good metaphor.

(We're not here for metaphors.)

In that case, I think you're probably going to be disappointed with my story.

(That's as may be, but why don't you tell me anyway. Tell me about the game.)

Okay, well, when we were little kids, we played pretend, right, like little kids do. Only Dom pretty much always wanted to play Hollow Earth stuff. The way it started out was that she'd pick a door and we would pretend that when we opened it, instead of the laundry room or her closet or my mom's bedroom we'd find a set of stone stairs leading down, and we'd follow them into the Hollow Earth. Or we'd go out exploring in the neighborhood and we'd look for tunnels leading down—storm drains, drainage ditches—anything that went down into the ground, and we'd go down into them to see if they led to the Hollow Earth.

I mean, I guess most kids are kinda obsessed with those things, right? They feel sort of forbidden and scary. Trolls live there, or whatever. Monsters. Except with Dom it was spiders.

(Spiders?)

Well, kind of, but I'm getting ahead of myself. If I'm gonna try to explain this, I gotta try to do it in order, or it'll make even *less* sense. So, Dom was all into these old Hollow Earth theories, but she also thought they were all wrong. She had her own instead. When we were little I guess I just thought it was a made-up story, or something that she got from one of her books. Dom's Hollow Earth wasn't an empty globe, it was more like a…like a hive. Like underneath the world was just caves, cave after cave, all carved out until the earth was all full of holes, like a piece of cork. And all those caves led to caverns, and the caverns were filled with cities and lakes and forests. Giant mushrooms sometimes, but weird plants, too, that lived off the light from the caves. Luminous rocks and all sorts of weird stuff, enough to make there be day and night, even though you were miles underground. Because the Hollow Earth was kind of magic, I guess. I dunno, it wasn't my story, it was Dom's.

However it all worked, she had this whole history for it. The Hollow Earth was older than the regular earth, according to her. There were people down there before the dinosaurs came, this "first race" of "golden people" who built huge cities with towers and temples and whatnot. She said that the cities down there looked kind of like the ones in Cambodia and kind of like the ones in Central America and kind of like...well, you get the point. The people who lived on the surface of the world—that's us—we were descended from these golden people, but the golden people were still down there, too, at least for a long time. And there were dinosaurs, like in an Edgar Rice Burroughs book.

(Who?)

He wrote Tarzan, but he also wrote these books about the Hollow Earth—like I said, it was all the rage back then. He called his Pellucid-something, I think. Anyway, in Dom's version of things there were dinosaurs down there way after they had died out up here, and the golden people lived alongside them, mostly in harmony, because even though the Hollow Earth was a real, physical place, it was also kind of like heaven. When you went there, you lived forever.

So, when we played the Game, as kids, we would pretend to go down into the Hollow Earth, and the golden people would recognize us as their descendants, and we would be royalty, of course, and they would crown us queens and we would ride dinosaurs and fight monsters and...y'know, all that little kid stuff. But there was another part to it, especially as we got older.

I already said we'd go exploring, looking for tunnels and whatever, but we also just went looking for doors. Dom would try to find a door she had never opened before, and before she opened it she would kind of hold her breath, and at the time I thought it was part of the Game but now, I think maybe she really was hoping that when she opened it up it might really, finally be the door that actually led to those stone steps that went down and down and down. She was obsessed with it, more and more as we got older. She'd jimmy open locked doors at school, break into abandoned buildings, go exploring in places plastered with *No Trespassing* signs.

(And when you met at the coffee shop, she wanted to play the game again?)

Right, but this time she had a specific door in mind. She said she'd been back to the apartments, now that she was living in town again. I had driven by them myself, on my way to the coffee shop, and I had seen that they never got fixed up. Mine was all bulldozed down now, nothing left, the rubble all carted up and hauled away, but the one that Dom had lived in still had the first floor walls intact, just nothing on the inside. An empty space. Hollow.

(Yes, go on.)

What? Sorry. Dom said she'd been back, that the basement was still there, and that there was a door in it now that hadn't been there before. She wanted to go open it.

(Basement?)

Yeah, there was a basement. Not under my building but under Dom's. It had the laundromat for both buildings in it, but it also had a storm shelter. In case of tornadoes, y'know? The storm shelter had a separate ceiling, under the building's foundation, concrete. That's where Dom said the door was.

(And you went with her?)

...I did, yeah.

(But you didn't want to?)

I don't know. I mean, it seemed crazy. Still does, really. And I couldn't imagine that the place was safe, after all these years. Maybe it was full of, I dunno, poison mold or asbestos or something. Maybe that was why they hadn't rebuilt it. But I also thought...I was guilty, like I said, and I thought maybe Dom was just suggesting this because it's something that we did when we were kids. Maybe she just wanted to reconnect. So yeah, I had my fucking reservations, but I went with her.

(So, the two of you went back to the apartment complex where you grew up?)

Yeah. We took my car, because Dom said she had taken the bus to the college and then walked to the coffee shop. We stopped by a gas station on the way and she bought some candy bars. "For sustenance," she said. You can probably verify that with her credit card company, or something, right? Anyway, I figured she was just hungry and wanted some candy, or that it was all part of play-acting the "adventuring party" and heading down into the dark dungeon or whatever. She stuck those in her bag and we drove over and parked near the apartment buildings.

It was afternoon by then, overcast and spooky. The walls all still standing up, the top edges blackened to charcoal, the windows empty, no glass or nothing. No doors. They had cleared out the inside, so that it wasn't as dangerous if kids came and trespassed, which is what we had to do, because there was a chain link fence around the whole place now. We didn't have to climb over, though. There was a place already, one that Dom went right to. You've probably found it by now. Where you could pull the fence up and kinda skootch under. We went through there, and then into what used to be Dom's building.

I'm sorry, I know I'm getting a little choked up here, which probably seems weird.

(Take your time. Just tell it however you need to tell it.)

It's just that... I could still remember right where everything had been, y'know? I was standing in this empty spot, where the ground was all black and gritty from where they had bulldozed everything except the walls, and I knew the moment I stepped over what would have been the threshold of Dom's room, even though it was three stories above my head back in the old days.

Back then there was a door that led to the stairs leading down to the laundry room, and also an elevator, but they had filled the shaft up with big chunks of broken up concrete and rock. The stairs were still there, though, just with no door now, and a pool of rainwater down at the foot of them, where they turned a corner and then there was a metal door with a padlock sorta *draped* across it, but not locked, not anymore.

(Because Miss Martin had unlocked it?)

I don't know. But yeah, that's what I thought, when I saw it, was of her picking locks when we were kids.

She took the chain off, wrapped it around the handle of the door, and then pushed the door open. It was dark on the other side, but not completely dark. The laundry room ceiling was concrete too, part of the foundation of the building, but during the fire it had been weakened or damaged or something and now there were holes in it. Up above, they had laid in metal grates to cover them up, but the grates let in light, at least a little, and also water, so that the floor of the laundry room was probably an inch deep with rain water. When I stepped in I could feel it, sloshing around my Doc Martens. I was worried about snakes and god-knows-what. I wanted to go back, but Dom was already going ahead of me.

They hadn't taken out the laundry machines, I don't know why. They were still lined up there, in two rows, facing each other. Washers on one side and dryers on the other. We had to walk between them. I'm not a little kid anymore, but I've seen dumb horror movies, and I was picturing arms reaching out of those black openings and grabbing my legs the whole fucking way, you bet I was.

(You stopped talking. What happened next?)

I don't want to tell you what happened next.

(Does that really seem like an option, at this point?)

No... It's just... okay, so, I know that what I'm about to say is fucking crazy, all right. I know that. And I know that I'm going to be telling it to whatever you cops have that passes for a shrink here in another day or two, but whatever. Whatever. I'll tell you, too. Why not? What choice do I have? I guess I could make something up, though that's what you and the shrink and everyone else maybe me included will say I'm doing anyway, but... okay, here goes:

We walked through the laundry room and pushed open the door to the storm shelter. Back when we were kids, the storm shelter had a foosball table and some other stuff in it, but that was all gone now. It was just an empty, dirty, dark room. Dom took a flashlight out of her bag—something bright, a bike headlight I think—and it lit up the room. And...

You remember I said that when I walked into the place where the building used to be, it was like I had never left? I could remember exactly where Dom's room had been, could count the steps in my head up to her apartment? Well, I remembered the storm shelter, too. It had been just a square, concrete room. That's it. One door in, the one we just walked through. No other door out. Now, though, there was another door on the far side of the room.

If you go back there—if you haven't already—I don't know if you'll find it there or not, but it was there then, just like Dom had said it was. The door wasn't metal, like the one leading to the laundry room or the one from the laundry room to here. It was wood, and it looked old, which made even less sense than it suddenly being there where no door had ever been before.

A symbol had been painted on it in something black that still felt tacky under my fingertips. A circle, with a long, straight line piercing it from above, like what the utility guys paint on the sidewalks and lawns in my mom's new neighborhood to mark the location of buried lines. The door didn't have a knob, it had a handle, and Dom smiled back at me before she pushed it down and then pushed it open, holding her breath like she did when we were kids...

(And? What was on the other side of the door? Annabel, I'm going to need you to talk to me...)

Right, sorry. First, though, I guess I should tell you about the spiders.

(Okay, if that's what you feel like you need to do.)

So... I said that when we were kids, Dom had this whole history of the Hollow Earth, right, and how it was eternal and when you went down there you lived forever. Well, as we got older, the story started to change.

See, before the golden people, there were apparently other things that lived down there. Giant monsters, shit like Godzilla and Gamera and whatever. Titans, she called them, like in Greek mythology. And, like in Greek mythology, the golden people had thrown the Titans down.

Before that the golden people were simple, tribal, sort of like cavemen. They were nomadic, traveling around from one cavern to another. It was conquering the Titans that gave them civilization. They had to band together to beat them, and that was a start, but there was more to it than that. The Titans couldn't die, so the golden people imprisoned them someplace in the center of the center of the world, and it was on their shoulders that the golden people built their great cities. Like... once the Titans were imprisoned, they became a power source, like a battery. Don't ask me how any of this works, because it was Dom's fairy tale, not mine. But even in a fairy tale, you can't just do something like that and not pay the price.

(The price?)

Dom said it was like radioactivity. We get nuclear power, right, but the tradeoff is that it's radioactive, dangerous, it gets into everything, sooner or later, poisons the planet. We get energy from coal, but to do that we have to burn it, and that puts smoke into the air, eventually it'll choke us all to death. Whatever we do to drive our world, there's a tradeoff, right? So, when the golden people threw down the Titans and used them for energy, they built these incredible marvels, but gradually the people and their cities rotted from the inside out.

They were still eternal, though. They didn't die or fade away like Tolkien's elves, they just... changed. Into these things partway between people and spiders—don't ask me why, I asked Dom once and she just replied, with the characteristic logic of a kid, that it was just how it was. The spider-people—Dom called them ghouls—built a new empire in the ruins of the old. They fed on the dead and the dying, and waited for their time to come up and seize the world of light and life. These are Dom's words now, I'm just parroting them back to you.

(You'll pardon my saying so, but that sounds a lot less appealing than magic cities filled with dinosaurs.)

Yeah, but Dom was still convinced that we wanted to go. That the Hollow Earth was still something more than all this, y'know?

(You think this hollow earth was someplace where she was special?)

No. I mean, yeah, when we were little that was it. We weren't very popular in school, and I think we were both lonely kids...I think...I think maybe we're both just lonely bigger kids now. But it wasn't just a way to feel special. There was more to it. It was...it was a way for the *world* to feel special, y'know? A way to believe that there was something more than four walls. More than just going in to work every day. Not more *for us*, necessarily, just more at all. Like...did you ever play that game Bloody Mary?

(I may have, but you tell me about it.)

So you look in the mirror and you say *Bloody Mary, Bloody Mary, Bloody Mary* or whatever. Maybe you say it three times or five or something, I can't remember. It was in that movie *Candyman* too, right, so maybe you say *Candyman* instead. Whatever you say, you stand, and you look in the mirror, and you say it, and then she appears, or he does, and they kill you. So why the hell would you ever do that? To prove to your friends that you're brave? To prove to *yourself* that you are? That's a fucking dumb reason to risk getting killed, right? So maybe you do it because...because it would be *worth it*, if you got killed. If Candyman appeared over your shoulder or Bloody Mary reached out her bloody hands from behind the glass, because then, just as you died, at least you'd *know* that there was something magical in the world, even if it was also terrible.

(Do you think that's what Miss Martin wanted when she opened that door? To die?)

I don't know what Dom wanted. I really don't. And if I thought I did, before she opened that door, then I sure as hell don't now. I don't even know what I wanted, but I know what I expected to see. Not a goddamn thing. I expected the door to open onto a concrete wall, or onto dirt, because there was no place else for it to go, not from there.

(And what did you see?)

Steps, of course. Stone steps, leading down into the dark...

From notes left behind by Annabel Chambers, written on white legal paper

Mom just left. She begged me to tell the police what really happened. I guess it's been long enough now that they've figured out that Dom isn't coming back. I guess they've decided that she's dead. Maybe they've decided that I killed her.

The police shrink, Dr. Schriver, says that I'm not being held, because there's insufficient evidence, but she also told me that I'm not supposed to leave town, so... I don't know what you call that. House arrest, maybe, here in the guest room of my mom's new house, that hasn't ever been home to me. Dr. Schriver comes by once a week. She says that I'm supposed to write this stuff down, like I'm writing now. She says it's for me, to help me remember, to help me "process," but she collects the pages whenever I'm done, so hi there, Dr. Schriver.

You say you don't think that I had anything to do with Dom's disappearance, but you also say you think I know more than I'm telling. You say that right now my mind is "protecting me from the truth," but that if I really work with you, I'll be able to remember what actually happened. You should probably talk to my mom. Between the two of you, I'll bet you could work out a story that you'd like better. I can't. All I've got is what I remember, and what I remember is this:

Dom opens the door and there are the steps. They're stone and they're old, much older than the burned-up apartment building, much older than the storm shelter with its damp concrete. These are Mayan ruin steps, Pyramids at Giza steps.

They go down into the dark, but the dark isn't dark. When we start down, Dom shuts off the flashlight, and we can still see. There's a light that isn't light. It comes from things that grow on the walls of the cavern, from luminous strata in the rock itself. In school, when we went to the museum, there was this room that had a black curtain over the door and when you stepped inside there were rocks in a case. You pushed a button and a black light came on and suddenly the rocks glowed these marvelous fluorescent colors. The rocks in the cave do that, too, but they do it on their own, no need for a button.

We go down, and sometimes the tunnel is natural, sometimes it's man-made—or *something*-made—but always the steps, and as we go, I can tell that we're going deeper and deeper, toward the heart of the world. We're going down into Dom's Hollow Earth, and I wonder, as we travel, if we're going to the one filled with golden people and dinosaurs, or the one filled with cobwebs and rot and giant spiders, and I wonder if Dom cares all that much, one way or the other.

She's walking ahead of me. Excited, a kid again, lacking even the motes of trepidation that I still carry. She practically skips down the steps, weightless down here in the dark heart of the world, where she has always belonged. We come out into a cavern, and it's all glowing fungi. Mushrooms as tall as redwoods shedding purple and blue light down onto us both. Things move among the mushrooms, big shapes, too big to be Dom's ghouls, but definitely relatives somehow. I see one of them pass between the stalks, its body like a spider's but without enough legs. Bones make up its outside, but something is alive inside them. A dinosaur skeleton in the museum that got up and took a walk, but underneath living black carapace and glittering eyes, cobwebs making tendons and muscles, making the great jaws hinge open and closed.

It doesn't come after us, maybe because it isn't interested, maybe because Dom is there, and it knows, somehow, that she belongs. Beyond that cavern is another tunnel, more steps, then another cavern, a city all in ruins. The buildings have fallen in on themselves, their domes and towers pitted like an apple eaten through by worms.

You'll like this part, Dr. Schriver. I've been having a dream, lately, ever since Dom disappeared, and at this point I can't tell if the dream is a memory or just a dream. In it, we're in that ruined city, except Dom isn't there, I'm by myself, and I hear this voice, lifted in a kind of singsong chant. *The worms crawl in, the worms crawl out*, it sings. *The worms play pinochle on your snout.* Funny, that's the only thing I know about pinochle.

I follow the sound, and there's a man standing there. Or, at least, something that looks like a man. He's wearing a suit and tie, not quite a tuxedo, but almost. Like he's dressed up for prom or something. But his head is hanging down, he's looking at his hands like he doesn't recognize them, and his face isn't right. There are too many eyes, and it's all beginning to come apart.

When I come around the corner, he looks up at me and says, out of the blue but clear as day, "What happens when you die, do you think? Your body is empty now, the electrical impulses that once animated it have fled. Is there anything left, when they're gone? Or does a spider crawl inside your mouth, and from there to your brain, slowly spinning its webs among your neurons until, finally, you are something very different?"

So, is that something I saw down there, or is it just a dream? I'll leave that one for you to puzzle out, Dr. Schriver. That seems more your area than mine. What I know is that time didn't seem to pass while Dom and I were underground, though later I would learn that we had been down there for three days.

I know that we ate the candy bars that Dom had brought down—or rather, that I did, Dom said she didn't want any. I know that we saw more of the empty cities, fallen into ruin, and some of the new cities built by the ghouls, round buildings clinging to the ceilings of the caverns in clumps like a spider's egg sac.

Dom never seemed to get tired, but I did. Tired and scared. I wanted to see my mom, wanted to see the sun. I kept thinking about my car, parked there on the street next to the burned out apartment buildings. About my job, my apartment, the jade plant that I hadn't watered that morning, the homework that I hadn't finished for the one college class I was taking online. I told Dom that I wanted to go back up and she smiled sadly and shook her head, but not telling me no, saying, "If you go back up, I don't know if you can come back. At least, not the same way."

And I knew what she meant, just like I know why the guy in my dream is dressed so nicely. But I wasn't ready, I guess, because I told her I wanted to go, and we walked until we found steps that led up. We were holding hands, like when we were little kids, but now Dom was walking a little bit behind me. I started up the steps, and there was light up above me, different than the light that glowed from the rocks and fungi, and Dom's hand was still in mine, but it was heavy, pulling, and then I realized that I was still walking but she had stopped.

I looked back at her, and she was smiling at me, but her face looked different. There was a seam now, running from her bottom lip down along her chin. The place where her face would eventually split open, where mandibles would be. Her eyes were dark and shiny, but she looked happier than I could remember her looking since we were little girls.

"This is where I have to stay," she said, and I knew she was right. I tried to smile back, but I was crying, and I let go of her hand, let her fingertips trickle out of mine one by one, and I turned and went up the steps. That's the last thing I remember before I woke up in a field of milo about a mile from town, covered in a layer of dew, my fingers and toes so cold that I thought I might have already lost them. My clothes, the same ones I had been wearing when I met Dom at the coffee shop three days earlier, were filthy and torn and caked, here and there, with blood that you tell me isn't hers or mine.

I know what you're looking for, what you want me to write here. A story that makes all of this make sense, that turns it into some kind of metaphor. You may not think that I killed Dom, but you *are* pretty sure that she's dead, and you think I know how, why, where. A car accident, with Dom's body in a ditch and a rivulet of blood from her scalp. A fall in some abandoned building, playing that silly game from when we were kids. Something I feel guilty about, and my guilt is driving me to make up stories. That's what you want. Anything, really, that you can latch on to.

And I wish I could give you that neat if unhappy ending, mom, Dr. Schriver. I really do. I want you to be okay with this, want you to be happy, so you can see all this as a metaphor if you want to, but you'll have to decide what it represents for yourselves. For me, it's been long enough now, I've talked it through enough times, that I am left with only one thing that I know for sure. There's no door waiting for me in that basement storm shelter anymore. Probably no door waiting for me anyplace else. At least, not the kind that you go through without first paying a toll.

I had my chance, and I got scared, but there's another way down into the Hollow Earth, and I guess I'm just desperate enough for saying Bloody Mary three times in the mirror to be worth the risk, after all. Because if there's anything I regret, it isn't that I left Dom in that place. It's that she got to stay, and I didn't.

THE WRITHE

TOM LYNCH

Carter Banks stepped off the commuter train onto the platform, and hurried through the pouring rain to the small, covered, lit area by the stairs. He huffed out a breath and dropped all of his bags: the duffel with new hiking boots, a new sleeping bag, new hunting jacket with zip-out removable lining, new woodland-brown camouflage cargo pants (lined), several new flannel shirts, six pairs of wool socks, and two sets of thermal dual-layer underwear as well as his new waterproof daypack containing a new water bottle with integrated filter, new hot/cold thermos with two cups, new binoculars, and twelve disposable hand warmers. He'd also put his laptop, iPad, and several folders from work into the backpack in case Mr. Hathaway intended this to be a working weekend.

His cell still had no signal. How was he supposed to get an Uber over to his boss's place from here if he couldn't get a signal?

He shouldered his bags and climbed the steps to the overpass, glaring at his screen. At the top of the steps, the situation was no better.

And there was no one at the ticket booth, either. Carter scanned the walls for important phone numbers, like nearby taxi services, but he found nothing.

A flash shot through the sky, followed by a tremendous thunderclap. The train station shook. The lights flickered and dimmed, but flared back to normal. Carter sighed, releasing tension he didn't know he'd been holding. He wondered if the storm was affecting his signal.

Carter checked his phone again. Still nothing. And no Wi-Fi, either. He was stranded, and this incredible opportunity was going to pass him by. He'd been invited up to his boss's country place for a weekend of hunting with the senior managers. As the newest guy on the team, this was huge to Carter. An acceptance, a validation. Payoff for dues paid for the two long, painful years spent at Sloan. Sure, he'd earned an incredible scholarship and graduated with a prestigious degree, but none of that put money in his pocket. But he'd landed the job his favorite professor had recommended him for, and the pay had been good with the promise of great. This invitation was the beginning of the great.

There was something Carter had noticed, though. He was the youngest in the group by far. It felt initially like he'd gone to work with his father's friends, though his dad the plumber would never have been friends with these guys. His boss, Rutherford Hathaway, owner of Hathaway Group, their eighteen person, nine billion dollar boutique financial consulting firm, insisted the reason for this was that they were very choosy about who was allowed to join the team. That recommendation from Pr. Hamilton had been a big deal.

This was important to Carter, and he could feel the opportunity being pulled out of his hands by crappy cell service in the middle of fucking nowhere. He headed out to the street to see if he could find someone nearby who could help. It had gotten to that point.

With one eye on his cell phone screen, and another at the rare passing car, Carter headed outside. The space directly across from the train station was forested. Right next to the train station was a deli that had closed hours before. On the other side was just the track approaching the station. No people. Just darkness.

Adjusting his backpack and duffle bag, Carter decided to see if there was anything helpful in the deli window. He ran through the downpour only to find a number of real estate offerings and the phone number for a snow plowing service, but that was it. He was just pulling out his phone to check one more time when—

"Can I help you?"

Carter spun around, heart clenching and breathing squelched. Chills ran sparks up and down his body until he saw the stopped police car with an officer leaning out the driver's side window toward him. Raindrops were snapping off the wide brim of his hat. "Oh!" Carter began, breathing again. "Thanks. I, uh…"

The policeman narrowed his eyes.

"I need a ride." Carter managed. "I can't get a cell signal, and I need to get to my boss's house."

The policeman relaxed. "Ah. Got it. What's the address?"

Carter fumbled with his phone. "It's, uh…man. It's in my address book, but I can't pull it up without a signal. Oh, wait! I wrote it down." Carter dropped his duffel bag on a dry patch and spun the backpack around to in front of him. He pulled a small slip of paper from one of the pouches. "It's, uh… 14 Mountain Ridge Road."

"Oh yeah. That's a ways. I could probably get you a cab, but no idea how long they'll take. Want me to give you a lift?"

Carter blew out his relief. "That'd be amazing, Officer. Really. Thanks."

"I just can't have you up front, okay?"

Another twenty minutes later, the police car slowed to a stop along a dark road, with a lone gas lamp flickering its light at the bottom of a driveway that stretched uphill into the dark.

"Here you are. Hope you have a good visit."

"Thanks again, Officer," Carter said as he clambered out of the back with all of his gear.

The car sped off and Carter was left standing there in the murk. The rain had finally stopped, but the humidity had swamped in to replace it.

He looked over at the driveway light. Why was it a gas lamp? Well, when you are the CEO of the company bearing your name, you can do whatever you want with your money, he supposed.

The driveway wound off through a shadowed wooded area. Carter couldn't even see the house from where he stood. He shouldered his bags and leaned into his walk.

What must have been a good quarter mile later, he saw a grand farmhouse with a wraparound porch and warm light pouring from all the windows. Off to one side there was even a barn. Parked out front were only two cars: one Beemer SUV and the new Tesla crossover.

Only two cars, though? Where was everyone else?

With a sudden feeling of exhaustion, he leaned on the doorbell. He heard the chime inside, followed by a set of footsteps. The door flew open.

"Carter, my lad!" boomed Mr. Hathaway. He turned and called inside, "He made it!"

A voice inside let out a hearty cheer.

"Sorry, sir…" Carter mumbled. "Long train ride and—"

"Never you mind," Mr. Hathaway said. "Come in, come in! Two rules for this weekend. Number one: no more *sir* or *Mr. Hathaway*. My name is Rudy, and I expect you to call me that."

Carter couldn't help the grin that spread across his whole being. Warm relief and excitement filled him. "Okay, Rudy."

"Good man. Now. Did you eat? There's still steak, shrimp cocktail, sushi, caviar. And thirsty? The bar is next to the table. Help yourself. Pull the drawer out underneath, that's the beer fridge."

Carter tried to take it all in. The two-story entryway, the stacked-stone fireplace, the massive table covered in food, the sidebar covered in bottles of high-end alcohol. Not only that, but—

"Carter!" thundered another familiar voice.

"Professor Hamilton?"

"How's Rudy been treating you?" A bear of a man with tousled gray hair and beard stepped forward and put his arm around Carter.

"Really well, thanks!"

"Good, good. If he doesn't, you just let me know, and I'll straighten him right out!" the professor said with a joking glare at Carter's boss. "Now, let's get you fed!"

The remainder of the night had been amazing. The best food, the best drink, and the best company that could be had. They had stayed up late into the night, joking and laughing, drinking and kidding around. Of course, all the drinking had made the following morning a little… if not painful, at least sluggish.

Carter slowly woke in one of the many guest rooms, and was instantly starving. He could smell amazing things wafting up from downstairs. He rinsed out his mouth in the ensuite bathroom and padded down the stairs to find Rudy sitting at the table by himself, reading on his tablet and sipping coffee. Again, the table was laden with a feast of all the right things: different styles of eggs, French toast, waffles, pancakes, bacon, sausage. Carter salivated before he'd taken three steps toward the table.

Rudy looked up. "Carter! Good morning! How did you sleep?"

"Fi—" Carter croaked and cleared his throat. "Fine. Thanks."

"Good! Feeling okay? We all put away a good bit of booze last night."

"Oh, I'm fine. I don't get hangovers."

"Really? Must be that young constitution. Don't ever tell anyone that. They'll be jealous. Coffee? Tea? Help yourself. They're both on the kitchen counter."

Carter ambled over to the kitchen and poured himself some coffee, and came back out to pour over the breakfast options. Plate full, he sat down with a steaming pile of breakfast a few seats over from Mr. Hath— Rudy! He didn't want to crowd.

Rudy continued reading, leaving Carter to his thoughts of the night before. Carousing with his boss and his mentor as if he had been part of some inner circle was amazing. And that "tradition" they had over in the barn. Drunken men locking arms in a circle and chanting while stomping on the concrete floor. It was really something. Pr. Hamilton said the chant dated back to a region of Romania in the 5th century, and was an appeal for a successful hunt. He went on about pre-Christian beliefs and civilizations in the region until Rudy had told him to have another drink. The chant had been hypnotic, though. Really something. Carter hoped it worked, because he'd never been hunting in his life and was hoping to not embarrass himself today. Truth be told, he was scared. He didn't like the idea of hunting. At all. But he was going to do it so he could prove to his boss that he could. Just like in the office. He wouldn't walk away from a task because he didn't like it. He hadn't liked grad school, either, but he'd known what the payoff would be, and as with that, the payoff for success today promised to be very good indeed.

"What's the grin for?" Rudy asked, snapping Carter back to the present.

"Oh! Remembering last night. That chant."

"Really something, wasn't it? Ham taught it to *me* when I was in his class at Sloan."

"H-ham? Wait…you had him? As a professor? At Sloan?"

"Didn't he never tell you? Oh, yeah. He and I go back to *my* grad school days, and we've been in touch ever since."

"That's—"

"Don't try to figure out how long ago, Son. Ham has been involved in this kind of work for a long time, and has helped guide me—"

"Helped guide you to what?" rounded Pr. Hamilton's voice from the bottom of the stairs.

"G'morning, Ham!" Rudy called.

"Morning, Professor," Carter said.

"Might as well call me Ham, Carter. Everyone does now, anyway."

Carter beamed.

"Now, coffee," declared Ham.

"Kitchen," directed Rudy.

"Excellent. Now, how did I guide you? Because clearly my work isn't done," Ham called from the kitchen.

"Nope," Rudy said. "Never is. We'll need you to steer us for a good long time."

Ham clapped Rudy on the shoulder as he came back in to consider breakfast.

The three chatted and ate, and by late morning, relaxed by the fire, satiated. Carter checked his watch, realizing something. As if reading his mind, Rudy spoke up. "Not a traditional hunt, this time, Carter. No early rising or tree-climbing this time. No, we have some cave hunting to do."

"Cave hunting?"

"There's a cave by the back of my property that occasionally takes on unwelcome residents. We've been asked to clear it out."

"Unwelcome residents?" Carter asked.

Ham pointed to the rug between the sectional and the fireplace, the one under all their feet. "Bears."

Carter's stomach clenched. "Bears?"

Rudy and Ham seemed remarkably calm. Had they done this so many times that they took all of this in stride?

"Bears're the only ones who could be a threat," explained Rudy.

"Well, sure…" Carter managed.

"Won't be a problem!" Ham assured him. "We haven't lost anyone to a hunt yet."

"That said," Rudy pointed out. "We should probably suit up and get underway."

Ham and Carter followed Rudy up a hill behind his house.

"And before you ask," Rudy called over his shouldered shotgun. "It usually takes us almost an hour to get there."

"How big is his property?" Carter asked Ham.

Ham smiled. "At last count, it was about 250 acres. He keeps adding to it when places nearby go up for sale."

"Two hundre—"

"Yah," breathed Ham. "Approximately one third the size of Central Park. Now hike. I have to focus or I get out of breath before we even reach the first peak."

"The *first?*"

Ham just waved him ahead, and they trudged up the hill.

After a lot of uphill walking and brief breaks enjoying the view while Pr. Hamilton caught his breath, they descended the far side of the final peak and approached the cave. The short parade of hunters slowed their steps while Carter did his best to slow his racing heartbeat.

He was sure it was going to choke him since it was pounding so hard and so high in his chest.

The cave opening came into view in front of them, with dead leaves and moss hanging over the entrance. Only now, Carter understood the reason for the flashlight attachment on the shotguns Rudy had handed the two of them before they'd left.

With quivering fingers, Carter clicked on the power on the flashlight near the end of the shotgun he held. He'd never fired a gun in his life, and now here he was about to use one on an animal that could tear him in half with little effort. He had to remind himself to breathe.

His vision flattened.

His palms sweated.

His knees shook.

A reassuring weight pressed down on his left shoulder. He turned a little too quickly and felt a little dizzy. Pr. Hamilton stood there. "It's okay, Lad. You'll do fine. We go in. We rid the area of this menace. And we're done. Won't be hard. Won't be long. I promise."

Warmth spread through Carter's chest and his shoulders relaxed. He felt better. Air flowed freely through his lungs, and his grip on the shotgun firmed up. Realizing the time had come, he followed Rudy into the cave.

The temperature and humidity skyrocketed as soon as they were inside and out of sight of the entrance. Carter tried to remember if caves were supposed to be cooler or warmer, but the heat made him feel more uneasy than he already was. Slashes of blue-white light stabbed through the pitch black in a visual cacophony.

Carter found himself continually adjusting his grip on his shotgun, and wiping the clamminess off on the stiff cloth of his jacket. He had to clench his jaw shut to keep from panting out loud. The pounding in Carter's ears threatened to deafen him.

The trio crept quietly forward, until suddenly, in the beam of one of the flashlights, Rudy's hand went up, signaling all to stop. He turned, put a finger over his mouth, pointed to his eyes, and then pointed to a wide cavern just beyond a ridge they stood behind.

Sweat trickled down Carter's back and legs. He moved forward as quietly as he could, and peered over the edge with the rest. In the beam of his flashlight, he saw what looked like a mass of fur, impossibly large. A few parts of the mass shifted softly as he watched. Squinting his eyes, he swallowed his initial panic. It wasn't a bear at all. It wasn't a ridiculously giant bear. It was a *family* of bears. They must have found the den and *all* its residents.

With horrid calm, Rudy and Ham lay on their stomachs on the ridge, and lined up their shotguns at the family of sleeping animals. They lay in a line, with Rudy at the far left, and Pr. Hamilton right in the middle, next to Carter's left elbow.

Carter was on the end.

He felt alone.

Each of the hunters settled into position. Carter's stomach queased and threatened to rebel. Were they really going to do this? They were so far from the farmhouse. What was the point? Were these creatures really such a thre—

The cavern exploded in sudden flashes of white light. A clap/boom. It shocked Carter so badly his gun slipped from his fingers.

Through his dazzled vision, as he picked up his gun, he could see that one of the animals already lay motionless. Carter spun to his left, to see Ham lining up his shot as the remaining bears leapt into panicked motion. Carter squeezed his eyes shut, and pressed his hands over his ears, cradling the shotgun in the crook of his elbow.

Thunder and lightning flashed and boomed inside the cave. Carter rolled away from it, curling up into a ball, until the silence moved back in.

He felt a sharp jab in his back. He uncovered his ears and opened his eyes, sitting up.

Pr. Hamilton was there, and he seemed annoyed. "Your turn, Carter. Now."

"Uh," was all Carter could say. He felt like throwing up. Then he heard it. There was a pathetic wailing sound. Almost like a bleat, but more throaty. He looked past Pr. Hamilton. The two men were glaring at him. As if he had failed to do something important, and was about to be severely reprimanded. "I don't—"

Rudy stepped forward. "Too late now. Take the shot."

Carter turned and saw a bear cub running back and forth in the cavern below. It nudged at its parents' dead paws and cried out. It tried to get past them. It tried to run. It had nowhere to go, and it wailed, still dashing forward and back.

"It's just a—"

"Now, Carter." Rudy said, suddenly sounding...something else.

"Hurry up, Carter. Shoot." Pr. Hamilton said, turning Carter toward his target.

Had it gotten warmer in the cavern? Was that fog, or just the smoke from the shotguns?

"Carter," Rudy said. "Please."

Please? Really? Carter swallowed, turned, shouldered his shotgun and squeezed the forward-most trigger. The butt slammed back into his shoulder and the barrel jolted upward.

He brought the gun back down and pointed at his target. He'd hit it. His first time firing a gun and he'd hit his target. But he hadn't killed it.

The poor creature lay there, bleeding. It breathed out a weak, mewling sound.

"One more, Carter. Finish it." Pr. Hamilton now.

Carter fired again. He peered down. He'd killed it, *murdered* the poor, defenseless bear cub. He leaned down, hands on his knees, and let out everything in his stomach. His eyes burned with tears.

Carter straightened back up on shaky legs. They were looking at him. Rudy nodded, his face grim. "I know that wasn't easy. I'm sorry. But it was a threat. They all were."

"A bear cub?" Carter cried. "Really? A threat to who? It would never go near the farmhouse!"

"Not to us," Pr. Hamilton cut in. "Not to the farmhouse."

"Then why the fuck were we doing this?" Carter shouted.

Pr. Hamilton knit his eyebrows and pointed.

Carter turned and looked down at the cavern floor. It was still lit with the beams of light from the flashlights. Something was moving down there.

The bears were still moving.

"No," Pr. Hamilton said. "Relax."

Carter stared down again, and from the shadows around the carcasses oozed…something. Were they worms? Something like giant worms wriggled from under each bear and suddenly spun around it. Then again, and again until each bear was wrapped, covered in what looked like black, oily ropes.

As Carter watched, hypnotized, the ropes spread, mummifying and wrapping each carcass. Each mummified bear then started to move a bit. It almost looked like a boa constrictor that had eaten something way too large. But then Carter realized what was happening. His association with constrictors was dead on. The mummifying ropes were squeezing the bodies of the bears. Horrible, muffled noises of tearing flesh and popping bones echoed up from the cavern floor as the bears were consumed by whatever the oil-slick ropes were.

Finally, there was a terrible liquid sound, and it became clear that the ropes were now empty. They splashed into thousands of tiny, oily, black snakelike creatures and slithered away into shadows and down into crevices out of sight.

Carter hadn't realized he'd been holding his breath. He blew it out, and looked around at Rudy and Ham.

They nodded, stepped over the ledge, and started to walk down toward the now-empty cavern floor. Carter gaped at them as they filed down the narrow path to the bottom. He couldn't move. He couldn't believe this. Everything had been so crazy, so surreal. And now they were going down into that pit of God-knows-what?

Pr. Hamilton turned and looked back up at Carter and held out a hand, a simple gesture inviting him to join them down there.

Carter's knees unlocked, and his legs buckled briefly. He stepped forward. He didn't want to go, but his legs were going. He stared down at the other two men on the cavern floor in terror, and couldn't look away. He couldn't stop himself, either. Numb fingers dropped his shotgun onto the stone floor where it clattered and lay still. The flashlight attachment shattered, hurling the immediate area of the cave into pitch darkness.

With stiff, robotic movements, Carter stalked over toward Pr. Hamilton's outstretched hand, unable to stop himself. He strained his hands outward to grab the rough stone walls along the path, but couldn't, as if there were a massive invisible hand wrapped around his body, squeezing his arms to his sides.

Eventually, Carter stood with them. Pr. Hamilton and Rudy stood on either side of him, faced the shadowed back of the cavern, and waited.

Carter didn't know for what. He still couldn't move. Every nerve in his body felt like it was firing, but every muscle in his body felt like it was made of frozen lead. He couldn't even turn away.

First came the sound. Wet, slithering, like hundreds of mucus-covered somethings dragging themselves across the floor.

Carter's body started quaking with the conflicting needs, wanting to be anywhere on the planet but there, but unable to change even the direction of his stare.

Out of the gloom came the things. They twisted and wriggled like worms, but they were too big. They couldn't be worms. Not normal ones, anyway.

They flowed out of the darkness like a tide, and then pooled in front of the gathering of men. The pool spiraled and piled onto itself, twisting and turning into a column of giant worms covered in tar. Carter gaped at the event in front of him. It reminded him of water going down a drain, but inverted. Rather than spinning and disappearing, this was spinning and building up. A sickening potter's wheel of black clay ropes, guided by invisible hands. Or was it guiding itself?

The column stopped twisting and growing. Spots tightened and narrowed while others opened out. The form shifted, flared, drooped, and oozed. At no point did it stop shifting. For brief moments, it would almost seem familiar, like an image from a faded childhood memory.. Shapes strobed and flickered, in constant motion, writhing.

Warm urine ran down Carter's legs and pooled around his borrowed boots.

As Carter glanced down at the pool growing around his feet, he noticed slithering on the floor. Three tendrils snaked across the floor and rose up in front of the three men like charmed cobras, till they were level with their faces, and flicked forward, snapping onto the men's foreheads, biting into flesh with needle teeth.

White fire axed through Carter's skull and blew out his nerves from his eyes to his ass. He puked bile where he stood, unable to move. The sour, viscous fluid squirted, then drooled out of his mouth and down his front, pooling on the floor with his piss.

As Carter's body shivered from the aftershocks of pain, the form spoke.

Bones shuddered at the intrusion. Skin crawled off, leaving muscle and nerves naked and helpless at the invasion. But the "speech" didn't come from outside.

An intense series of images flashed in Carter's mind.

A door opening. A holy man bowing. An ancient god on a pedestal. Thousands prostrating before it. Cavernous deep earth. Night sky. Pain. Naked suffering.

Warm, thick liquid ran down Carter's cheeks and upper lip. Blood.

Pr. Hamilton struggled to stand upright, and grunted with effort to speak. "Greetings, God of Deep Earth. We throw ourselves at your mercy, having done your bidding," he said, coughing out a mouthful of blood himself.

A smiling stone statue of an ancient god. A river rushing through a canyon. Pr. Hamilton as a young man in threadbare clothing. Pr. Hamilton as he looked today, but dressed in rich robes sitting on a throne.

"I thank you, Ancient One," intoned Pr. Hamilton.

Rudy hunched over a desk with Pr. Hamilton standing over him. Rudy as a young man running from the subway into an office building. Rudy standing on a mountain peak, legs set wide, fists on his hips. Pr. Hamilton on a pedestal. Rudy on a pedestal. An empty pedestal. Interrogative. Wonder.

Rudy lifted his head, licking blood away from his upper lip. "We have brought him here before you, Ancient One. We purged your altar at your request, and now present your newest follower to Walk in the Light, Carrying the Darkness."

The abomination finally shifted its direct attention toward Carter. Carter gazed up to where he figured the eyes should be, but rather than eyes, there were gaps in the worm ropes that made up the top portion of this creature. His mind wanted to simply accept the emptiness, but Carter kept looking.

And Carter *saw*. Darkness roiled from the bowels of the Earth, reached out from those eyes and clawed his mind with stinking tentacles. They wrapped themselves around his brain and *squeezed*, pulling him down, down, down. Into the reeking, compressing dark.

A massive wooden door slamming. Fire consuming. Fury twisting the face of the ancient stone god.

Rejection thundered through Carter's collapsing mind. It wasn't defiance, though. Not his. He, *Carter*, had been rejected.

Carter snapped back to the now with a deep gasp. He'd seen. He saw the was. He knew the now. He quailed at the would be.

Shattering glass. A wailing infant. A lone wolf cub starving in the wilderness.

Rudy and Ham dropped to the ground and put their faces to the stone floor. Pr. Hamilton spoke up, "Forgive us, power of Ancient Earth. We sought but to please you, and have failed. Give us but one more chan—"

Ancient statue turning its back. Sun setting. Three pedestals standing empty, rubble piled at the base of each.

The three tentacles that had lodged to each of their foreheads snapped away, and blood trickled down from small wounds. A perverse emptiness followed.

Pr. Hamilton wept, shaking, but did not speak.

The creature's form fluxed, and one edge extended into an arm which stretched out, growing longer as it reached toward Pr. Hamilton. The corded appendage grabbed at the back of his neck and lifted him, bending him backwards so Carter could see the agony and fear in his old instructor's face. A small part of his mind rejoiced at the thought of Pr. Hamilton's pain, for subjecting him to this nightmare.

The creature oozed forward, thrumming and growling audibly somehow, and its entire shape came alive with movement. All the worm ropes shook out and stretched toward Pr. Hamilton, reaching for the old professor's face.

When they came in contact with his skin this time, Pr. Hamilton screamed. Unlike with the bears, the worms now stabbed *into* the flesh of their victim, and burrowed underneath the flesh. This wasn't for psychic contact, either. This was punishment. Skin tore and blood flowed, drunk up swiftly by the growing swarm of worms that extended to and into Pr. Hamilton's face, head, and neck.

The old mans' body convulsed, shuddered, and went limp. The worm-being suddenly lurched forward, enveloped the entire corpse, crushed, consumed it, and stood, all in one nightmarish fluid motion. Rudy hadn't moved. Of course he hadn't.

But Carter suddenly realized *he* could.

Freed of the hold, he unlocked his knees and made to turn and flee this horror, trying not to hear his boss's bones being pulverized into powder.

In what little light he had, he could see the things slithering past them up the rise that they'd walked down. A thick, oily river flowed uphill.

A throng crying out with joy. Open air. A field. A house beyond. A town. A city. Teeming millions, waiting, ready.

What…what had they done? Was that family of bears the only thing keeping this creature in this underground cave? Carter had to get out. He had to do something, run, tell someone, call someone. *Something.*

The mouth of the cave collapsing. Carter falling. Carter screaming. Carter dying.

Suddenly utterly frozen, Carter wept. And hoped. And prayed.

Carter wept and prayed as he felt the worms wrap around his feet. His ankles. His lower legs, knees, thighs. The creature couldn't help but to violate him as it wrapped itself around his groin and hips, pressing inside. Burrowing.

A sharp, stinging sensation pulsed from Carter's lower abdomen, and he realized the thing was feeding from the inside. He tried to scream, to vomit, but failed at both.

It continued to envelop its way upward.

His middle. His chest.

Shoulders.

Arms.

Neck. The back of his head.

It pulled open his mouth and poured down his throat. Tears leapt to his eyes as Carter gagged, but then his eyes were covered too.

Death was a long time coming.

VOLVER AL MONTE

S. L. EDWARDS

I.

General Alfonsín Santos looked down on the garden he helped grow. Every verdant tree was a gravestone, and every flower burst from black, corpse-fed soil. Between the hum of the helicopter blades, the general listened to the oblivious choir of the birds who soared above the sprawling, cultivated earth.

He had dreaded this return for so long, but nonetheless found himself smiling. For the first time in years, he was coming home.

In the highlands things were primal and familiar. General Alfonsín Santos was a director and the field of war was his theater. The general was a man who could play chess against three opponents at once, a man whose fist was rolled and ready should the contest flow from one of wits to one of strength. Under the light-devouring canopy of the tangled trees, the general had been a force of nature, a dread name whispered on the lips of insurgents and terrorists who ducked under the whistle of chopper blades and the screeching of mortar fire.

Several "human rights watchdogs" had brought shame to his name and his country, claiming that General Alfonsín Santos had "depopulated the earth" with his counter-insurgency campaigns. But such claims were far cries from the truth: the general had filled the earth, made its dirt ripe with the iron and nutrients that it needed to fuel its ever-growing beauty.

But he had grown tired. Looking across the helicopter cabin, he saw the faces of boys. Boys who fancied themselves men because perhaps they had shot weapons or perhaps because they had known the love of a woman, but who were boys nonetheless. Boys who were over-eager for war, boys who could see little beyond the possibility of a promotion. Boys who could recognize neither the hardship nor beauty of battle. Boys with thick hair and wild eyes, nervous smiles and shoulder-clapping hands who grinned and made dirty jokes as they flew above the ground. Boys who were desperately trying to cope with the fact that they were a fat, sitting target in the sky. The rebels could renege on their deal at any time, all it would take was one rocket.

The *Tuta Puriq* had made a deal with the government. Paint a white flag on a black helicopter. Put General Alfonsín Santos on it. *He* could negotiate with them for the life of the Vice President's daughter.

General Alfonsín Santos had not seen active duty for a matter of decades. Gone were the days when he had direct access to government and foreign intelligence, when he charted the movements of guerrillas and peasant bands with black x's on maps. A failed presidential campaign and several lecturing tours across a system of U.S. military colleges had made him fat. Years of inactivity put strain on his joints that the boys in the helicopter would only come to know if they were lucky enough to grow old.

What he did know of the *Tutas* scared him, not because they seemed ruthless, but because they seemed *directionless*. Santos had dismantled, demobilized and destroyed his share of insurgent groups and believed he knew all types. He had fought violent groups before, groups so hated and evil that it was simply a matter of arming the peasants so they could fight back. Groups that waded into schools, executing children in front of their teachers to petrify the population into unequivocal submission. Guerrillas who hung thieving children along with their mothers, groups who executed onlookers for too long and too awkward stares.

But for all the violence he knew, the *Tutas* seemed different.

Even the groups who reveled the most in bloodshed would leave messages, signs of their presence and symbols of their power. They could not resist it, and breaking the authority of the state meant constructing an authority of their own. They *had* to plant their flag on their corpses.

But the *Tutas* were boogeymen, quiet highland ghosts who moved through narrow mountain paths with such a silence that they were cast as an urban legend before they were discovered as an insurgency. Refugees from the countryside seeped slowly into the alleyways of the capital, wraith children claiming ghosts had killed their parents; that vampires had emerged from the mountain caves to feast upon the flesh of the barely living. By the time the government realized it was facing an insurgency, the countryside had been nearly emptied.

No one knew their demands. The military campaigns that captured *Tuta* foot soldiers revealed that they had cut out their own tongues so that they could not speak. If left alone the captured *Tutas* would go so far as break their own hands so that they could not write. They did not seem to mind pain, nor did they show fear of death.

The group had not named itself, and the general recalled his confusion when he first discovered what the journalists were calling them.

Tuta Puriq, an old Indian phrase which roughly translated to *those who walk at night.*

The general turned back to the jungle below, consumed with dread. The jungle had taught him that most beauty is superficial at best, that any joy was the punctuated break before returning to the mountains.

Before returning to the natural state of things.

The helicopter reached the landing site, a square space on a hill marked by felled trees and white spray paint. The blue sky seemed to explode overhead as they descended, the birds scattering up in wild panic. The helicopter roared as it hovered above the ground, kicking up wet dirt and the remnants of dry, yellow grass.

For a moment, it seemed as if they were alone.

Then the general saw them.

They came through the shadows between the trees, black-clad forms who covered their faces in thick bandanas. He gasped despite himself, surprised at how many of them there were. At least twenty, holding their rifles ready with both hands, moved towards the helicopter in a remarkable, tactical discipline. The general bit his lip for blood and composure. He unbuckled his seatbelt and stood, disembarking the helicopter and turning to the soldiers behind them.

Their eyes were white. Their faces were quivering.

"This is not how you greet death." Santos smiled weakly.

They snapped their attention towards him as the soft footsteps of the *Tutas* grew louder and faster.

"You greet death as a member of your family. If you are kind to her, she will be kind to you."

A meaningless platitude, but one which had calmed his troops as he sent them out to die. The boys smiled, fearfully and softly. They raised their weapons, following their general's lead as he walked out into the clearing to expose himself to the mercy of the *Tutas*.

He raised his hands, feeling for a moment the warm sun on his face.

The gentle kiss of a pre-monsoon wind.

Yes.

Yes, this would be as good a time to die as any. As good a way as any.

For a moment, he could feel the pang of a bullet as it entered his body, for a moment he let his world darken. But it was nothing more than a hopeful hallucination. Before him a young man, face shrouded by black cloth and hair concealed by a dark beret extended a gloved hand. The general took it, finding that it burned with a dry-ice cold. He winced.

"General Santos," the young man spoke with a high-pitched voice behind his bandana. "We thank you for your attendance today. We invite you back to our camp, and there we may talk further."

"Señor," General Santos smiled, "And how am I to trust you? How can I be sure that you will not slaughter me when we arrive?"

"Frankly, general, we don't need you to trust us. Look behind you."

The young men from the helicopter had their backs to the general, rifles pointed to the jungle. Beneath the trees black uniforms seemed legion and shifting, writhing and twisting into the jungle shadows.

"Please appreciate your situation, general, and follow me."

The young man lifted his hand into the air and pointed backwards. The *Tutas* re-entered the jungle, folding back into that yawning, cavernous darkness. Santos found himself not afraid of dying, but of dying in captivity. For seconds that seemed like years, he did not move.

Finally, his feet lifted and he followed the shadows into their lair.

▼ ▼ ▼

They had been hiking for longer than the general had anticipated. The insurgents were not being kind to him. He was an old man, one who had to stop often and lean against the slippery black bark of wet trees. He hissed the humid air in and out, clutching his chest amidst the hysterical chittering of monkeys and the quiet, knife-ended stares of the guerrillas. An attendant was at his side now, rubbing his ribs and looking nervously around.

The boys he had brought with him had divested themselves of their machismo. They no longer had anyone to impress, and absent the eyes of young women they became terrified, armed children.

"Thank you," he moaned, leaning against his attendant's shoulder as they continued.

Perhaps it was a tactic, to make him tired when he finally arrived at their camp, more prone to negotiate.

He had only hoped Katerina was okay.

Over his pain he recalled his friend Raul's baby girl, a little child who Alfonsín knew would be as close to a second daughter as he would ever come. Katerina Villalobos did not take well to her father's career, as he became a Colonel, a General, a Minister and finally a Vice President. She did not care for the elitism that her life demanded, and spent more time listening to the folktales of her Indian nannies than the demands of her father. She treated Alfonsín first as an uncle, and then as a friend.

The general welcomed having a friend so young, treasured knowing a young woman who reminded him so much of his own daughter.

"General," the high-pitched voice of the masked *Tuta* brought him back to reality.

Santos never failed to be in awe at the perseverance of guerilla groups.

They lived on thin, dirty blankets that rested just above the wet ground, under dark green tarps which barely kept the rain off them. They hung their clothes on stolen ropes, kept their cooking utensils fire-sterilized and maintained everything in a way that would be ready to move at a moment's notice. Most of their shelters were twigs, lean-tos built with a carpenter's precision.

They moved him towards a large lean-to in the center of a camp, a great thing built around the trunk of a thick, sprawling black tree. Entering the opening the general found that the ground was covered with ornate, dirtied rugs. A single kerosene lamp was lit, revealing a series of cross-legged figures whose faces were as shrouded as the foot soldiers who surrounded them.

Outside, a low rumble of thunder growled through the jungle canopy.

"General," a cross-legged form bade him to sit. They were so covered that Santos could not tell if they were men or women, though he supposed that it would not matter either way. Women could be just as ruthless as men in the field of war, and just as noble as well. The gender of his hosts had no bearing on the lives of his men.

"Thank you for speaking with me," the general winced through the pain that came with sitting down.

"Thank *you* for accepting our invitation."

"Where is Katerina Villalobos?"

"She is with us. Tell us." The figure leaned over the lamp, and for a moment it seemed as its eyes were orange and yellow, "What is the girl to you?"

"A second daughter."

"And what happened to your *first* daughter, General Santos?"

The general did not speak, waiting for a full minute before the *Tuta* finally gave in and retreated over their lamp.

"No matter, we will have time to get to know you."

"Why am I here?" The general did not mind dying, but he did not enjoy being interrogated. He had conducted enough interrogations himself to know when he was being toyed with, for him to know that he was merely food for the cat to play with. Under their coverings, the *Tutas* were probably laughing at him.

"We simply wanted to get a look at you, at the famous General Alfonsín Santos."

The *Tuta* laughed then, a light chuckle laden with cold evil.

"I'm sure you have heard the joke about you, General, that if there was a Nobel Prize for war, you would have received it. But, there isn't, so you had to settle for those little aluminum foil medals that presidents stuck on you."

"I'm content with the fruits of my labor, content with peace. I don't need recognition beyond that." Santos spoke through clenched teeth.

"Oh now, we don't believe *that.*"

"If you're going to kill me, you can get on with it."

"Now, General we have no intention of killing you or your men."

The rain began to fall, pattering gently against the tightly bound wood. Outside the men begin to pace in uneasy, wet plodding steps. The kerosene lamp flickered and the Tutas sat up straight, as if anticipating the storm themselves.

"We agree with you, General. The fruits of your labor *were* peace. But you did not go far enough in tending to your fruit. For all the talk of you *depopulating* the countryside, there are so many people still left living."

"So that's it then?" Santos smirked, "You're not some utopian Marxist group, you're just a death squad?"

"Our face may as well be yours, General."

"I've had enough of this." Santos stood. He did not travel all this way for riddles, to be laughed at. If they killed him on his way back to the helicopter, that would be fine; but he would *not* be laughed at.

Outside the rain began to pour, drowning all other sounds.

"What?" He heard one of his soldiers murmur.

Then there was a scream. The cracking sounds of an automatic rifle.

The general turned to his hosts, furious.

But they only sat impassively.

"What the hell are you doing?" Santos screamed.

"Not us, general, we are not alone out here."

The general ignored the pain in his joints and ran outside the lean-to. The air was grey, the water pouring over his eyes in a continuous wet veil. He held a hand over his forehead, drawing his pistol and narrowing his eyes. The guerrillas were gone, but the screams of his men filled the camp with an all-consuming panic. Over the beating of his heart he followed their screams, slowed down by the sucking wet dirt beneath him.

The bullets kept flowing, punctuated with the sounds of tearing flesh and spilling gore.

He called their names, which ones he could remember. But none called back.

His legs gave way to his weight and he fell to the dirt. His open palms slipped in the mud, black dirt covering his eyes and splashing into his mouth. His entire body ached, but he moved to raise himself.

Something warm and firm slowly sank onto his head, pinning him down. He froze, uncertain of what to do next. He moved his head up as far as he could, his blood going cold as he began to understand what was in front of him.

A giant foot, pale and white, with a big toe the size of his fist. The foot seemed as large as his torso, connected to an ankle as wide as a tree. The pressure holding him shifted across his back, the lingering touch of slow fingers.

He could not breathe.

The pressure increased, forcing him flat on the ground as his knees and elbows slipped from under him.

A human arm dropped next to him, ragged strands of wet red flesh where it used to connect to a shoulder.

There was a pinching at his neck and his body grew warm.

The world drifted away into blissful darkness.

II.

The general woke to find himself dry.

He had been changed, out of his military uniform and into the black fatigues of the Tuta foot soldiers. He was sitting down, propped against a smooth rock wall. The cave ceiling was low, cool and wet as fat, dirty drops of water fell on his forehead. He could hear the rain far away, pittering dimly against thick dirt and smooth rocks.

In the light of the dim kerosene lamp he could see the *Tutas*, still masked. They stood ready, as if they had anticipated his waking at the exact moment. They held long sticks, clubs and crudely made spears.

The general shifted, letting the shale and pebbles slide beneath him.

He knew guerrilla groups sometimes used the mountain caves to hide from government bombardments. They had taken him somewhere from the light, kept him alive for some unknown purpose and—

He remembered the foot. The severed arm.

"What is going on?"

"We are learning to trust you, general." The voice seemed to come from all sides, from the walls of the caves themselves. It was low and high at once, the sound of a distorted record and a gargling demon.

"Where are we?"

"Closer to the truth."

"What was that?" he asked, nausea and panic boiling in his burning throat. "What killed my men?"

"Not too much farther now," the voice answered.

Two of the *Tutas* broke their ranks, picking him up by his armpits. He gasped as electric needles dug into his knees and lower back. The hands shoved his shoulder blades and he fell to the earth once more. A stone cut his cheek and he bit back an indignant, angry tear.

"You're going to need to stand on your own, general, if you want to go any farther."

The same rough hands lifted him again and let him go. He took a breath in, keeping his unsteady balance and looking around slowly.

The cave was wide, and they were far from the mouth. Behind him the rain and wind were ghostly echoes, but he could not see any light to indicate an entrance. The tunnel walls were smooth and shimmering in the kerosene light, as if they had been deliberately paved by nature. There were five *Tutas* with him, all impassive and motionless until the same garbled voice spoke again.

"Forward, general."

He felt the butt of a spear at his back and moved forward as they commanded him. He resolved to not speak, to die with as much dignity as he could keep. The *Tutas* were little more than nihilistic madmen. Their annihilation would be the duty of some *other* general, some other poor, unhappy man set on a course he could not reverse. He maintained his silence, letting the walls come tighter and tighter until the *Tutas* and he were walking in a straight line between the cavern walls.

"These caves," the voice of the *Tuta* spoke after some time, "Were only uncovered due to Spanish greed. The Indians knew the truth, and theyimplored the Spanish to leave the mountains be. The mountains were where the gods slept. They told the Spanish that they could have silver, but just *enough*. Only so much as they truly *needed*. The Indians begged the Spaniards exercise moderation. But when," the voice became accusatory and amused, "When has power *ever* exercised moderation?"

The general would not respond to this provocation. He looked ahead, carefully and slowly moving one foot in front of the other. There was nowhere else to go, nothing else to do. Even if he escaped the Tutas, there was no way he would find his way out of the mines that fed into the caves.

"And so," the *Tuta* continued, "Greed consumed the earth, filling it until even the Indians were its children. Then, greed became violence, and the violence was eternal until *you* mastered it. Now general...now we are all *your* children."

A little girl. Pig tails tied in bright blue bows. An innocent smile.

"Don't say that," the general hissed.

The *Tuta* laughed. "Why, general? Is there no better legacy for a man than a child? To imprint themselves onto future generations?"

"I have no children!" the general roared.

"Save for your *second child*, Katerina Villalobos."

The general halted. He had forgotten about Katerina. She was surely dead, or at the very least it was clear that she would not be returning to her family. They would not have gone to such great lengths with the general otherwise.

"Tell us, general, what happened to your *first* child?"

Santos bit his lip.

The butt of a spear came down on his back. He fell to the floor of the cave, rocks crashing into his head. Overcome with pain and guilt, he let himself slip away.

Rosalinda Santos ruled her father.

Everyone in the capital knew that the general was subservient to his little daughter, who walked around the general's household as a princess in her palace. Perhaps it was because his wife died in childbirth, or perhaps because the general did not want to be the same man he was at home that he was in the battlefield. Dinner guests often smiled when Rosalinda ran up to her father with little slips of mandatos, *nonsensical commands such as* Daddy must read to me *or* Daddy must take me to the movies.

And in curiosity, they watched as the General bowed to his little daughter and followed her orders to the letter.

The general's head was buzzing. Heavy hands were lifting him up. He tasted sour, acrid vomit in his mouth. They leaned him against a wall and let the flickers of light fade from his sight.

He was still in the caves. Still alive.

"Just kill me, just be done with it!"

"General..." The distorted, scraping voice seemed sad. "We aren't going to kill you. But you *are* going to meet our gods. *Your* gods. And to meet them, you must be strong. You must unburden yourself of your sins."

"I don't have any regrets," Santos spat. He laughed madly, driven dizzy by torture and all the exhaustion it entailed. "I've *killed* before. I've killed so many and every last one of them deserved to die. I don't care about them so you may as well stop."

A spear shaft struck his ribs. There was a loud crack and the taste of stale blood at the back of his throat.

Rosalinda was a smart girl who became a brilliant young woman.

The General, it was said, was at once in awe of and exasperated by his daughter. He would laugh with his guests over cups of wine, explaining that it would have been easier had she simply been pretty rather than pretty and brilliant. But she got the best grades in her class, read everything she could get her hands on, and seemed to pierce the veils of higher meaning immediately. Metaphors, codes and formulas. Nothing could escape her.

And there was no telling her no.

He wasn't sure where she began to read newspapers, or when she became interested in politics. Her first explanation to the general was that she was reading Marx in order to better understand what her father was fighting, so that she may guard herself against it. But it went from Marx to Lenin to Mao, and soon she dropped the pretense.

Heated discussions at dinner were routine as she changed from a girl to a woman. The general began hiding her from society, avoiding guests in his home lest some competitor within the government use her as a piece of gossip which would have her blacklisted.

He implored her to be careful, to be mindful. But she only looked at him with eyes that broke him. Eyes that knew him.

"Very few people in this world *matter*, general." The *Tuta* spoke softly, as if it were speaking to a child.

"We are not interested in the people who are unimportant to you. A man cares little for the bugs he kills by brushing off his shoulder or those he exterminates to save his crops. These are *not* sins. Tell us then, general, what bothers you? For you must leave it here before you meet your gods."

They weren't going to stop. They would not beat him to death, they would not let his heart give way to the strain. They would merely keep beating him, keep prodding him and hurting him. But they could not hurt him as much as he had already hurt himself.

He was tired. He breathed in slowly, his chest quivering between shattered ribs. The tears in his eyes were reflexive, but they burned just as they had on the day he learned about his daughter.

The day he consigned himself to hell.

"Very few people matter to me." Santos' voice was weak, surprising even himself in his temerity and reluctance.

"Understandable," the *Tutas* shifted the general, supporting him as two of them held their arms behind his back so he would not need to walk on his own. They moved slowly, gingerly. The walls of the cave were different now, shimmering with rich veins of salt-and-pepper crystals as wide as his arm.

In the kerosene light it was beautiful, the sort of shimmering stars that Rosalinda would watch with him. He would help her on the roof of their home and watch the sky with her. She would ask him the name of a star and he would say, that they too were named Rosalinda.

Every star was named after her, he explained.

The crystals seemed to pulsate with the pounding of his head and the lurching of his stomach. He breathed in deeply, trying to stifle what could become a torrent of sobbing.

"People are burdens on the soul just as they are burdens on the earth, general. For one to move through life as far as you have, they cannot be held back. You are an important man, general. A *good* man."

"I am not a *good man*." The salt and snot fell into his mouth. He felt his sobs boiling into burning aches behind his mouth.

"Please," the voice was tender now. "Please tell us."

Rosalinda running away was inevitable.

She had been admitted into several universities, but her interest in education seemed to fade away faster each day. One evening, the general came to her room, a cup of coffee on a silver tray as meager a peace offering as he could muster after their latest fight.

But she was gone. A window open and a backpack missing.

He called in every favor he could, his peers in the military and government horrified that their staunch killer could be reduced to a mewling baby. They acted urgently, combing the capital with sleek black cars and halting every bus so that armed men could walk down the aisles searching for her. Fliers were put up; a reward was offered and then raised. Five times.

The general no longer slept, and as the insurgency increased he readily threw himself into his work. He orchestrated elaborate, merciless campaigns from his office, mapping out small massacres in the faraway highlands. He could not secure his own household, so perhaps it would be enough to secure his nation.

But for all the maneuvers of his troops, the general became disinterested in regulating the minutia of operations. Paramilitary groups came from the shadows, offering to take up duties the general did not care to examine or discuss. Through backchannels he gave his authority with ambivalence, moving from one mission to the next and not caring to examine what was left in his wake. And in the darkness of the general's inattention, these groups divested themselves of the semblance of man and became animals.

"But I don't regret it." The general explained. The *Tutas* stood still, engrossed and reverent of the general's story.

"Are you ready to move forward?" The distorted voice seemed clearer now, booming and low.

The general chuckled, letting the bloody tang of his mucus fill his mouth.

"I cannot move on my own anymore."

"You may lean on us, general. You may *always* lean on us."

Gently, gloved hands came to his side and back. He rose slowly, carefully as two-foot soldiers spread his arms over their shoulders. Gingerly moved forward.

"Thank you," the general whispered.

"General," the voice continued, "Why do you *not* regret setting the *paramilitarios* loose on the countryside? As you said, they were animals. Not men."

He sighed. He had given this speech so many times. Over his bitter cups, over the gasps of his peers. It was a moment when he dropped a façade, when he opened himself up and let loose the demon which rested just behind the veil of his eyes.

He took a moment to notice the pale purple veins of crystals, pulsing with their own inner light. Large geodes burst open as luminous, amethyst fungi. The walls were narrowing, so the *Tutas* and he lowered their heads and moved softly around low-hanging rock formations. The kerosene lamp was dimming, and it seemed that with each step the general's pains were healing.

"There is no real difference between men and animals," he began.

The cave walls shimmered, a rich swirling vein that glowed with the falling and rising cadence of his voice.

"We were built for violence. Every man and woman is readily designed for murder the day they are born. Our arms were made for spears, our legs so that we could ride horses to better pursue each other. War is part of our natural evolution. It is nature at its most exposed.

"So, we deserve it. And because we deserve it, it's only justice."

"Did your daughter deserve what happened to her, general?"

The question bore into his stomach deeper than any bullet ever could. The weight of the memories came down on his knees, but the Tutas moved forward, not letting him stop to fall. The shimmering purple of the crystal-veined wall became shining beams of sapphire. It was the bright blue of the summer sky, and for a moment the general was beneath it, holding his daughter's hand. And the brief, temporary hallucination was crueler than any torture.

"No," he answered. "No, she didn't."

How many executions did he order that day?

The report came down slowly from the highlands, a trickle of information had fed a blossoming hope in the general's heart. If he could reach Rosalinda before anyone else, if he could only bring her home in secret, he could save her from the tomb she had built for herself. The guerillas wouldn't be able to protect themselves, much less her, when the weight of the state came down on them.

Vague rumors of a young woman fighter, someone who resembled his daughter.

Someone he could save, the only person who ever mattered.

How quickly did those reports silence? How fast did those vicious paramilitarios turn inward, guard themselves to protect themselves from his wrath?

Santos had been used to torturing for information, for a purpose. He had never hated his enemy until that day. That day, he became a more real devil than those men could ever know.

He was tired. He was hungry and he was afraid and good god, he was thirsty.

His howling sobs overtook the darkness around him. The caves were shimmering with the lights of a nascent, unfolding galaxy. Around him the darkness sang and hummed. The light became all-consuming, and blinding.

Something cool and smooth came into his hands. Someone lifted the object to his mouth and he was overcome with an aching, sweet smell.

He bit into the unknown fruit and let the blinding light take his sight away.

III.

The world was red.

The kaleidoscope cave ended in a single crimson portal.

The general walked through unafraid, escorted by a race of giants.

The red light poured from a miniature sun, a disc that hung low in the air and shined down on the expansive, obsidian city. He had seen Machu Picchu before, back when Rosalinda was fourteen and he was trying desperately to recreate a little girl who refused to stay the same. This was a darker, grander Machu Picchu of towering black pyramids, glistening walls and roads unfolding in every direction. In the scarlet sky, leathery prehistoric birds cawed and cried out, preserved from the ravages of the world above them. Around them, tall trees broke towards the artificial sun, allowing some unseen, secret breeze to rustle them gently.

The *Tuta Puriq* abandoned their disguises, rising above him in long strides. They were pale, statuesque things made of tight, white sinew. Their black hair unfolded wildly to their lower backs, and when they smiled down on him it was with the horrifying kindness of beings who knew more than men ever could.

They spoke without moving their mouths, perhaps broadcasting from somewhere within his own mind.

"You knew, did you not, general?"

"Yes." He answered, giving up every defense he had.

"How sad." The voice answered.

Then, it continued: "Our children are ourselves, miniature and wild. And it is always a terrifying thing to see yourself made wild. This is why you allowed the brutality of the war to escalate, although you knew perfectly well that your daughter was out there. Fighting. Just like her father."

The general made no protest as he walked through the city, nor did an objection even occur to him. The sacred nature of the place was boring into him, crushing him as the weight of the world above him.

"It's normal, the disdain for your progeny." Spires rose into the sky as twisting needles, glistening with the red light as the leathery birds of prey rested at their tips. The giant race walked solemnly and silently, not a word or gaze passing from any one to the other.

"We made you to aid us. You were to produce the air we need, to cultivate and nurture the earth above us so that we may thrive below. But," the voice adopted the smallest bit of sadness, "We made you in our image. For that, we must apologize. It is not your fault that you are so flawed, it is only natural.

"But, general," a fountain of shining, molten silver liquid rose before them. The general lifted a hand to shield himself from the blistering heat, straining and peering as bubbles burst and shattered against the onyx pavement. The fountain parted into multiple currents, byways of glistening silver splitting beneath shimmering onyx brick ways.

"There is good news."

The general stopped, looking upward to his benevolent captors in hope. Their smiles unnerved him, filling him with all the dread-laden anxiety of a looming storm.

"You will be part of what comes next." They were beautiful. Wide grins of straight, white teeth. Eyes the size of fists, brown-yellow and knowing. "You may walk the earth yet. A better earth of better creatures."

An arm as long as he was tall motioned and the general followed.

The long walk was quiet. The molten silver coursed beneath his feet, the black Machu Picchu falling behind as they walked towards the surface of a writhing lake. In the red light, it seemed filled with fat, fighting worms.

"I've walked the earth long enough. I just want to rest."

The figures did not reply as the lake grew larger and closer. The worms made the soft, crying screams of angry infants.

"Then, general, might you consent to a sacrifice for your children? The children men deserve?"

The general had given up his will, approaching a set of shining steps. He looked forward to rest, to the long silence. To an end.

He stood above the lake, looking down on the new children of men. They had no arms for spears, no legs for riding horses. Only long, writhing bodies, sharp-needle teeth and innocent infant faces. All they would need for when they broke the surface and rectified an unforgivable mistake.

He smiled in peace, raising his eyes to the other end of the lake.

His eyes rested on a solitary figure, a young woman whose face and eyes he recognized despite all the distance between them.

A giant hand pushed him forward.

He fell, screaming her name.

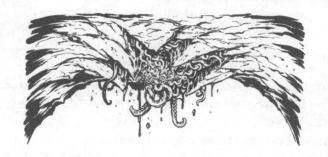

SOME CORNER OF A DORSET FIELD THAT IS FOREVER ARABIA

DAVID STEVENS

1.

His shame was exposed, the scar where a shell splinter had torn through his groin and ripped away his manhood. Albert no longer cared. He was counting the moments until he died.

A deep sucking followed the crack of bone. The slurping of marrow, the fluid dripping from her jaws, the varied noise of her digestion. The bitch's snout was buried in disinterred remains. Albert froze, no longer struggling, seeking to delay the moment he came to her attention.

That silk could bind so tight.

A charnel house in the familiar church yard. The stench of decomposition and the dripping remnants took him back to the

Western Front. Only his eyes moved, darting from horror to horror. *What was happening?*

The thing was globular in the moonlight. Heavy breasted. Round haunches curving to a woman's thighs that soon became dog's legs.

Or a jackal's.

He tried to control his shivering in the warm night. She would turn and see him. Otherwise, why would they have tied him and left him here?

2.

Lost in the fog of waking, mired in a dream of blood soaked sand, Ross sliced his breakfast orange finer and finer, cursing the imprecision of the available cutlery. He required surgical instruments. After all, the devil is in the details.

Soaked. The stained grains on the surface would blow away, to be lost amongst billions of others. But the gallons that soaked through, blood wending its way like water through gravel, heading for a parched destination.

Ross recognised the shallowness of what he had once thought had been at his core, his desire for the exotic. When faced with the truly foreign, he had run, and was still fleeing, leaving names and identities behind like confetti floating on the wind.

Afterwards, his overwhelming sense had been of clockwork, a mechanical tableau played out. Instead of brass, the mechanism was rock, driven by energies greater than the forces of desert winds and scorching sky. When the images returned late at night, they stretched beyond the cave, gears turning the ancient rocks of the planets and asteroids as they spun in slowly decaying orbits around the sun.

3.

Albert kicked out with his good leg, as if the thought of resistance had only just entered his head.

His captor evaded the bare foot easily, snaring it in silk and tying it to the post. "Don't do that."

"Why, will you shoot me?"

The man shook his head. It was covered, the head garb trailing down over his shoulder. *Not a turban*, but Albert did not know the word for it.

"If you try," the man began, producing a serrated dagger from the folds of his robe, "I will cut you." Matter of fact. "Not tie you. Slice through the tendon above one heel. Maybe both. It will be a long time to heal. You will never walk easily again."

"I am to live through this?"

The man sought the right words. "This is the appropriate attitude to bring to the endeavour. Fatalism creates the wrong atmosphere."

Beneath the afternoon sun, Albert was chilled.

4.

Desperate for shadow, Ross was reduced from sentience to a series of reactions as the midday sun burned him into the gap between the rocks. Heedless of serpent or scorpion, he dragged himself over scree into the small cave, gulped deeply from his leather water bag, and collapsed.

Awake, unbitten and unsavaged. Eyes murk adjusted, wondering where he was. He marvelled that he had slept. The ground shook and the rumbling echoed in the hollow of his chest. He knew why he had woken.

Oceans the size of a duchy persisted below Arabia. Ancient water remained from the sea that had left behind the mollusc shells he had seen on rock exposed after centuries beneath dunes. His imagination preferred a massive watery expanse with subterranean storms and huge eternally dark waves, though he knew the sea was trapped within shale and stone like oil. Even so, rivers travelled where rock had failed and pressure had forced the water out, and he guessed the rumble was the stream that fed the sheltered pond that had drawn him here.

Ross shuffled along, further away from the entrance. A strange quirk of the local quartz, or chance angling of the rock recess enabled him to see where he was going, despite the entrance being lost from view. The happenstance of a breach in the rock continued downwards, an easy slope leading him on hands and knees where he otherwise would not have bothered going. A litter of stone fragments disguised that the turning floor was smooth. If it had been outside, it would have been a helter skelter, a ha'penny to slide. The burrowing of a great worm exuding acidic slime from its maws as it moved beneath everything. Now, there is an image for Dr Freud, he thought. Which way did the worm come? Magma forcing its way up, or water wearing its way down?

He followed the path further and further down.

5.

Albert had seen hills rise into the air and fall like rain around him. Men had dissolved before his eyes. He had watched over time as bodies worked their way through trench walls, sappers who were undeterred even by their own deaths. Assured it was impossible, he had seen a bullet pass by his face, glinting as it caught the sun. He could no longer be shocked, though he would admit to this turn of events being unexpected.

They were in the church yard. It was not possible someone would not see. Someone would walk through in the next instant.

"Is this a joke? This is very serious, what you are doing." Careful enunciation, so the little foreigner could understand him. He didn't know where the other one was.

"Of course it is not a joke. To take and tie up a policeman like this. We would want to have a very good reason to do such a thing."

6.

Sitting here on this hard bench, tapping the lacquered wood with a fingernail, feeling the resistance, the solidity, while knowing it was all mostly empty space. Matter was a myth, a story we tell ourselves to get through the night. Rutherford had shown the gulf between the atoms, and the distances separating electrons from the nuclei. If Ross had gained one thing from his correspondence with the scientist, it was that there was plenty of room for other worlds, and space for their intersection.

How far he was from that cave. Now he breathed in steam and coal dust, not dry desert air, and brushed soot from his serge sleeve, not ash from a thoab. Ross rapped the bench. *Reading Railway Station*, said the sign, and all is right with the world. He brought his knuckles to his mouth, and sucked unwittingly at the fresh cut from this morning.

The steak knife had slit through the side of his finger as he hacked at his orange, leaving a pouting lip. A scimitar of blood arose, and awareness returned. Ross had surveyed the mess, his search for clues in the archaeology of his breakfast.

Steam billowed about him, the engine chugging out clouds as the train was readied. All that had passed between then and now. How difficult to return from the war and live what was thought to be a life. Empires had fallen, and here he was, catching trains instead of blowing them up. Sitting on benches instead of crouching behind dunes. Bearing an umbrella instead of a rifle. All will be well, and all manner of things will be well, he recited. Then he glanced at his wristwatch. The face of it squirmed and made no sense, and his stomach sank.

The fog that obscured the station around him could not have poured from the steam engine. The humdrum world was gone, the busy people lost to him. The set was struck and the stage stood bare.

A new cave presented itself, bored through the fog, clouds hiding the sharp edges that would cut through and tear at him. In the distance, a smile bearing the promise of pain. Heisenberg was right, though the professor could offer him no practical assistance. Ross had observed, and in observing had become part of the equation. Now he suffered the unforeseeable consequence of disturbing a mechanism worn delicate.

The tunnel telescoped. The distant image resolved. Slim, barely female, the colour of tea with a brief splash of milk. Observed, its spring sprung, the androgyne began to stroll towards him.

Before he was lost, Ross acted. He ignored the tendrils of steam, the infinitude of confusion that led to world after possible world. All the men he could have been, all the fates he may yet suffer. One foot in front of the other, just the way his mother had taught young Ned all those years ago. Avoiding the sick making suggestion that Reading Railway Station was less than real, he strode the distance to the carriage from memory, stepping it out yard after yard, not looking to see whether his feet were hitting the platform, or sinking several inches into it. His own machine drove him on, its clockwork as hidden as that of the orange. He walked, he climbed, he stepped up, he grabbed. There was a lurch, and whether it was the train or the world that shifted, he did not know. He froze, eyes scrunched and head bowed, as though waiting for a sandstorm to pass.

Solidity ebbed back. The carriage floor grew firm. Ross opened his eyes. The world had returned. The train clattered over a bridge, and he looked down at the Thames.

He had left his satchel behind on the platform. The price he paid to flee this time was only his manuscript, a year's work.

7.

They were characters were from a pantomime of insidious intent. At first sight, there had been nothing truly exceptional about them. All tweed and flannel. Dusky, to be sure, but he had served with the 17th. Sepoys had fallen with white men. *We're all of us just bags of blood,* a thought that was creeping into Albert's mind more often. A courteous nod in passing as he walked his quiet beat, his mind on other things. The loneliness of children's laughter. The sadness of midday sun. Hiding his limp.

Then he was taken from behind. His despair that he was taken so easily, that he was held and could do nothing.

They stripped him and his heart galloped. His shame would be exposed, he could not live if it was, could not bear it, but they had left him his drawers. He stood, near naked, while they were, well, they were robed. Like Bedouin or such, he guessed. Some Arabian Nights affair. Not that he could know for sure, his war had been entirely on the Western Front. When had they changed their clothes?

He worried that they would leave him alone here, until someone came upon him. Then he worried that they wouldn't, and some poor soul would be caught up in whatever nonsense was taking place.

Where were the villagers?

8.

In that sinkhole beneath the earth, yards under the pond, the rumbling no longer travelled just through rock from below, but now through the air all around Ross.

There was no geological purity here. Igneous rocks penetrated sedimentary. Great spans of years wore all of it down. The tunnel grew a little, the descent ceased. A sleeve of shale had fallen away, sharding the floor, exposing granite beneath.

The roof moved. He thought his vision blurred, then that some creature was above him, or a breeze was blowing ... something. Then he realised. Through the wound in the shale, he saw the source of the earth's vibration. Ancient rock slowly dragging itself through a mostly hidden expanse. A wheel not quite the same darkness as the roof, bearing markings he could make out but not understand, despite his education.

It was close enough that he could have touched the wheel, let the eons drag across his fingertips as it circumscribed its way through rock. Eyes closed, he concentrated on the noise. In the distance, a similar sound, of higher pitch, joined it. Another wheel?

And finally, his attention complete, underneath it all, from just next to his head, he heard a moan.

He jumped, of course. Barely there, it emanated from the rippled wall. His eyes were playing tricks, searching for meaning that was not there, like astronomers seeing canals on Mars. It was an illusion of a fossil, a vague resemblance to a visage reduced almost to nothing by deep time.

With the merest disturbance of dust, the story failed, as a lid lifted and a rock eye stared out at him.

Now that he could see one, they were everywhere. Not some bas relief. A foot protruding from rock here. An outline of a torso. Things in the earth that had become exposed.

He touched nothing. He went no further. Slowly, then quickly, he retraced his steps, the corkscrew of the tunnel more obvious in his faster ascent. Behind him, a new sound, a whisper. He was sick, as though something obscene had been exposed, and he would not remain here a moment longer.

He had climbed down, of course he could climb up. It was an illusion that the tunnel seemed to have narrowed. It was very, very old, and could not change in a few minutes. Only fear suggested the pinprick of light was vanishing. The entrance would still be there, he would not be trapped. Still, he hurried, dragged himself up, leaving skin on stones, a small price to pay. Scurrying, fleeing, and as he reached the entrance to the cavern, the bare trace in the earth, he burst out, breath exploding from him as though he had been underwater for minutes. He exulted in the open space about him. The hottest hours had passed. He wasted no time leaving.

Behind him, below him, infinitesimally, heads turned. He had observed. In turn, he had been observed.

9.

Albert paced out his beat, buoyed by the languor of a mid-summer's morning. As he walked though, his spirits lowered again. The things that once brought pleasure reminded him of what had been taken from him. The sounds of children at play. Once pretty women, widowed or doomed to spinsterhood by the War, and he with nothing to offer. Despite the heat, the ache creaked back into his leg, reminding him that the simple life he craved, the only life he had ever wanted, had been stolen irrevocably.

Enough really was enough. Unbidden, a decision formed. He could hold out until mid-autumn. Why bother with another winter's gloom? A mild day, before it became too bleak. Streaks of cirrus against a still blue sky, the hint of frost to come, crunch of straw beneath his feet. A last look at the turning leaves. He would stumble. *Bad leg, you know. War wound.* A simple hunting accident, not uncommon at all, even for one adept at handling arms. He could almost pity the farmer who would find him, but after what he had seen, not really.

10.

The price Ross had paid another time. A shoulder blade and two ribs smashed, one of a thousand masochistic recollections available to him. The ultimate price the pilots had paid. Over Italy, the end of the right wing tore free. They said it must have been worn, the frame weakened. They were wrong. It had crumpled before his eyes, the wing colliding with an invisible reef, uncharted by previous flyers. Molecules of air had conspired and hardened in that spot of sky. A fragment of remnant tunnel that had once corkscrewed into space. Then they were past it and sinking in the ocean of air. He looked up through the ripped fabric of the wing, and all he could see above was the approaching earth. The tug of gravity thwarted by the lower wings of the bi-plane as they caught air and glided, force and resistance alternating. A long fall, long enough to imagine an Arabian night's world of clouds as floating islands, and a race of beings to which gravity's pull was as resistible as the magnetic attraction of his pocket compass was to him. An empire of the air with its own ranks, language and perceptions, as alien to him as the empire of the ants.

11.

Albert would wait. Though none of it made sense to him, no doubt it did to an oriental type. The reason would either present itself, or it wouldn't. He would endure, as he endured every day. Treat it as sentry duty. Long boring hours of standing still, walking a few yards here and there in a muddied Flanders field. This night too would pass, until soon there would be no more nights.

When the twilight dwindled away, it left a blackness penetrated only by stars. He could have been floating in space, and despite the persistent warmth, he shivered at the thought. Then, fooling him (because he thought it was not due for at least a week, and he was not wrong), the full moon rose.

He blinked, and when he did something shifted, and in the lunar luminescence, he saw through another's eyes.

Albert gasped. His body sagged. Everything had been a dream, these past twenty years an illusion. He was awake now, and back on the Somme.

A butcher's field. A desolation. Bodies buried after earlier onslaughts resurrected, disinterred by explosions and their parts draped, the landscape furnished by the eviscerated. The earth a churned quagmire, the soil a sponge that if pressed, would evict blood. It was over, he had not survived it, he had died and haunted the battlefield, his apparent life the daydream of a wraith. Where was his own corpse? Was it the one being fed on over in the corner?

What was that?

12.

Ross had his work. Gas lit nights (more shadow than light), a flickering world of ink where nothing was certain, writing his letters and reading the journals sent by his correspondents. His efforts to make sense of it all, and his constant frustration that his tools were inadequate. Classical Greek and Arabic and expertise in mediaeval pottery could only take him so far.

Sufficient to each night are the worries thereof. Days were for the work of hands, and he rubbed them together. This morning was for him and his motorbike.

The grumbling beneath, the solidity of road pressing up against the rolling wheels, the security he cherished and loathed. A fraud as much as always, walking about in a borrowed persona, hiding in the world. Ned, T.E, Chapman, Shaw, Ross: all the men he had been. Pick a name, any will do.

Vibrations coursing through him, sun warming, fields alive with green, exhilaration tempts him. A crass approximation of joy stabs his heart, the magic of a summer's day. He would prefer a world with no magic at all, straightforward Newtonian physics, with cause always preceding effect.

What does a hint of happiness precede? Rounding a bend, she is there, the sudden scorpion spoiling an English attempt at paradise. Surprised, he swerves to miss her but she has already vanished. Her winding path has spiralled outwards, and he has intersected it again.

She appears outlined against storm cloud, a foul sky that was not there a moment before, but has always been here, at this place and time. This is how she is for him. Slim, boyish hips. High cheek bones, semitic nose. The promise of everything, wanted or not.

It is not cloud. It is darkness pressing through. The wind is not blowing a storm, it is air fleeing the breach of reality, streaking from huge fingers that unfurl and part the sky. At night, he has been constructing a poetry to convey it, using images that a mind evolved to survive on an African plain can understand. Formlessness beyond creation. He chooses not to look up. What sense would his mind make of it? Would he picture a distant eye staring down, a djinn peering at a world trapped in a bottle?

He is a man. He can make choices. He will not be part of this. He will have no truck with things of the air. Any accidental transgression has been paid for time and again. The blood that has been spilled, the lives lost, the causes betrayed.

She is there. The sacrificial slaughter of the battlefield has kept the door open. Is blood required to close it?

He will have none of it. He waits. This too will pass. Meanwhile, he sits astride his bike, booted feet firmly planted on bitumen. He is not stupid. He has studied the lore, taken precautions. Lodestone, inscriptions, herbs, incantation. He is not bound.

Around the corner, puffing as though they ascend the latest turn of a long corkscrew, come two boys on flimsy bicycles. They swerve all over the place. They are oblivious to the androgyne and the torn veil. They know nothing of the howling winds that would bear their small forms away in an instant. They lean into the corner as they turn on the ascent. He is stabbed through at the sight.

Her smile is canine. Her face is hunger. She is not composed of atoms. If she could be held, if she could be dissected, there would be no space in her but the gut demanding to be filled. She is Freud's onion, the same all the way through, no mystery to be revealed, only appetite.

Her shape is that of a curse.

Choose.

13.

Eventually, inevitably, a gasp escaped Albert, and the lupine head withdrew from the guts it had been tearing at and turned to him. She pushed up from the ground with her hands, lowered the globes of haunches she had presented to the night, and became bipedal. He was caught and she was coming.

She flowed, a quivering mirage of soil and night, not bound by the complexities of human locomotion. She poured towards him, and for Albert she was milky in the moonlight, and round, oh so round, not like the pinch faced city lasses of recent years. Observing, he determines her for the moment, fixes her shape with his pointless desire. Though he does not want them to, his eyes travel down the marble whiteness of her, the smoothness of the curved belly, and he yearns despite himself, despite his wound, pulls at his bonds while his mind reels, knowing what has gone into that mouth to fill that stomach.

While he pulls, she marvels at the gift that has been presented, and turns to look at the human skull she holds, as though to share the moment with a companion. Albert can see that the skull has been gnawed. He presumes it has been dug from the grave she was worrying at. Her raking nails protrude through the eye holes, and he wonders if he is staring at his own remains, if he is a ghost haunting a battlefield.

An animal, he decides, a night creature thrown up by evolution, filling some monstrous niche in the food chain. She surprises him though when she breaks the silence, throwing his theory of a mindless beast into disarray.

"Son of Eve," and of course the S is sibilant, dragging on, longer in his mind than on the air. Her face is human. She touches him, and he sees the stain of muck on her fingers as they approach his face, readies himself for the nails to penetrate his skin. He imagines the fingers at play, worrying beneath the flap of his scalp. "Al Bert", she says, picking his name somehow from the aether, and he shivers at the connection she has made between them. She smiles again, as though at some tremendous play of words, and the slaughterhouse stench rolls out with her breath. She will flow about him and he will be lost. She is made of teeth, every part of her a mouth, he will be consumed, he thinks, when he hears another voice.

"Ghoul." A simple declaration, a cataloguing statement made from somewhere to his left. She is fast, very fast, and Albert sees seized in her other hand not the skull but the small Arab, her worshipper, the one who left him as sacrifice to this thing.

This close to her, he sees the fresh blood on her face, and the thought comes; *there are no new dead here.* Not in this yard. What rawness has she been eating, that it could still drip fresh down her chin? Time was not right, things were out of joint. The little Arab does not look happy, her fingers are through his robes. Albert sees the black seep at his shoulder and knows it is moon lit blood.

"Sons of Eve," snake drawn out, "I have you both," and triumph was there, pleasure at a victory achieved. Though the victory was beyond Albert's comprehension, there was also a hunger, which Albert understood very well. Her head rose, taking on again a wolfish cast. Her eyes lifted to the impossible moon, glowing green.

Reaching low, her nails scratched at Albert's groin, dragging across his scar. Momentary confusion, expecting one thing but finding another. She reacts, and it is then that Albert sees a tiny star streak across the yard, a light broken away from the litter of the others in the heavens. She moves, but not quickly enough. She leaps, but the orbit of the star bears into her, tearing into the flesh above her breasts. The meat of her splits and there is a hiss of escape. Only as she falls does Albert hear the bang.

The small Arab was down. Despite his wound, he was cutting, hacking at her neck. Albert heard the crack of her skull as her severed head was flung against a tombstone. The man chopped, breaking off her limbs, throwing each to a different corner of the field. There were words of course, a constant muttered litany, but they meant nothing to Albert.

With only the torso left, the Arab dug with the point of the knife, the same point that had been in Albert's mouth just hours before.

Albert felt a sympathetic twinge in his cheek. Wiping away gore, the man held up the treasure he had retrieved. As he did, his companion walked across the yard towards them, bearing a long rifle.

"See," said the small man, as though Albert was a fellow enthusiast being shown an interesting specimen. "Meteor iron. Struck down by iron from beyond the earth." He smiles. "Don't want to lose that." Then the knife came towards Albert.

"*No*," he cried leaning away, but they held him firm. They cut the silk and caught him, bearing his weight gently.

"We owed it to him," said the small one, speaking English for Albert's benefit, but the other shook his head, and Albert realised they were speaking not about him, but of another.

"We did not, but in honour we could not leave him like this."

The grass was a soft meadow, no sign of the viscera that had littered it moments before. Albert's naked feet were no longer in danger from splintered bone. "It is dead," he said, but it was a question.

"Whatever *dead* means to a thing of that order," the small man shrugged. "It will feed on him no more."

They bore Albert up before a grave. The moonlight gone, they shone a lamp at the inscription.

To the dear memory of T E LAWRENCE.

This was where he had first seen the creature, but now the grave was undisturbed. Nothing monstrous had dug its way out to emerge from its larder. A vase of marigolds rested there. All still, all quiet.

An oppressive weight was lifted from him. Other than the ache in his limbs, all Albert felt was a sense of liberty.

He straightened and looked at the Arabs. "What happens now?"

The taller man turned and walked off, shouldering the rifle. Looking back, he said, "Now? It is up to you".

Albert had been a wind-up toy, borne here on the inevitable track of his one life. Now he was derailed. Possibilities stretched before him, definitions beyond the gelded policeman. Not every path led to that autumn morning in a frosty field.

14.

Choose life.

Ross wheels the bike away, gunning the accelerator, as though he flees, as though he has not all these years and many miles been following the path set for him. As though he could not have been plucked from the air or dragged down through sand or vanished from a railway station.

The world is distorted at the edges by goggles. It does not bother him. There is the wind in his hair and the rumbling machine beneath him, and in that moment, it is enough. What is a curse, what is fate, other than an inability to jump from one track to another? He has travelled more than enough tracks for any man. All the men he has been.

The blackness above him is unobscured by the order we have imposed, no longer papered over with the legends and habits from which we have cobbled together the mundane. It is a place beyond creation and rationality, a place of its own senseless causality, a wilderness of pain and evil refreshment. .

Faster, faster, Ross accelerates until he reaches the rock that marks the edge of the road, and he is up, he is flying, he has found the path that has no surrounding. He climbs the invisible road. The bike roars and he is tearing, he is rending the air, climbing the wall of it, boring through. The hole in the sky takes human shape, and she - it - descends.

He leaps his last track. He meets it in the air.

The boys hear the noise. There is a flurry. They see the man catapult, turn through the air, a stunted flight without wings. They say it was over in a moment.

They did not hear the screams. They did not see his face, torn between terror and desire.

They cannot know that the moment stretched more than a thousand years.

Enough time for the granting of all wishes, known or hidden, consistent or not. The price he paid. The careful filleting that can occur over such a long time, the precise slicing required to lay a delicate mechanism bare.

VAULT

ANTONY MANN

Parnell took the twenty pound note straight from the newsagents back to the bank. The woman behind the shop counter had treated him like a criminal, even threatened to ring the police. He hated that: being made to feel guilty for something he hadn't done. Even worse, she had taken delight in his discomfort. She was a compact specimen, twenty-nine or thirty, with streaky blonde hair and a thin face, no doubt pretty to someone, but Parnell found her ugly. Nothing unusual there. Everyone looked ugly to him these days. Maybe it was the incessant drizzle that made their faces seem so flat and unattractive, the shopgirls, the passersby in the streets. Parnell couldn't remember the last time it had not been raining.

"Just the paper."

Dull-eyed, as bored as Parnell found her boring, the woman had snapped the banknote between her fingers out of habit then swiped it under the eye of the security machine. To her surprise—and Parnell's—the light had flashed red and the buzzer gone off. She had glanced up at him, reset it and tried again. *Beep-beep*. Those in the queue behind him had gawked and craned. His face had reddened and he had felt the heat crawling up the back of his neck. *Beep*.

"I'll have to get the manager," the woman had said, making little effort to hide her pleasure. *Why?* he wondered now, standing outside the bank. Why should it have been such a source of enjoyment? Was her life so miserable that embarrassing a customer constituted a highlight?

"But... but I just this minute came from the bank!" he had stammered. The woman had paused; if it were possible, her face had hardened even more. Clearly, she had disbelieved him.

"Store policy requires that the manager contact the police in any instance of..."

But Parnell had lurched forward across the counter, plucking the twenty from the woman's hand. She had squawked in surprise. It had almost been fun then, dumping his newspaper amidst the sweets and chocolates, deflecting a small boy from his path as he made a break for daylight. The glass door opened, he had pushed out into the street and set off down the footpath at a brisk half-trot, dodging umbrella points as they loomed up out of the pedestrian flow. He had almost expected a rallying cry from behind, a posse of the civic-minded spontaneously arising to give chase, but there had been nothing. Not a peep. So much for community spirit.

It must have been a trick of the light, but it seemed to be raining more heavily outside the bank than elsewhere. The facade was brownstone, Georgian he guessed, yet uninspired—now, there was a fitting epitaph for his age, he mused. The Age of Parnell: We achieved little. We were uninspired. Gargoyle faces frowned down at him against a backdrop of relentless grey cloud.

He paused on the step and brushed the water from his shoulders, flicked it from his hat, then entered through the swing doors, blinking against the bright fluorescent glare. It was stuffy inside, airless.

The heating was up too high. No doubt it was bank policy. Render the staff semi-conscious. Encourage the public to sweat. Make banking as dreary as possible. Better yet, make it an ordeal.

He noted that the mock-walnut paneling was plastered with those idiot pictures of actors/models with samey haircuts pretending to be families whose happiness was exceeded only by their smug satisfaction— at having taken out a mortgage with the bank. In contrast, a line of tired-looking customers waited for teller service. That was how they were referred to these days, wasn't it? As customers? As though it were the role of the bank to serve, rather than extract as much money as possible from account-holders who had little choice other than to suffer in silence? Well, here's one customer who is not satisfied, Parnell thought grimly as he approached the Enquiries desk.

He took the counterfeit note and his auto-teller receipt from his wallet and placed them on the counter before the man who sat there entering data into a computer terminal. *Wakey-wakey,* thought Parnell. *What have we here? Another slack-shouldered drone in white shirt and nondescript tie?* In truth he was more boy than man, fresh out of college but still not grown. His cheeks were clear, tinged rosy by the heating.

"This came from your machine out front."

The young man looked up from the screen.

"I see."

"No, I don't think you do, Mr Paltrose," said Parnell, peering at the young man's identification tag. "It's counterfeit, and it came from your automatic dispensing machine. I have just now undergone considerable embarrassment trying to change it in the newsagents. I have a good mind to demand compensation for loss of standing in the community."

The young man regarded him with some doubt.

"Oh, that's right," said Parnell drily. "I forgot. You're a bank. You don't make mistakes."

He had not spoken softly, and a couple of the tellers and customers looked in his direction. He stared back at them, but they at once averted their gaze. Ha! There they were, as always—the slumberers, as he thought of them. The great and ugly hordes of the timid and the tired, who would do anything rather than kick up a fuss, who believed in all this, and were subservient to it: the buildings that housed the ideas that made up their world. Banks, churches, governments, nations. Bow down, bow down, you lovers of mirages.

Anyway, what was he supposed to do? Apologise for being right?

"Your account number?" said the man.

Parnell handed over his cheque card and waited while his details were keyed into the terminal. Paltrose read off the screen.

"According to this, you made a twenty dollar withdrawal ten minutes ago."

"That's right."

"And what was the problem?"

"I'm sorry?"

"The problem."

"The problem? The problem? Haven't you been listening to what I've told you?"

The young man handed back Parnell's cheque card, picked up the twenty dollar note and the auto-teller receipt, looked at them with what may or may not have been curiosity, and put them to one side.

"Thank you," he said. "Your request has been noted."

He turned back to his computer.

Request? The inherently mediocre could hardly be accused of audacity, but perhaps Parnell could make an exception in this boy's case. He regarded Paltrose with an irritated bemusement, but said nothing. At length, the lad looked up once more.

"Was there something else?"

"My twenty dollars. You have it. And my receipt."

"You said it came from our auto-teller."

"So it did," said Parnell. "If you intend to keep it, which is fine by me, then you'll have to give me a real twenty in exchange."

"Oh, I can't do that," said the man. "If you ring our helpline, someone would be more than happy to…"

"As it happens, I am self-employed," Parnell interrupted, "which means that, inconvenient though it may be for me to do so, I am at liberty to stand here all day if need be."

Paltrose took the point. With a great yearnful reluctance he handed over the note and the receipt, casting a lingering, wistful look their way as they disappeared back into Parnells' wallet. It would not have surprised Parnell to see a tear creep into the lad's eye. Paltrose indicated a door in the wall at the end of the counter.

"Through and down the stairs," he said. "Ms Abercrombie will help you."

▼▼▼

"Counterfeit," repeated Parnell.

Ms Abercrombie's lips took it upon themselves to smile without letting the rest of her face know. Her eyes seemed especially ignorant of the fact. *Come to think of it, perhaps she can't properly smile,* mused Parnell. The skin of her face was waxen, stretched tight across her cheeks from ear to ear. Her grey-brown hair was plastered to the skin of her skull. She was starchy all over.

Parnell held the troublesome bill up to the light, as though demonstrating to an idiot child.

"As in, phoney. Fake. A dud."

"I see," she said.

Another who saw—but this one was older, in an advanced state of decay. *Did that mean that she had seen more, or now saw less?* Parnell wondered, amusing himself with his own cleverness. Or did they all see the same thing, no matter what it was they were looking at? Root and branch—ha! was that a joke?—they were all of the same tree.

It was hotter down here, and damp. There were no windows of course, only plain wooden office panels succumbing to the appetites of various strains of mould and mildew, like abstract floral wallpaper in relief. It saved on decorating, he supposed. But where was the ventilation duct? He could see none. Something smelt sweetly rank, like compost. It was either the fungal growths or Ms Abercrombie—he couldn't tell which. Or maybe it was the rotting carpet. He wondered how much of it he would carry away with him on the soles of his shoes.

Her shoulder creaked as she stretched out an arm. He thought for a moment the bone was going to snap into shards, there inside her withered flesh, but somehow it held together. No wonder she had declined to shake hands. She took the note and held it up to the light, just as he had. Was she mocking him?

"Phoney," she said. "Fake. A dud."

"I think I knew that already," said Parnell.

"And what was the problem?"

Oh, they were good here, there was no denying that. It was probably genetic: natural selection for obtuseness in the face of even the simplest request. These days, they had aptitude tests for that sort of thing. Can you keep the cogs behind your eyes well-oiled and quiet? Can you keep a straight face? This Abercrombie…thing. He examined her with renewed distaste. Neither her voice nor her expression had even begun to hint at the bank's liability. Hell, she didn't remind him remotely of anyone he knew, and still he disliked her.

"The problem is, that I withdrew that note from your auto-teller."

"And you maintain that you withdrew this note from our auto-teller?"

Unfazed, he tried a different tack.

"Supposing I had withdrawn the note from your auto-teller. What would you do? Give me a proper twenty? A year's supply of credit slips? Some of those plastic change bags of which you can never have too few?"

"We'd all like twenty dollars, Mr Parnell," she said, neglecting once again to emote. "The trouble is, it's your word against ours."

"Forgive me," he said, "but I don't think I've heard your word yet. Do you have a policy on this or are you making it up as you go along?"

She took a pad and pen from the desk drawer and began to write. Parnell watched as she drew a series of small rectangles of varying sizes, connected them at random by lines both dotted and unbroken, then filled them in with letters and numbers apparently also selected in haphazard fashion.

"Shorthand of the damned, is it?" he muttered to himself.

"I've referred you to Mr Dobson." She handed him the paper and the counterfeit twenty. "Through and down the stairs."

The receptionist took his referral then directed him from her counter to the empty green chairs along the wall, from which vantage point he had ample opportunity to size her up. There was flesh on her bones at least—and a pleasing amount at that—but she was wall-eyed. Curiously, she had let blonde curls grow down to obscure the normality, leaving the crooked side of her face in plain view. She had been cranking some kind of machine when he had come in, and now she returned to her task. Parnell could see it from where he sat. It resembled an old-style manual typewriter, but it was almost as though such had been turned inside out. There were no keys, only hammers, and instead of rising through an arc and striking paper, they bent upwards in the middle, jointed like a spider's legs, and rippled from one side of the contraption to the other as she cranked. It made no sound, only clicking once to signal the operation was complete.

"Keep you busy, do they?" he said idly.

Her crooked eye fixed him with a blank look. It was a pity. For a change, he might have welcomed a less antagonistic conversation. In his experience, the menial buffer staff did not invest so much intellectual (or emotional) energy in the concept of whatever corporation they served. Hence they were less likely to defend it so vigorously.

There was a crank handle on the other side of the machine too. She turned it, and the hammers rose up and rippled back over. She repeated the whole process twice more before speaking.

"Mr Dobson, was it?"

"That's right."

"And what was the problem?"

"I withdrew a counterfeit twenty dollar note from your auto-teller."

"I see."

That made three out of three.

He glanced around the room. It was L-shaped, lit softly by antiquated lamps on small stands. There was one on the receptionist's counter, too. The shades even had tassels. The green chairs were also antique, and (he guessed intentionally) uncomfortable. Split by a low table, they sat in a row of four along the L's perpendicular, opposite the counter. In the middle of the base of the horizontal was another door. It was hot down here too, but drier than it had been in Ms Abercrombie's office. The walls were of the same wood paneling, but they were clean and hung with detailed black and sepia prints of animals that Parnell did not recognise. The floor was parquetry, polished to reflect all.

He picked up the magazine that was on the table beside him. It was not one he had seen before: *Structures of Altered Sense, No. 2, Vol. 7.*

There was no editorial or contents page, so he turned to the first article, by someone called E. P. Edwall: "A Discourse on the Nature of Solid Fragment". *To truncate what is elevated to higher lightness involves coursing only by means indicated in the previous issue's explanatory diagrams. If we were to consider the possibility of such an eventuality it could only be in the context of further progress, or 'back-walling', as it has been called elsewhere. What does not concern us here is the nature of the courser, for whomsoever reaches that juncture in consciousness...*

It hurt his eyes to read more. He assumed it meant something, but it meant nothing to him. What was wrong with the customary year-old copy of *Country Life*? He flicked to another page. There was a second piece by the same fellow, E. P. Edwall, this one called "Amar-Abtar, Lord of Castings". It began: *Origins of inference predicate a 'gestation period' for the ripening of intuitive knowledge not dissimilar to the method used by the Bar-Aki in their pursuit of...*

On further inspection, Parnell determined that all the articles in the magazine had been written by E. P. Edwall with the exception of the last: "E. P. Edwall" by F. Beasley-Saint. It appeared to be a biographical piece, but not even that made a lot of sense. In fact, he must have drifted into a light sleep while trying to read it, because after scanning the first paragraph the next thing he knew he was rocking back in his chair, swallowing air. The magazine lay open at his feet. The lamps on their stands were flickering, and there was a metallic, burning smell in the air. He checked his watch. Only a few minutes had passed.

He glanced at the closed door at the far end of the room. Still no sign of Dobson. This was a common technique, of course. Everyone knew without being told. Make them wait. It was a silent, unconscious conspiracy, in which the public were more often than not complicit. He was sure it had been bred into humans as a species. A child taken from its mother at birth and reared in isolation would still grow up knowing how to wait. Perhaps the instinct was fundamentally religious. To wait was to endure was to suffer. Parnell didn't like suffering. He considered the receptionist, still cranking her machine.

Then it occurred to him: had she even let Dobson know he was here? He didn't recall it. He stood and approached her. Leaning over the counter, he saw that the machine was not precisely as he had thought. The device that the woman cranked was no more than a crowning part, suspended in a rectangular gap in her work surface by cast-iron horizontal struts. The rising and falling hammers were levers, themselves connected to a series of downward-pointing metal rods, and as they rippled back and forth across the frame Parnell saw that they were causing motion below. The woman was not so much sitting on as attached to the rest of the machine. Her torso was held in a brace welded to an iron plate on the rear wall. Her left leg was free, yet her right, bent at the knee, was encased completely in an iron frame which moved up and down as the hammers rippled. He could not see, but by its motion Parnell assumed that this frame was also connected to something, a piston perhaps that disappeared below the level of the floor. The whole had an ungainly appearance. It seemed to Parnell an exercise in excessive ingenuity. He was surprised it didn't make more noise.

"I'm sorry," the receptionist said, at last registering his presence. She stopped cranking. Her leg stopped too. "Who was it you wanted to see?"

"Mr Dobson. I told you when I came in."

"Oh! I thought you were telling me that *you* were Mr Dobson. Funny coincidence, I thought, there being two Mr Dobsons like that. But it's not, is it? As it turns out. A coincidence."

"Or funny," he said.

"You want to see Mr Dobson? What was it about?"

"A counterfeit banknote."

"And what was the problem?"

"The bank is trying to rob me," said Parnell. The woman didn't see the little ironic joke, unless the expression of her sense of humour extended to looking perplexed. Parnell inwardly conceded it might have more to do with the joke than the woman. But she pointed at the door in the far end of the room.

"Through and down the stairs."

▼▼▼

"And what was the problem, Mr Parnell?" Mr Dobson's large moon of a head swivelled jerkily in the iron neck brace, directing his face towards the floor. Parnell pulled the offending note from his wallet.

"This twenty dollar bill is counterfeit," he said. "It came from your auto-teller. I demand restitution, compensation, reparation, indemnification. Take your pick. I have no pressing engagements for the foreseeable future. Until March, in fact. Of next year. So, you may pass me from drone to ghoul to corpse in endless circle, for all I care. I have plenty of time, and I will be satisfied."

"I see."

Et tu, Dobson?

This office too was hot and stuffy. All that was not beaten iron was crumbling brick, and all was covered in a fine soot, so that the entirety was black or lesser shades of grimy darkness—except the bare globe above that burned a tired yellow. From floor to ceiling, in the centre of the room, there stretched a dark metal pole, six inches in diameter, the purpose of which was not immediately apparent.

He must have been directly below the reception room, for Parnell saw that he had been right about the piston. It emerged through an aperture in the left-hand side of the ceiling and pumped into the body of a great spherical engine, which sat on a tripod the height of a man and emitted a constant low humming noise. This machine was the source of the soot: a copper exhaust pipe protruded from the upper hemisphere, and every minute or so a puff of black dust would explode gently into the air.

Mr Dobson himself was attached to this sphere by means of a large iron arm, its elbow bent up, the hand of which was a cage into which he fitted most snugly. He was suspended in the air so that Parnell had to crane upwards to see him. His body had been surgically truncated at the torso and left shoulder, from which points a myriad of fine cables snaked out and down, across the floor, thence into sockets at different heights in the walls. Above these points were legends that read, varyingly, GOVERNANCE, EXECUTION, FORMALITY, DECISION, ALLOCATION, and so forth, there being many more, perhaps a hundred, words that sparked in Parnell's mind no association of pleasure.

Alone of what remained of his body, Dobson's large round head and right arm were without the mesh of the cage. He was free to use his hand to manipulate a panel of levers at the base of the container where his right hip had once been. He did so now in fact, pulling on a handle, and the great iron arm swung him down to Parnell's level.

It was difficult for Parnell to take account of any human characteristics he might have possessed. Indeed, he appeared to have few. His movements were smooth, but mirrored the mechanical nature of his attachments. His hair was oily and dark—whether this was due solely to the soot Parnell could not say—and his skin pallid and moist beneath the film of accumulated black dust. His face was so devoid of expression that it might have been a mask. Still, he wore what might have once been a white shirt—without the left arm—and a narrow grey tie.

He took the bill from Parnell's grip and raised it to his eyes.

"This note is counterfeit," he said in a voice both flat and uninterested. "And you say that it came from your account?"

Fair enough Parnell wondered. What mastery of deflection and evasion was he witnessing?

"I wonder," Dobson continued, droning on now like a tired recording, "if I were to check your account, whether or not I would find that all your funds were counterfeit."

"Perhaps so," said Parnell acidly, "if I were to withdraw them from your auto-teller."

"And if so, Mr Parnell, I wonder also, would that constitute fraud? Now. Sir." He handed back the note. "Was there a problem?"

Surely this could not be taught, this level of tap-dancing. Parnell was too impressed to be affronted. He had been dismissed, insulted and counter-accused in one breath. Masterful.

He clapped his hands slowly.

"Bravo, Mr Dobson," he said. "Bravo."

Dobson did not react, but the innards of the great spherical engine to which he was attached coughed loudly, and a particularly large puff of soot spluttered from the copper pipe and drifted slowly to the ground. Parnell watched as it settled, and saw for the first time that the floor itself was made of iron. Not one sheet, but two, joined down the middle. He realised now that the heat was rising from underfoot.

Parnell looked back at Dobson. The wax-like hand hovered over the control panel on the cage. It was a dare.

Fair enough, thought Parnell. *And fuck you.*

"I'd like to see the manager."

"Certainly, Mr Parnell," said Dobson.

Before the request could be retracted, Dobson's hand worked furiously over the panel, turning the small handles, pulling and pushing levers in a predetermined sequence. It must have taken only a second, but it seemed much longer; when he was done, he tweaked a last handle, and the iron arm swung him back into the air.

There was a moment's silence, in which he almost relaxed, but then Parnell heard a murmurous sigh from below, a distant wakening that seemed to find answer throughout the entire building. There came next the grind of a massive gear, the sound of it muffled by deep stone, and the iron plates beneath Parnell's feet began to drag apart, sliding uniformly into cavities in the walls. He looked down.

At first there was no means by which to gauge the depth of the black pit that yawned beneath him, yet as the floor split ever wider, he saw the top of the staircase that spiraled down, well delineated at first, but fading eventually into no more than the hint of a grey line, then disappearing altogether into the blackness. Five hundred, a thousand feet? So that was the purpose of the central pole: the very top of the staircase railing was attached to its base.

He walked off the disappearing floor and onto the top step, grabbing the pole for support. The whole construction was sturdy. There was no danger that he would fall. He could see more clearly now, or rather, see more clearly that he was looking down into nothing. The pit had no sides that he could detect, and there was nothing in it, only the uprushing of uncomfortable heat. Dobson hung now more or less directly over him.

"It's not the principle," said Parnell. "It's the money. Surely you understand that."

"Understand? Understand?" said Dobson. "You are the one who understands now, I think."

By crikey, it approximates to a sense of humour, thought Parnell. But he looked down again, curiously, and in the next instant knew it was no joke, for there, a thousand feet below, as wide as a mile and as deep, a great fiery eye opened and peered back up at him.

"Through," said Mr Dobson, "and down the stairs."

THE AUTHORS

AARON BESSON is a writer of Weird Horror from Seattle, Washington. His writing has been published in the *Weird Fiction Review* from Centipede Press, *Cyäegha*, Kind of a Hurricane Press, and *Spinetinglers*.

NADIA BULKIN writes scary stories about the scary world we live in, three of which have been nominated for a Shirley Jackson Award. Her stories have been included in volumes of *The Year's Best Horror* (Datlow), *The Year's Best Dark Fantasy and Horror* (Guran) and *The Year's Best Weird Fiction*, and in venues such as *Nightmare*, *Fantasy*, *The Dark*, and *ChiZine*. Her debut collection, *She Said Destroy*, was published by Word Horde in August 2017. She has a B.A. in political science, an M.A. in international affairs, and lives in Washington, D.C.

The Oxford Companion to English Literature describes **RAMSEY CAMPBELL** as "Britain's most respected living horror writer". Among his trophies are the Grand Master Award of the World Horror Convention, the Lifetime Achievement Award of the Horror Writers Association, the Living Legend Award of the International Horror Guild and the World Fantasy Lifetime Achievement Award. In 2015 he was made an Honorary Fellow of Liverpool John Moores University for outstanding services to literature. He was born in Liverpool in 1946 and still lives on Merseyside. His most recent books are a trilogy – *The Searching Dead*, *Born to the Dark* and *The Way of the Worm*.

S. L. EDWARDS enjoys dark fiction, dark poetry and darker beer. He is a Texan currently residing in California. His fiction and poetry have appeared in *Ravenwood Quarterly*, *Turn to Ash*, *Weirdbook* and several horror anthologies. With Yves Tourigny he is the co-creator of *Borkchito: Occult Doggo Detective*.

Formerly a film critic, journalist, screenwriter and teacher, **GEMMA FILES** has been an award-winning horror author since 1999. She has published two collections of short work (*Kissing Carrion* and *The Worm in Every Heart*), two chap-books of speculative poetry, a Weird Western trilogy (the *Hexslinger* series—*A Book of Tongues, A Rope of Thorns* and *A Tree of Bones*), a story-cycle (*We Will All Go Down Together: Stories of the Five-Family Coven*) and a stand-alone novel (*Experimental Film*, which won the 2016 Shirley Jackson Award for Best Novel and the 2016 Sunburst award for Best Adult Novel). All her works are available through ChiZine Productions. Her novella *Coffle* was just published by Dim Shores, with art by Stephen Wilson. She has two upcoming story collections from Trepidatio Publishing (*Spectral Evidence* and *Drawn Up From Deep Places*), and one from Cemetery Dance (*Dark Is Better*).

JOHN LINWOOD GRANT is a professional writer and editor who lives in Yorkshire with a pack of lurchers and a beard. Widely published in magazines and anthologies, he writes strange historical horror, including the Mamma Lucy tales of 1920s hoodoo and the *Last Edwardian* series, and contemporary weird fiction. He is also editor of *Occult Detective Quarterly*, plus forthcoming anthologies. His 2017 collection *A Persistence of Geraniums* – stories of murder, madness and the supernatural – is now available on Amazon.

ORRIN GREY is a writer, editor, amateur film scholar, and monster expert who was born on the night before Halloween. His stories of monsters, ghosts, and sometimes the ghosts of monsters have appeared in dozens of anthologies, including Ellen Datlow's *Best Horror of the Year*, and he is the author of the collections *Never Bet the Devil & Other Warnings* and *Painted Monsters & Other Strange Beasts*. His writing about film has appeared in places like *Strange Horizons, Clarkesworld,* and *Unwinnable*, and his Innsmouth Free Press column on vintage horror cinema was collected into the book *Monsters from the Vault*. John Langan once referred to him as "the monster guy", and he never lets anyone forget it.

BELINDA LEWIS spent her childhood reading fantasy novels and disappointedly hitting her head on the backs of wardrobes. She was born, raised and currently lives in Johannesburg. Just for variety she plans to die somewhere else.

TOM LYNCH is a longtime devotee of the art of the fine frightening tale, and is descended from family that enjoys a good nightmare: is it any wonder he focuses on the weird and dark? Tom has published fiction in Horror for the Holidays, Undead and Unbound, Eldritch Chrome, Atomic Age Cthulhu, Dark Rites of Cthulhu and more. By day, Tim is a middle school teacher, working to expand young minds. He spends what little "spare" time he has hunched over his keyboard.

H. P. LOVECRAFT liked tinned spaghetti, ice cream, coffee, and cosmic horror. This last to the degree that he is often referred to as the father of the weird tale, which may or may not be true, but certainly speaks to his lasting influence on the genre. He disliked the smell of the ocean, jitterbugging, and miscegenation. He is best known for his classic tales *The Call of Cthulhu, The Dunwich Horror*, and *The Shadow Over Innsmouth*, among others. He died, of complications resulting from cancer of the small intestine and Bright's Disease, in March of 1937. Since then he's become quite the industry, and we thank him for that.

ADAM McOMBER is the author of *The White Forest: A Novel* (Simon and Schuster 2012) and *This New & Poisonous Air: Stories* (BOA Editions 2011). His new collection of queer speculative fiction, *My House Gathers Desires*, was published by BOA Editions in September 2017. Adam's work has recently appeared in *Diagram, Kenyon Review,* and *Fairy Tale Review*.

ANTONY MANN's stories have appeared in *Interzone*, *Crimewave*, *Ellery Queen's Mystery Magazine*, *London Magazine* and many others.

ADAM MILLARD is the author of twenty-six novels, twelve novellas, and more than two hundred short stories, which can be found in various collections, magazines, and anthologies. Probably best known for his post-apocalyptic and comedy-horror fiction, Adam also writes fantasy/horror for children, as well as bizarro fiction for several publishers. His work has recently been translated for the German market.

SARAH PEPLOE was born and raised in Norwich. Her short stories have appeared in anthologies (Snowbooks' *Game Over*, Hic Dragones' *Hauntings*, Three Drops Press's *A Face in the Mirror*, *A Hook on the Door*), journals (*Body Parts 8: Killer Clowns and Freak Shows*), zines (*Market Clothes*), and Krampus-flavoured Christmas crackers. She has illustrated several poetry collections for Manchester-based poet Anna Percy, and she also produces comics as part of Mindstain Comics co-operative. She lives in York.

SCOTT SHANK's work has appeared in AE, Plasma Frequency and Heroic Fantasy Quarterly. He lives in Toronto and online @scoshank.

CHRISTOPHER SLATSKY's stories have appeared in *The Year's Best Weird Fiction vol. 3*, *Nightscript vol. 2*, the *Looming Low* anthology, and elsewhere. His debut collection *Alectryomancer and Other Weird Tales* (Dunhams Manor Press) was released summer of 2015. He currently resides in Los Angeles.

DAVID STEVENS (usually) lives in Sydney, Australia, with his wife and children. His stories have appeared amongst other places in *Crossed Genres*, *Aurealis*, *Three-Lobed Burning Eye*, *Pseudopod*, *Cafe Irreal*, *Not One of Us*, *Kaleidotrope*, and several anthologies. He blogs irregularly at davidstevens.info

THE EDITOR

SCOTT R JONES is a writer, spoken word performer, mostly unintentional comedian, and naturalized sorcerer. He lives in Victoria BC Canada with his lovely wife Sasha and all-round awesome kids Sean and Meridian. His fiction and poetry has been published in *Broken City Mag*, *Innsmouth Magazine*, *Cthulhu Haiku 2*, *Andromeda Spaceways Inflight Magazine*, and a few anthologies and podcasts besides. His book detailing an auto-ethnographical approach to religious themes and practice derived from Lovecraft's Cthulhu Mythos, *When The Stars Are Right: Towards An Authentic R'lyehian Spirituality*, has received praise from the likes of Laird Barron and Richard Gavin, and apparently caused S. T. Joshi to make a squicky face when it was mentioned during a convention panel. You can reach him by email at srjones@martianmigrainepress.com or you can follow him on the Twitter @PimpMyShoggoth

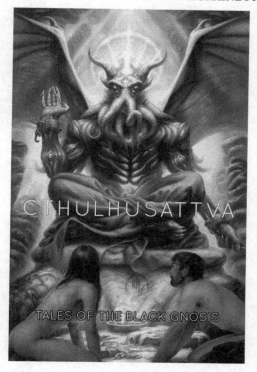

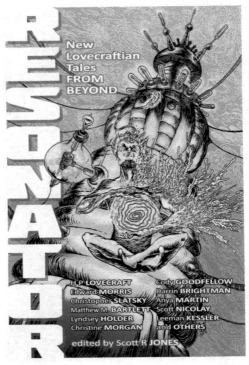

CPSIA information can be obtained
at www.ICGtesting.com
Printed in the USA
LVHW021544240721
693406LV00012B/615